ALSO BY THOMAS GRATTAN

The Recent East

IN TONGUES

IN TONGUES

THOMAS GRATTAN

MCD · FARRAR, STRAUS AND GIROUX NEW YORK

MCD

Farrar, Straus and Giroux

120 Broadway, New York 10271

Printed in the United States of America

First edition, 2024

Library of Congress Cataloging-in-Publication Data

Names: Grattan, Thomas, 1974– author.

Title: In tongues / Thomas Grattan.

Description: First edition. | New York : MCD/Farrar, Straus and
  Giroux, 2024. |

Identifiers: LCCN 2023050758 | ISBN 9780374608187 (hardcover)

Subjects: LCGFT: Gay fiction. | Novels.

Classification: LCC PS3607.R3774 I5 2024 | DDC 813/.6—
  dc23/eng/20231107

LC record available at https://lccn.loc.gov/2023050758

Designed by Patrice Sheridan

Our books may be purchased in bulk for promotional, educational, or
business use. Please contact your local bookseller or the Macmillan
Corporate and Premium Sales Department at 1-800-221-7945, extension
5442, or by email at MacmillanSpecialMarkets@macmillan.com.

www.mcdbooks.com • www.fsgbooks.com

Follow us on social media at @mcdbooks and @fsgbooks

3   5   7   9   10   8   6   4   2

FOR DAVID

Later, he looked back on this time as if he had caught a severe illness which left its mark on him for the rest of his life.

—TOVE DITLEVSEN, "THE UMBRELLA"

PART ONE

I

On the night Alan, my first serious boyfriend, dumped me, I lay awake on the couch I called ours, though he'd been the one to pay for it, waiting for anger or sadness or relief to come. What showed up instead was the suspended feeling that captures me from time to time even now, like flinging myself from a diving board so I'm not rising or falling but still. That weightlessness stayed as I packed everything worth taking into a pair of duffel bags and stole two hundred dollars from the drawer where Alan kept cash. It held steady as I drove to a dealership, its cars' windshields laced with frost, and sold my own, lingered as I hitchhiked to the bus station where I waited in line behind a woman who took forever at the ticket counter, the clerk's mustache trembling with annoyance as she asked one question, then another, a custodian next to us smacking a mop up and down. But then another clerk showed up, sharp lines around her mouth and eyes, and said, "Next." And, as my bags and I made it to the counter and she asked, "Where to?" my descent began, so I said the first and maybe only place that came to mind, one I'd never been to before.

For that daylong bus ride from Minneapolis to New

York, stillness switched to falling, though as we passed bill-boards about all-you-can-eat buffets and abortion, as towns came and went with aluminum-sided sameness, I itched with the excitement of not knowing where I'd land.

Where I finally landed was an apartment in an attic above a garage in Bay Ridge, Brooklyn, a job stocking shelves at the Food Land across the street. Car exhaust crept through the apartment's floor, so I left the windows cracked open and moved the sofa—a pullout, according to the landlord, though its pullout mechanism had rusted itself closed—next to the window. But the apartment was cheap. The landlord hadn't even asked for a security deposit. This was a sad relief, cheapness my only horizon. As I lay on that sofa each night, light from the *Food Land* sign searing through my window, I wanted to return to that line in the bus station and name some other city instead. But I would've been met with disappointment anywhere, been shocked by it, too. That was me then, surprised by results as inevitable as a math problem's solution, most due to how easily and often I jumped, with no plan for what I'd do once I'd thrown myself into the air.

At Food Land I stocked shelves and organized inventory under the supervision of a man named Thor. And though the job wasn't what I'd hoped for, its boring purpose was all I had to hold on to, so I took it seriously. I made sure labels on cans were perfectly straight until the repetition of graphic and word (*Baked Beans, Baked Beans, Baked Beans*) felt like art. Kept the back area so clean that even Thor, who I sensed didn't like me, grudgingly said, "You're making it harder for the mice," his compliment a warm hand on my cheek.

A few weeks into that job, I asked one of the cashiers a question. She looked shocked.

"I didn't know," she said. Her name was Marcy.

"Didn't know what?" I asked.

Marcy had small features and wore a product in her hair that made it look perpetually wet. She admitted that they'd all thought, with my dark hair and pale skin, clothes a cheap approximation of what was fashionable, that I was from some country that used to be part of Russia and "ended in -stan," curse words being my only English.

"I know a lot of words," I answered, then told her I had something to do in the dairy case.

I saw Marcy again an hour later, both of us in the store's back alley on a cigarette break. The dumpster's rot perfumed the air.

"I still can't believe you speak English," she said.

I answered with a series of complicated English words— *onomatopoeia* and *incumbent* and *lackadaisical*. It had rained earlier that day. Water plinked from a gutter.

"You're weird," Marcy said, then asked where I was from. I told her.

"Maybe what's weird here is normal there," she said.

"You sound like a philosopher," I answered.

"You sound like you're making fun of me."

"I wasn't making fun," I said. I hoped Marcy and I might become friends. I had no friends in New York. Spent days off from work walking until blisters collared my heels, or smoking too much and lying on the couch, wishing the apartment had come with a television. "I was weird in Minnesota, too."

I returned from my break. Thor saw me and said, "Was looking for you."

Thor seemed eternally annoyed. He could rest several boxes on his gut and called everything, from a person he didn't like to a difficult stain, a faggot. This was how he talked, though I also sensed it was his way of letting me know he was onto me. Each time he said that word, I picked up more boxes than was comfortable or deepened my voice. My attempts at passing only made it worse.

"There's meat," he said.

Thor spoke in as few words as possible. Whenever I asked for clarification, he said the same words again, sometimes louder.

I walked to the cooler, saw it was low on stew beef, and went into the back to get some.

At home that night, I was unsure if I wanted to jerk off or cry. I did both, half-heartedly, waking up hours later to a shivering light. The *L* in the *Food Land* sign was beginning to go. The next day, I saw Marcy and said, "Welcome to Food And." She looked at me like I had something stuck in my teeth and was deciding whether or not to tell me.

One night after work, I took the subway to Prospect Park. I walked into the woods where men met for sex, one of the few things then that offered me a break from failure's blunt noise. If I found someone who was game, it was usually rough and fast, the men haggard-looking or so masked by hoodies and baseball caps that I felt more than saw them. That night, I met a man with sunglasses on. I began to hum a song about wearing sunglasses at night but he squeezed my jaw with one hand, used the other to lower me to my knees. His dick filled my mouth. Small stones knifed my shins. He came and stepped away, dick bobbing in front of him. "Thank you," I said, but he didn't answer.

As I walked out of the park past half-empty bars and brownstones with bikes chained to their fences, it hit me how dangerous what I'd just done was, even more that I didn't care. I got on the subway, my throat sore from the way it had been used, and said—I did an inordinate amount of talking to myself then—"Well, *that* got the job done," though a few minutes later, the train stuck between stops, its bald fluorescents giving everyone a jaundiced hue, I added, "What job is that?" and a man across from me looked up with such disgust that I wondered if I'd been talking for longer. For the rest of the ride I gorged myself on the self-pity I'd grown up with, one I'd first mimicked, then made my own. "It was my special skill," I told a boyfriend years later. He'd smiled with polite embarrassment, then changed the subject.

A few weeks later, Marcy pulled me aside. I'd been in the freezer for an hour, my toes and ears numb. Her hair product smelled like synthetic watermelon.

"His real name's Vince," she said. "He thinks the Thor thing is funny."

"I don't get it," I answered, though I did, impressed he'd kept the ruse going for so long.

I went to check in with him, calling him Thor several times in our conversation. Each time I said it, his annoyance rose a notch and I wondered if he'd hit me, wanting it almost, a sign that I'd rankled myself into importance.

"Thor," I went on. "I'm finished in the freezer. Wondering if you have anything else for me to do, Thor." Messing with him was so enjoyable that for a moment everything grim about my life loosened its grip.

"Why are you talking that way?" he asked.

"The way I talk, Thor," I answered, then told him I'd be out back, breaking down boxes, which I did while smoking. That made me feel dismissive and sexy with an edge I'd always wanted, just as some people dream of being taller, how others want only to live with an ocean view.

But then the heaviness that sometimes got me returned. At work, I moved slowly. I hid in the staff bathroom, washing my face with frigid water until it ached. On days off, I slept until it was dark. When I was awake, I'd smoke and eat toast, lying on the sofa I pretended was a bed. There was crying sometimes, even more the wish that I could weep, for catharsis to move me past the dullness that made it hard to open my eyes all the way, the sense I'd been dumb to have expected more than this job, this apartment. I thought to go back to the park's woods, but that felt as stupid as Food Land and the emails I wrote to friends back in Minnesota filled with lies about my job and apartment, about the way I felt when I moved down city streets. One night, a trucker dropping off pallets of frozen food offered to sell me some weed and I bought it, smoking it until sleep bludgeoned me and I had a dream I vaguely remembered where Alan and my father were eating sandwiches together. I woke up to a knock at my door. It was Marcy, telling me I was late for work, asking if I'd quit.

"I didn't quit," I said.

I showed up at Food Land a few minutes later, eyes still crusty from sleep. I waited for Thor/Vince to tell me to wash my face, but he moved around me nervously and my indifference turned powerful, a spill that managed to get everywhere.

Halfway through my shift I said to him, "I know your name isn't Thor."

"Good for you," he answered. "Cantaloupe."

"Good for you," I said to the cantaloupe as I stacked it. I said it to Marcy, too, when she told me she was heading home. "Good for you," I told a lady who saw me pick up several boxes and said I was stronger than I looked.

I went behind the store to smoke, listened to the squeaking traffic of rats nosing through the trash.

"Good for you," I said, kicking the dumpster and walking back inside.

I got an email from Alan. He made no mention of the money I'd taken, but told me he'd started dating Ryan, his manager at the bank where he worked. I didn't want Alan back, but felt an acid annoyance at the thought of him and Ryan on our couch. Him and Ryan making food together, him and Ryan all eye contact and platitudes as they got close to coming. I tried to convince myself that Ryan was an idiot, though the few times I'd met him I'd appreciated his sly humor and great hands. *Hands off to you*, I wrote Alan back. Alan answered right away that he thought I meant *hats off*, and, in the internet café I spent too much time in, me and a bunch of cabdrivers sending emails or slyly scouring message boards for hookups, I said to no one in particular, "Hats and hands." A man next to me looked over. I gave him a thumbs-up. I wished he'd looked back with knowing interest so I could have invited him over for some fun on my formerly pullout sofa, the lights from the wavering *Food Land* sign pulsing against my apartment's walls in a way that sometimes reminded me of the ocean, other times of electrocution. But he turned to his monitor, grumbled something in a language I didn't know, and I wrote Alan back, *You're right, as usual*, and waited for him to answer, though he did not, and later I was surprised that I'd thought he would.

On days off, I started to ride the subway. Sometimes on those rides I got caught staring and had to look away fast or pretend I was reading an ad above people's heads. Other times I'd find a seat and fall asleep, waking up on the far edge of the Bronx or Queens.

One night, awake when I should have been asleep, I heard a noise outside and hoped it was Thor/Vince. Though I wasn't especially attracted to him, there was something in his manly indifference I found appealing. I peeked out my window. A man pissed between parked cars. My heart hurried as if I'd done too much coke, so I got dressed and took the subway into the city. It was two in the morning when I walked into the first rainbow-adorned bar I could find.

The bar was sparsely populated. The few beautiful men there looked either bored or tired. One of them said hello to me.

With no other questions coming to mind, I asked what he did for a living, wincing at the thought of being asked the same thing.

"Art director," the man said.

"I don't know what that means," I told him, and dropped an ice cube into my mouth.

He smiled, as one might smile at a pukey baby, and told me he saw a friend he needed to say hello to. I chomped my ice cube into smaller pieces.

The night ended with me in a Honda, giving and getting an unsatisfying hand job from a man who didn't bother to take off his wedding ring. In that car afterward, crumpled paper towels bouqueted at our crotches, the man said, "I wish you could come home with me."

"Your wife might have a problem with that," I said.

He wiped off his dick, asked me to throw out his paper towel, and kissed me sweetly. I took his hand, held it to my throat. He looked startled and pulled his hand away.

On the subway ride home, I fell asleep, was woken up by its conductor, telling me the train had reached its last stop and was out of service. "You okay?" he asked, a question so kind I felt myself tearing up, wishing I didn't cry so easily, wondering if there would ever be a time when the biggest thing in my life wasn't difficulty. My self-pity was large then, though maybe it was fear, the call and response of those two feelings so seamless it was difficult to distinguish follower and leader.

At work the next day, my sadness gathered momentum. I stayed in the cooler until I couldn't feel my fingers. Tipped over a pallet of canned vegetables, one can exploding, the floor of aisle six a riot of grayish peas. I found Vince, told him something was off with my stomach, that I needed to go home.

Instead, I walked. I moved through unfamiliar neighborhoods, the signs written in Chinese characters, passed store entrances wreathed in purses, others crowded with trays of fish on ice. I turned in the direction I sensed would lead me to my neighborhood and thought of the man in his Honda the night before who'd looked at me like I was an unbelievable prize, his attention a wave to carry me for a time.

But then, walking past me, was Thor/Vince. He wore a pleased, mean smile as he asked, "Feeling better?"

I nodded. I also started to cry. I thought to kiss him just to see what he might do, though the thought of kissing someone who hated me turned everything bleaker. But, before he had a chance to walk away, I wiped my eyes and said, "Yes, I *am* feeling better," which was as much a lie as his Scandinavian name. Then I asked him where I was.

In my second week of wandering, I stumbled onto a dive bar. Young people with grubby clothes and perfect teeth filled its booths, its walls weighed down with taxidermy and kitsch. Behind the bar stood a woman with long red hair finagled into a pompadour and a large chest, arms collaged in tattoos. When she gave customers her attention, they looked pleased. When she laughed, its throaty rattle rose above the miasma of music and conversation. Sitting at the bar, nursing a beer and a basket of stale popcorn, I found that I wanted her attention, too. Someone said something dumb; she smiled and told them to fuck themselves. A man commented on her shirt and she answered, "Didn't know it was open season for talking to strangers about their bodies," then poured him an overly foamy beer. She mixed and muddled without a pause in conversations. When certain songs came on, she hummed along. I left her a large tip in hopes that she'd remember me.

I returned a few nights later, trying not to watch her too much. When I find someone interesting, I spend a lot of time collecting the vocabulary and rhythm of their gestures. This looking has gotten me into trouble. Once, in fourth grade, the closest thing I'd understood about my interest in men and boys being a special attention I paid them, one of the Mikes in my class slammed me against a wall before I realized I'd been staring. But the bartender caught my eye, smiled, and though it wasn't about sex for me, something in me looking, her looking back felt like seduction.

At the bar's far end, a drunk couple played checkers. The man dropped a checker into his beer, fingered it out, then placed it on his tongue, like a communion wafer.

"You two good?" the bartender asked. The man nodded.

Kitschy watercolors crowded the wall behind them: boats and sunsets, landscapes featuring buffalo and industrious streams. Glasses clanged as the bartender washed them.

I was thinking of going home when she placed a fresh beer in front of me.

"On the house," the bartender said, and smiled.

In that smile was the tingle I'd hoped New York would bring me, that sense of vaulting into the air.

"Checkmate," the man at the other end of the bar said.

"Wrong game," the bartender whispered.

"This is nice of you," I said, lifting the beer in cheers.

"I'm nice sometimes. To my kind anyhow."

"You mean the gays?"

She nodded.

"So this is in solidarity? Like a queer beer?"

She answered with a deep laugh and asked my name. I told her, and she said hers back—Janice—then went on about the only other Gordon she'd ever known, a Mormon in her middle school who couldn't stop staring at her chest.

"Gordon the Mormon," I said, and pointed to her cleavage. "You had all that, even then?"

Janice pressed a hand to each breast. "Blessing and a curse, these ladies."

"These ladies have names?" I asked.

The checkers woman waved to Janice, who nodded, then handed me paper and a pen.

"Start a list," she said, touching her breasts again. "Names for us to consider."

I wrote down old-timey ones like Gertrude and Millie and Pearl. Janice came over, looked at the list, and said, "I knew I liked you, Gordon."

A few minutes later, Janice's girlfriend arrived. She was rangy, her haircut almost identical to mine.

"This is our new friend Gordon," Janice said.

The girlfriend clapped a hand on my back and told me her name was Meredith.

"You don't look like a Meredith," I said.

"That dumb observation will cost you a cigarette," she answered. I gave her one.

The man playing checkers knocked over his beer. Janice walked over with a cloth and spray bottle, told him he'd need to clean up the mess himself.

A look passed across his face suggesting he'd challenge her. Instead, he cleaned.

I spent the rest of the night telling Janice and Meredith stories of Food Land and my terrible apartment, the utilitarian raunchiness of my exploits in the park. I talked more than I had in months, stories burping out of me about Thor/Vince, also Marcy, who'd recently admitted she had a crush on me.

"Does she not have eyes?" Meredith asked.

"You still don't look like a Meredith," I said.

She put out a hand. I gave her another cigarette. Janice asked if I'd decided on names.

"That one's Delores," I said, pointing to her right breast. "The other's Gertrude. Gertie when she's in the right mood."

"Where did you come from, Gordon?" she asked.

I thought to tell her about the handful of third-rate towns I'd grown up in, my mother and me nomads after my father left, but wanted to come up with a better answer. I went to the bathroom. Getting back, I found another beer waiting for me.

"Queer beer," I said.

"Gordon," Janice answered.

I almost teared up at the way she said my name.

I ended up sleeping on an air mattress in her apartment, as trains to Bay Ridge were out due to construction. Meredith went to bed. Janice helped me inflate the mattress, sat next to me when it was full.

"You always bring random patrons home?" I asked.

"I wouldn't call you random," Janice said.

She picked up my water glass, sipped.

"I remembered you," she said. "That first night you came in, you noticed everything. The people at the bar, the art on the walls."

She handed the glass back to me.

Janice's apartment was narrow and dark, though she tried to offset its gloom with a frayed green love seat, a kitchen table painted robin's-egg blue.

"So you're not random," she said, and asked me questions I answered in detail about the first boy I'd been with, the few semesters of college I'd muddled through before money and men and boredom got in the way. I talked about meeting Alan at a party, the comfortable rhythm we'd found, the ending I hadn't seen coming.

Janice and I went onto the fire escape to smoke (one of her few rules was about indoor smoking). She told me about a friend she'd fallen for in high school, her surprise in realizing she was attracted to women. "Like how Alan ended things and you had no idea," she said. "But a good surprise. Also scary."

The sun began to rise. In an apartment across the way, a woman slept close to her window. We saw her shoulder, her dark hair on a pillow. Janice told me she'd never seen her awake before.

We ran out of cigarettes, and I braced myself for Janice telling me she was heading to bed. Instead she took my hand and we walked to an all-night deli to get cigarettes and egg sandwiches, the two of us smoking and eating on a bridge over the Gowanus Canal. Its stink was strong, even on that cold morning.

Back at the apartment, we found Meredith awake, coffee made and waiting. She kissed each of us on the lips, and I wanted more of their easy affection. More of Janice and me smoking until our throats hurt and walking down early-morning streets whose only other life was rats and the stray cats chasing them.

We sat at the kitchen table, knees knocking into one another's. As the sleep I hadn't gotten ached behind my eyes, Janice told us she was thinking of getting a roommate. She was mostly at Meredith's, she explained, though I could tell from Meredith's expression that this roommate idea was news to her. I was thrilled at this development, even though the room for rent was more a hallway, one she had to walk through to get to her bedroom. When Janice tells the story now of how we became friends, of her offering me a place to live within hours of our meeting, she always explains that she'd been able to tell right away that we were a match, how when we talked as night lost out to morning, a sturdiness emerged that she'd felt only a few other times. I felt that sturdiness, too, the thrill at our mutual excitement, how in staying up all night and saying whatever came into my head I felt saved for a time.

I moved in two days later. And a week after, at Janice's urging, I gave notice at Food Land. "I have nothing against working at a grocery store, Gordon," she said. "But I think you want more." Janice, Meredith, and I huddled at the bar that night, brainstorming a list of possible better jobs. Meredith crossed off *baker* as I had no baking experience, also *waiter*, listing the things I'd dropped in the short time she'd known me. Staring at the whittled-down list, quitting turned into a mistake.

"Wait," Meredith said. She pulled the phone from behind the bar and dialed.

Janice often said that Meredith and I—with our meat-less arms and square jaws—could pass for siblings. Janice was our opposite, soft where we were angled, the first person I'd met for whom the word *zaftig* made sense. On the phone, as Meredith mumbled no and yes several times, a pleased expression bloomed across her face. She hung up, handed me an address, and told me to report for duty the next day.

"What sort of duty?" I asked.

"I have an ex who runs a dog-walking service," Meredith told me.

Meredith had exes in most fields that came up in conversation, a fact I found impressive and a concern. I sometimes wonder what would have happened had Meredith been friends with an architect or caterer instead, if everything that came after was the result of the bread crumbs she'd laid out for me to follow.

Janice returned from serving a customer, shook her head and called me sugar when I tried to pay for our beers. She was always calling me names like sugar and hot ass, words I held on my tongue and tried to believe.

"I just got Gordon a job," Meredith said.

"I've never walked a dog," I added.

"You do know how to walk though?" Meredith asked.

She spoke gruffly, a loyalty underneath she did her best to disguise. I saw her goodness in the way she said hello to old ladies on the street, in how once, when they didn't know I was awake, I watched her mouth move up Janice's arm in careful succession.

I pulled Janice's fake-fur coat off its hook and draped it over my shoulders. I walked the length of the bar wearing the sour disinterest so many men in this city claimed.

"What are you doing?" Meredith asked.

"He's walking," Janice said.

She came out from behind the bar, took the coat from my shoulders, and performed a model's strut of her own. She passed people playing board games, the taxidermied boar's head with beads dangling from its tusks, before returning the coat to my shoulders, watching as I walked again. As she and I kept going, gaits more outlandish each time, Meredith tried to bury her amusement.

A few customers eyed me strangely. A straight guy who was always there, who flirted with me, but just enough to let me know the limits of his interest, waved a dollar at me. I took it, pressed it between my pretend cleavage, and laughed at the audacity Janice unearthed in me.

A customer asked Meredith what was going on.

"Walking, it seems," she answered, then moved behind the bar, making him a drink as if she worked there.

The next day at the dog-walking company, Meredith's ex was so relieved I'd shown up that she only asked if I was legal to work. An hour later, she introduced me to Sandra, whose route I was taking over. Sandra seemed to sense I didn't know what I was doing, though she was nice about it. She offered pointers, telling me which dogs would love me no matter what, which I'd have to dominate with my words and actions.

I did the route by myself the next day, moving through apartments the size of houses and brownstones packed with museum-quality furniture. I bought a disposable camera and took pictures of some of the grander places, trying to get a shot of me in those homes. One captured the top of my head. Another a washed-out shoulder. In the only picture that showed my face, my eyes were closed. Looking at it, I understood something Alan had said to me early on, the two of us in bed after an enthusiastic fuck, the excitement of being with him so caffeinated that I was ready to go again. He leaned close, lips red from kissing, and said, "There's something lonely to how you look, you know? Like a junkyard dog."

I told Janice that story after my third dog-walking day, the two of us on the fire escape, splitting a cigarette. We sat close to stave off the cold.

"I don't know about that," she said. "But when we're walking you always look at the ground or above people's heads. When men look at you, you need to look back."

In the apartment across the way, the sleeping woman turned onto her shoulder.

Years later, after the rise and fall of all of this, after the countries I'd ended up seeing and the job I'd been handed then managed to lose, Janice asked me for the umpteenth time about that moment at the bus station when I didn't know I was going to New York until I said the words. I was visiting her and her wife on a cool October day, Janice's belly beginning to round with what would turn out to be her older daughter. We sat on her porch, cups of coffee warming our hands. Janice squinted, showing off a dubiousness she rarely pointed in my direction though when she did it was all I could see.

"And you had no idea you were going to New York before you said it?" she asked. "Like when Alex asks what I want for dinner and I say Mexican the second it comes to me?"

"Exactly," I said.

"But this wasn't ordering dinner."

"I know."

Most of my decisions felt the same to me then, choosing to have a third cup of coffee or dropping out of college or moving in with Alan all answered with the same two words: "Why not." When I tell Janice this now, I cast the me of then as naive, as if my current version sees the way I'd stumbled through my younger years as dangerous and strange. But I still like to think back to that line at the bus station, its air heavy with floor cleaner and exhaust, when the bored clerk looked at her nails and asked, "Where to?" and both of us waited to see how I would answer.

2

In most places I only saw dogs. It felt strange to be left alone in such lavish homes, to use bathrooms larger than my bedroom. I was told by Sandra about the Warhol in one place, the sofa in another that originally belonged to a French monarch. So when I walked into the town house on Morton Street on my fourth day and found a slim, older man wincing at me, I held up my hands and said, "Dog walker."

"Do you think I'm going to rob you?" the man asked. He raised his hands, too.

"Letting you know I come in peace."

"You must be Gordon," the man said.

He had white hair, but his eyebrows were thick and dark gray, lifting to assertive arcs as he came forward to shake my hand. The dogs jangled at our feet.

"I've been able to tell that they like you," he said, wincing again. "An ease they didn't have with Sandra. She had terrible energy."

I didn't know which of the owners this was—Philip or Nicola—though with his Puritan paleness, the puckered droop of his face, he looked more like the former. On the wall behind him hung a large, monochromatic painting.

"I don't want to keep you," I said, leashed the dogs, and left.

The dogs and I walked to the West Side Highway, crossed to its path tracing the river. A few once-forgotten piers were being turned into parks. Others were rotting and ignored. The dogs liked the old piers best, as did I. Something in their creaky abandonment gave me an end-of-the-world calm.

One of the dogs took a shit. They were both King Charles spaniels, their coats white and burnt sienna. The dog looked at the stinking pile (that day, also burnt sienna), then at me.

"Everything matches," I said as I scooped it up.

Wind wound down the Hudson, the sky dulled by clouds. The dogs lunged at a seagull.

A man jogged past in a tiny pair of shorts, his back's architecture showing through his shirt. I tried to catch his eye, wanted closeness rather than distance, a sense I could see things and have them, but he didn't look back. The dogs and I crossed the street.

"Philip was right," a different man said, when the spaniels and I returned. He put a hand on my cheek. This should have felt strange, but I liked the attention, along with the smell of his cologne.

"Philip and I don't usually agree," he went on. "On the menfolk."

I started to blush. He seemed to grow amused. Nicola. He was tanned, with a long, stately nose, his dark hair punctuated by silver streaks. Like many of the rich people I'd started working for that week, I understood that he was older than me, but—with his well-preserved shine—I couldn't sense how much.

"Sandra told us you grew up on a farm," Nicola said.

"Minneapolis," I answered.

"Isn't that where they grow all the corn?"

"I don't know."

"You don't?" Nicola said, voice high and fey. He spoke with a hint of an accent, looked younger than Philip by a considerable margin. "A lovely piece of corn," he added, touching my cheek again.

The dogs retreated to their beds. I hung up their leashes and wrote in the notebook they kept which one had done what business while we'd been out and about.

"I've never met a Gordon," Nicola said.

"I've never met a Nicola," I answered.

Nicola's expression turned pouty.

"Never met a Nicola," he said loudly to Philip, who sat at the kitchen's pristine island, eating a grapefruit. Nicola poured himself some coffee.

"You've met a Philip before, I imagine," Nicola said.

"I think so," I said. "Definitely a Phil."

"Well, this is definitely *not* a Phil."

I wanted them to keep talking, the way they spoke a music whose time signature I couldn't quite catch.

"Sandra also mentioned that you just got here," Philip said. "To the city, as it were."

"A few months ago."

He didn't say anything more, so I added that it was nice to meet them.

"You don't want coffee?" Philip asked. "Nicola, get him coffee. Where are your manners?"

"I'd love one," I said. "But I'll be late for my next dog."

Philip winced again. I began to understand that that was how he smiled.

"You'll have to stay for coffee next time," he said.

"Such a lovely piece of corn," Nicola added.

"You already said that, dear heart," Philip said, then went back to dismembering the grapefruit in front of him.

———

I finished my last walk, eager for a post-work cigarette. But checking my pockets and bag, I discovered I was out. I passed a man smoking on the street. He had thick arms and an assertive, muscular chin. Smoke rose from his mouth in a ghostly plume. Channeling Janice, I smiled and slowed and tried to catch his eye. When I did, when the shift in his expression signaled interest, it was a new kind of hunger I felt, also a new way of being fed.

"You don't have an extra one of those?" I asked.

He pulled one from his pack, placed it between my lips. The lighter sparked against his thumb a few times before it let out a lick of flame.

"You're a cute little thing," he said.

"I'm not little," I answered.

I am average height, was skinny then in the unforced way of people in their early twenties, but often referred to as small (a friend once told me I had a short personality).

Looking at the man's inflated chest and arms, I considered walking away, though knew I wouldn't.

"Let's go," he said.

I followed him down a street, its middle a rash of cobblestones. He took a final drag, threw his cigarette into the air, a somersault of sparks before it landed. I flicked mine into a gutter. We walked into an office building, his hand on my back as he nodded to the security guard and guided us to the elevator, which we took to the eleventh floor. My pulse fluttered against my neck.

We walked past empty cubicles and into a large office, shining plaques crowding one wall. He closed the door, held my shoulders, and turned me so I faced the window.

In seconds, our pants were at our shins. The sex I'd had since moving to the city had been so unremarkable that I turned hard right away. My hands pressed against the window. Downtown's skyline glittered, the lights at the top of the Towers blinked. I heard the condom's damp unraveling, felt an unnerving burn as he moved into me roughly and without warning, though I breathed deeply, working to feel what was good underneath that pain until good won out. His fingers clawed my hips. He grunted out obvious filth about what he was giving me, how much I wanted it. "Shh," I answered, and the man pushed himself all the way into me. I let out a barnyard noise. He wrapped one arm around my waist, another tight on my throat, kissing the back of my neck with the force of a bite. Good feeling grew larger, pain hovering just underneath. I pressed my forehead against the window.

Afterward, the two of us pulling up our pants, I asked if he often brought people to his office for sex. In the dim room I could only see his outline. His belt buckle chimed as it clasped closed.

"This isn't my office," the man answered.

I waited for him to explain, then thought of the confident nod he'd offered to the security guard, the way he'd hit the elevator's buttons as if he'd done it thousands of times. His deceit seemed wondrous then.

"So you wouldn't know where the bathroom is either," I said.

He kissed me and left. I wandered until I found a bathroom. I walked around the office after, stopping at a cubicle. Tacked-up pictures showed friends at a bar, a dog in a sweater. I slid a few pens into my bag. On a notepad I wrote, *I just had sex here.*

"Can I help you?" a voice asked.

A man moved toward me, holding a vacuum at his hip. I wondered if he'd watched us a few minutes before and called the police. Arrest had been a fear of mine since childhood. I'd assumed that each street I'd jaywalked across, the seconds of soda I'd snagged at self-serve places would lead to unwanted contact with the law. That fear went hand in hand with an indignation I felt all the time but rarely showed. Still, the excitement of what had just happened, the man I'd been able to seduce with a look and a question left me too giddy to care about the police or the office this man had to clean or the rain that had begun tapping against the windows.

"Just leaving a note," I answered.

Back downstairs, I wished the security guard a good night.

"You too," he said, with warm familiarity. He was good

looking enough that I would have flirted with him had he seemed game. I thought of my old job and apartment, of Alan's breakup monologue where he insisted that the most reliable part of me was the certainty I'd let him down. I didn't care about any of it now.

Outside, debating whether to run to the subway to stave off the rain, I felt something against my legs: the spaniels from Morton Street, Nicola attached to them.

"You!" he said.

"Just finishing work," I answered.

"You don't work in that building."

Nicola stood under a large umbrella. At certain angles, he was handsome. At others, he had the overlong countenance of a cartoon villain. The dogs—Alice and Lola—tugged on their leashes.

"Busy bee," Nicola said. "Do you drink wine?"

"I drink a lot of things."

Nicola and I shared his umbrella. We passed warmly lit brownstone windows, chandeliers and elaborate cornices centered on ceilings. Rain landed on the pavement in juicy pops.

We found Philip sitting in the living room, a painting behind him that Sandra had commented on when I'd shadowed her. "You probably know them," she'd said, and named an art gallery Philip and Nicola owned and ran. But I knew little about art, nothing about the couple apart from the fact that they were wealthy, the gallery part of that wealth, or at least what made it interesting.

"Look what the dogs dragged in," Nicola said.

"Nicola fancies himself a comedian," Philip told me.

He spoke with baritone benevolence. I wanted him to keep talking.

"We're here for wine," Nicola said.

We walked into their kitchen filled with stainless steel appliances and open shelves. Bowls sat in sculptural stacks. A wall of windows showed off a terrace and garden. Philip uncorked the wine with elegant efficiency.

"Tell us about corn," Nicola said. His smile was blinding.

"What's this corn nonsense?" Philip asked.

"He's from the corn state. Minneapolis."

"Dear heart, that's not a state," Philip said. "And even if you'd said Minnesota, I'm not sure corn is on the menu there, as it were."

Philip seemed older than I'd first suspected. Wrinkles framed his mouth, his knuckles patterned in bunched skin. Perhaps noticing my noticing, he dropped his hands under the counter.

"Corn is so American," Nicola said.

"Nicola's not, in case you hadn't figured that out," Philip added.

Nicola rested a hand on my shoulder. "I found this one with some muscle monster."

"How did you know about that?" I asked.

"I'm not dumb," Nicola said, offering no further explanation.

I blushed. But Philip smiled, lifted his eyebrows, and unleashed a staccato laugh, and I sensed they didn't care, that, if anything, what I'd just done with some man who smelled like horses raised me up in their esteem.

"Everyone used to do that," Philip said. "Sleep with this

or that person, often several at a time. It's a wonder any of us survived. Did you even get his name?"

Before I could answer that I had not, a cell phone on the counter rang. They were an anomaly to me then, something Alan had ranted about, citing radio waves, brains blooming with tumors. Philip picked it up, covered the receiver, and turned to us to whisper, "It's Deidre Holmes."

"Of course," Nicola said, then saw my confusion. "But why would you know who that is? A nice thing about having a farmer in our midst. Reminds us how our world here is itsy bitsy."

Nicola finished his wine, looked down the hallway Philip had disappeared into, and thanked me for stopping by. I finished my drink in one gulping swallow. Nicola opened a closet, pulled out a rain jacket, and handed it to me.

"You need to dress for the weather," he said.

"I'll bring this back tomorrow," I answered.

Nicola shrugged, said it looked nice on me. The jacket was a shimmery gray.

Philip reappeared, asked if I was leaving already.

"Nicola lent this to me," I said as an answer.

"I'm sure he's outgrown it anyway," Philip replied.

"Philip likes to tell me I'm fat," Nicola said.

Discord hung between them. Then Nicola laughed and Philip held out a hand, to shake mine ostensibly, though I saw a bill folded between his fingers. "Thank you for taking such good care of our girls."

Once outside, I found that Philip had given me a hundred-dollar bill, enough for a bounty of groceries, though I'd use it instead to take Janice to a restaurant we otherwise couldn't afford. Rain clapped against the sidewalk and streets, and people without umbrellas or rain jackets ran for safety. I pulled up the jacket's hood and walked in my regular rhythm.

Getting home, I saw our apartment through Philip and Nicola's eyes: the rust-hinged cabinets, the wall behind the stove infected with stains. The love seat crowding our living room where Janice sat reading a magazine. She asked if I had cigarettes.

"Of course," I said.

The rain had stopped, so we climbed onto the fire escape. Light from a nearby F train flashed in and out of our peripheral vision.

"One of the richies gave me this," I said, touching the jacket.

"Let you borrow it, or gave gave?" she asked.

In the weeks I'd known Janice, she'd become, among other things, my mentor. She stopped me each time a man checked me out and I didn't notice, telling me I needed to always look at who was walking by. Now I shared the story with her about the cigarette I'd asked for, the sex it had led to, and she squeezed my shoulder as a coach might after some hard-won point had been scored. Water dripped down the fire escape's banister.

Back inside, Janice scrambled eggs that we ate on a shared plate, covering them with hot sauce so that my eyes watered.

"Sugar," she said. "Next time tell me you don't like it so spicy."

I wiped my eyes, spread more hot sauce across the eggs, and took another bite.

"Oh," Janice said. "Some old man is on the machine for you."

"What old man?"

"Not the guy who just fucked you, I hope."

It was Philip. Janice went to her room to gather clothes for a night at Meredith's. Her packing up left me sad, embarrassed, too, at how quickly I'd come to consider her a basic need.

The phone rang several times before Philip answered.

"Good evening. This is Gordon Wagner, your dog walker," I said.

"So formal, young man," Philip said.

"The dogs need more walking?"

"Tomorrow is fine for all that. But we're wondering about your plans for Friday."

Through her opened door, Janice threw a bra into her bag.

"No important plans," I said.

"Good," Philip answered. "We're having a little dinner."

I pictured myself at their table, conversation pinging back and forth about artists and foreign countries. It felt thrilling, terrifying, too, all the land mines I might unwittingly step on.

"We're hoping you might help us out," he said. "You'd be well compensated."

"Oh. I'm not much of a cook."

"This will be more arranging."

I felt dumb mistaking his call for an invitation, wrote *arranging* on the notepad next to our machine. In her room, Janice tossed clothes around, trying to locate something.

"I'm fine at arranging," I said.

"We knew you would be," he replied, adding that he'd see me then before hanging up.

"Who was that?" Janice asked.

"One of the richies who gave me this coat."

"Or let you borrow it," she said. "He wants it back?"

I didn't want to tell Janice about the party, felt surprised by choosing not to, so I answered, "Dog-walking things," adding, "Tell my sister Meredith I said hello."

Janice gave me a kiss. Her leaving for the night felt like a larger exit, the easy gift of her presence taken away just as fast. I teared up. She rested a hand on the back of my neck, asked what was wrong. I thought to tell her about the note I left at a random woman's desk, how that woman might find it and feel disgusted or that she was being made fun of. Of how, had I not found the bar on a night she was working, I'd still be in Bay Ridge with Thor/Vince and Marcy and the apartment whose fumes I was sure would lead to early cognitive decline. But, still in the raincoat I'd been lent or given, I said, "I just get sad sometimes."

"Why I like you, hot ass."

"My ass is just lukewarm," I said.

Janice kissed my forehead, my eyelids.

"You want me to stay?" she asked.

I did, but said no, told her I'd go for a walk and make wild eye contact.

"Oh," she said. "There's another message for you on the machine, too."

Janice left. I hit play. It was my father. I hadn't talked to him in close to a year. He explained with annoyed surprise that he hadn't known about my move. "I called where I thought you were living and your friend said you were in

New York, that he didn't know how to get in touch with you. I had to call your mother, which was, well. But she and I agree on this New York business. Call me back, please."

I went into Janice's room and lay on her bed, trying to remember the moment when I'd seen the handsome man smoking and, rather than stare at the ground, looked right at him. But thoughts of my father interrupted: early years when he was wildly silly, eyes gleaming during a week Mom "needed a break from us" and went to her sister's. It snowed the night after she'd left that time, and Dad told me we needed to explore. I was eight or nine, easily wooed by his playful carelessness.

We'd piled into sweaters and coats, walked down the middle of streets usually clogged with traffic. Snow transformed parked cars into soft-shouldered hills, muzzled our neighborhood's usual honking horns and loud music and growling arguments. We walked past a playground and into a park. I was thrilled at this adventure, the timidity I usually clung to falling away for a moment.

But then Dad insisted that we walk to the river. Even at my young age, I understood it was too far, our adventure losing out to the beige monotony of obligation. Snow fell harder. A few abandoned cars sat in the middle of the street. My face and fingers ached with cold, my jacket soaked by the snow's weight.

"Dad," I said.

"Almost there," he answered.

It took him several seconds to realize that I'd stopped walking. When he turned around and saw snow past my knees, anything brave and certain in him deflated. I felt the sharp embarrassment of having a parent whose difficult feelings surfaced so easily and often, who cried when he lost a job or if he and Mom were stuck in some fight. Dad's mouth hung dumbly open, and I fought the burying worry that I was just like him.

"Let me carry you home," he said.

Dad had a bad back. He breathed with wet effort when he moved faster than a stroll. But he liked to pretend, thinking it lifted rather than deflated me.

"I'll walk," I said.

Back at the apartment, cold's ache having spread to my feet, Dad told me to get undressed and went to fill the tub. I climbed in. The water's warmth itched and squeezed. As an oily skin of soap spread across the water, my father promised me meals we couldn't afford, movies Mom wouldn't let me see. I lifted a wet hand, placed it on his knee. It left a mark on his jeans. Dad kept talking, about a camping trip we could take, the sleeping bags he'd buy, the propane stove we'd cook on. I filled a cupped hand with water and dropped it onto his lap. He went on about the constellations he'd show me, the new kind of dark I'd experience. I sliced my arm across the water. A wave lifted from the tub and onto his face and shirt. Dad didn't move. Water dripped from his nose and chin, flattened his hair so I could see his red scalp, veins roping up his forehead and under his sideburns.

"You aren't stopping me," I said, livid and ashamed and scared that he'd let me keep going until our bathroom flooded and the water broke through to the apartment downstairs where a lady lived who banged on the ceiling whenever my parents fought or we walked with shoes on.

"I figured you were getting even," Dad said, then went to get me a towel.

In my Gowanus apartment, I walked to our bathroom. Though cluttered with lotions and makeup, it was clean. I wondered if my father, now having found the Lord, had also stopped letting people douse him with water or say they needed a break from him. I dialed his number. He didn't pick up for several rings. When he finally did, his startled hello reminded me that it was late, that I'd woken him up. He said hello again and again, his annoyance more potent each time. I hung up and hoped he didn't have caller ID, though after so many years of near poverty, the idea of him with anything beyond the most basic need was funny to me in the way I see most things as funny and sad at the same time.

I went onto our fire escape to smoke. The woman across the way was awake for a change, her face so different than I'd imagined it. "Hey," I said, but her window was closed. I tried to memorize what she looked like awake, so I could tell Janice the next time I saw her.

3

Some dogs wound around my ankles or jumped on me as if I were a lover thought to be lost at sea. Others eyed me with princely indifference, only leaving the apartment if I dragged or carried them. That day, the talent agent's Pekingese growled when I tried to put on its leash and the handbag designer's Lhasa apsos stopped in the middle of a crosswalk, refusing to continue.

In an elevator after my last walk, a famous actress my mom was obsessed with stepped in just as I was lifting an arm to sniff out any obvious odor. She looked surprised. Then her expression flattened. Perhaps because I equated fame with familiarity, or because I'd never been close to a celebrity before, or because of Janice's advice to engage when I wanted to retreat, I said, "One of those days."

In movies she played downtrodden women. What was most remarkable about her now, apart from the fact that she was quite small, was how clean she looked. I was so used to her hardscrabble version that her blown-out hair and simple dress felt almost like drag.

"If it's any consolation," the famous actress said, "I can't smell you from here."

"You're my mother's favorite," I answered.

Her face fell, with embarrassment or annoyance. In the lobby she left first, greeting the doorman by name. I went to a deli to buy cigarettes and deodorant, jamming them into my bag with the dark clothes I'd packed and my one nice pair of shoes.

Philip and Nicola's was quiet and cool, the floor a gleaming sea. The sofas anchoring the living room looked both crisp and soft, the light from the ceiling fixtures warm and even. Everything—from the pillows on the sofa to the bowls shining on shelves—seemed intentionally spaced, each a point in some invisible geometry. The house's quiet seemed by design, too, and when I walked in and said hello, I realized I was whispering. Philip ushered me into the kitchen.

"If people ask, you're a friend, helping out," he said.

He stood on one side of the kitchen's island; Nicola and me on the other.

"So I make people drinks?" I asked.

"Only if you want to," Philip said.

Nicola nudged my shoulder with his own. He was forty-seven, I'd discovered a few days before, when I dropped off the dogs and found his passport on the dining room table. He looked over at me now, a spray of superficial wrinkles rising around his eyes.

"So when it's time to eat, I'll stay in the kitchen?" I asked.

"You're not the help," Philip answered.

"I feel like I'm being dense."

"You're a friend who helps out," Nicola said. "You have

some drinks. Talk to people as you chop things, tell them
you like to cook. A bit of a lie. But a small one."

He'd told me earlier that week that he was from Mi-
lan. His father owned a handbag factory there and thought
Nicola being around so many purses had led to his love of
men. "As if we're in it for the purses," Nicola had said, "and
not the cocks," all with a sense of performance that made
me appreciate rather than believe him.

Philip put the duck in the oven and asked me to chop
garlic. His brow dropped into a sharp V.

"Is that what you're wearing?" he asked.

"I have other clothes," I said, and pulled the black pants
and button-down from my bag.

"You'll look like a waiter," Philip told me. "Come."

The next floor of their house was sparsely furnished,
paintings centered on its walls. I passed a bathroom with
a glossy-looking tub, then walked with Philip into what I
guessed was their bedroom. On a mantel sat photographs
of them at a younger age, Philip benignly handsome,
Nicola stunning. It was strange to see what age had taken
from them, what it would steal from me someday, too. We
stepped into a closet as large as my living room, where
Philip instructed me to take off my shirt. In the cool room,
my nipples stood at attention. I worried he'd mistake this
as interest then wondered if I could make myself interested,
but Philip was busy digging through a drawer. He pulled
out a gray T-shirt, its softness exceptional.

"Nicola's from a while ago," Philip said, as I put it on.
"He doesn't throw things out, thinks he'll fit into them
again one day."

Philip's side of the closet housed white shirts and gray

pants, boots in a polished row. He walked me up to the third-floor bathroom.

"You can change in here," he said. "Shower, too, if you're so inclined." He must have sensed my embarrassment, because he added, "It might make you more comfortable."

I closed the door and climbed into the shower, used soaps that smelled smoky, medicinal. I got so involved in the shower's assertive water pressure and the products at my disposal that I lost track of time. Remembering where I was, I got out, dressed, and rushed downstairs.

Philip stood alone in the kitchen. He told me I looked much more comfortable, then asked me to chop the garlic again, this time smaller. Nicola came back with flowers and said, "Such a clean farmer, you are."

"Should I tell people I'm your dog walker?" I asked.

"That shouldn't come up," Nicola said.

I showed Philip the newly chopped garlic. He purred out the words "young man" and asked me to make sure the wineglasses didn't have spots. I polished each one, held them to the light to be certain.

"Look at you," Nicola said, and laughed so heartily I could see his cavities and the red bend of his tongue.

Guests began to arrive at eight. "Our friend Gordon," Philip said, introducing me to a man named Marcus with a movie star face and a stout, toddler body.

"I just opened some red," I said.

Marcus lifted a glass toward me.

Within twenty minutes, six other guests had arrived. "This is Friend Gordon," Marcus said to each of them and squeezed my arm. I admired his directness, was put at ease by his flirting. He was on his third glass of wine.

Guests watched as Philip and I chopped and assembled. Steam rose from a pot in a gurgling column.

"You're a chef?" a woman named Audrey asked.

"Just like cooking," I answered.

"You live nearby?" she asked next.

"Gowanus," I said.

"Like the canal?"

"Like the neighborhood."

"I didn't know people lived there," she said, waving a toothpick. "You're an artist then?"

"No."

Her torrent of questions left me flustered.

"And how do you know Philip and Nicola?"

"The third degree, Audrey," Nicola interrupted. "We met him in the neighborhood. He's a lovely new friend."

I found out later that the guests were art world bigwigs. But that night I was too busy trying to straddle the line between helpful but not the help, between being polite to Marcus when he rested a hand on my back without further encouraging him.

Just as people moved to the table, a painter named Pavel arrived. He had a thin, insect-like handsomeness that grew strange when he opened his eyes wide. He sat between Audrey and me, a fleck of paint on his forearm. The rest of him was so carefully put together that the paint felt more accessory than accident. He spoke with a slight accent that came out mostly in his emphasis. (In New York, I'd experienced more accents than I ever had before, the ones in Minnesota variations in a hard-voweled series.)

Pavel passed me the beans. One of the guests raved about the duck. "It's just so special," the man said. I took some beans, passed them.

"You have paint on your arm," I said.

"Oh," Pavel answered, but made no effort to look.

"You're not from here?" I asked.

"Los Ange*lees*," he answered.

Audrey asked Pavel about his new work.

"There's a show planned for autumn," he said. "I'm with Philip's gallery now."

Nicola started in on a story about a painter they all knew who was livid with how a museum in Berlin had hung his work.

"I saw that show," Audrey said.

"I heard they painted the galleries an army green," Marcus added.

"More like pea soup," Audrey corrected.

The guests laughed at jokes I didn't understand, tossed names back and forth I didn't know and kept mentioning a place that sounded like an herb. I went to the bathroom, sat on its lidded toilet, and wished I was at the bar with Janice, where no one talked about painters or wall colors or things with price tags in the millions. Coming out of the bathroom, I found Nicola waiting.

"Sorry, I didn't realize you were out here," I said.

Nicola eyed me with pleased amusement.

"All this talk about paintings and art fairs," he said. "This person's gallery. That person's collection. I find it boring, and it's my job."

"I'm not bored," I answered. "Feels more like people sharing inside jokes."

I sensed Nicola evaluating me. I wanted to be liked by him, even more for him to find me interesting, though I had no idea how to make that happen. Laughter rippled through the dining room. Nicola's eyes stayed on me.

"I saw a famous actress today," I said, wishing I hadn't almost immediately.

Nicola put a hand on my cheek then went into the bathroom.

Back at the table, Marcus—drunkenness showing in the unfocused flatness of his eyes—turned to me and asked, "What do you think about pea soup?"

"I haven't eaten it in years," I answered. People laughed as if I'd said some witty thing.

Someone brought up a show everyone was raving about, though this person wasn't sure if it was amazing or trash. For the next ten minutes, they argued over it. Some agreed that it was spectacular, another person insisted that whenever a certain critic called something a revelation, it was more likely bathroom graffiti. I was amazed not only by the strength of their opinions, but also how easily, how certainly they materialized, when for me, a trip to a diner turned complicated when asked *How do you like your eggs?* and I wanted to answer that I liked them all ways. I also thought of pea soup, which my father had made for me a few times, insisting I'd like it, though I never did.

At the end of the night, Marcus lingered.

"The first to come and the last to leave," I said to him.

"*You* were first, Friend Gordon," he answered.

Philip sorted through leftovers. He seemed to do everything in their house—organizing, managing logistics, constructing complicated meals—Nicola's sole role to charm. What had hardened into regular handsomeness in Nicola had been delicate years before. Large Cleopatra eyes, a knife-edged jaw. Moments of that beauty resurfaced when he smiled a certain way or held his head at a particular angle. But it was all about placement now, and I understood the work it took for Nicola to disguise how time had had its way with him.

"No need to stay and help clean," Philip said to Marcus.

"Friend Gordon is entertaining me," Marcus answered.

He wanted to sleep with me. I wasn't particularly keen on the idea. It reminded me of the park, though at least there it had been a choice, often an excitingly seedy one. As Marcus watched me scrub the stove, I grew more unsure of how to extricate myself. His flirtation had anchored me for most of the night.

"You live around here?" I asked him.

He smiled as he said, "Chelsea," my question translated as interest.

"You're a very nice friend, to help clean up," Marcus added.

"No need to be coy," Philip said, and went to get Marcus's bag.

As soon as Philip disappeared, Marcus kissed me. His tongue pried my teeth open; fingers raked through my hair. His other hand pushed under my jeans and underwear, a finger jabbing at my ass with wormy determination.

"I know we asked you to be friendly to the guests," Philip said, having returned. "Marcus, he's actually the help."

I removed Marcus's hand from my jeans, stacked bowls back where they belonged as if a moment before I wasn't being fondled. Philip blew out the candles. Smoke slunk upward in lazy coils.

"I can wait for you outside," Marcus said.

He kissed me again with Philip only a few feet away, and this dinner suddenly felt like a joke I was the butt of. I missed Food Land in the same way I often, when faced with new, daunting disappointments, longed for familiar ones. I cleaned a wineglass, set it to dry. As acquiescence pushed me toward Marcus, along with a sense that I wasn't getting what I wanted but was at least getting something, what had seemed sturdy about the night turned rickety. I was about to tell Marcus I'd meet him outside, to walk with him to his well-appointed apartment, sex in exchange for soft sheets and drunken interest and the quiet sleep of a rich person's place, when Philip said, "Go home, Marcus," in a scolding tone, and Marcus left.

Nicola, who'd watched the end of this conversation from the hall, threw me a look of playful shock.

"I'm tired," Philip said. He looked toward the stairs rather than at me, disappointed at the stink I'd brought in, the outfit I'd mistaken for sophisticated, the flirtation I'd managed as badly as the Lhasa apsos earlier that day. I missed Food Land again, where no one thought twice about what I was wearing and people had assumed English wasn't my mother tongue. The stairs cracked as Philip walked up them.

"You *are* a busy one," Nicola said. "The muscle queen. Now boring Marcus."

"Busy wasn't my plan," I answered.

Nicola's amusement annoyed me. He poured each of us a whiskey.

"I think Philip's mad at me," I said.

"He's a grumpy drunk," Nicola replied. "I also think he's surprised. I mean, Marcus is low-hanging fruit."

As Nicola finished his whiskey and moved on to mine, I grew certain they'd call the dog-walking service on Monday and ask for someone new. Part of me wanted that, if only to turn this evening into a story of being wronged. Nicola walked me to the door.

"Just tell Philip you drank more than you'd planned to," he said. "He has a wealth of empathy for just that thing."

Nicola kissed me on the mouth. He let that kiss linger, or maybe the lingering was mine, then asked that I make sure the door locked behind me.

Rather than head home, I returned to Prospect Park. Its constellation of streetlamps glowed, the woods on either side of me smudged in shadow. I hoped someone would appear and, with a nod and a few explicit verbs, say what he wanted to do to me, allowing me to give in, one of my favorite feelings.

A man emerged under a streetlamp. He was old. His thin hair and reddish scalp glistened, and bugs stitched the air around him. He nodded. I nodded back, though I was disgusted at the thought of touching him, more horrified knowing that in my first New York months I might have swallowed that disgust and gone with him behind an elm or a maple. The man smiled. There was kindness in that smile that allowed me to imagine the hard pull of his need, the break from it he hoped to find. But going anywhere with him was an end I wasn't ready for. So when he stepped closer, I said, "Have a good night," and his expression hardened. He called me terrible names, his catalog of insults as impressive as it was mean. I walked back down the path, past woods where, in the breaks between this man's raunchy assault, I heard growled inhales of men already occupied. The man stopped shouting. Still, I wanted to get out of the park. Inside my backpack was an envelope from Philip and Nicola, three hundred dollars inside. I sprinted through a meadow in the expensive T-shirt Philip had given or lent me, knowing that, had anyone seen me just then, they would have guessed I was running from trouble, trouble I'd likely caused.

4

One night, I told Janice I'd never swum in the ocean. The next morning, we were on a train to the Rockaways, bathing suits under our clothes. Meredith came, too, as a witness.

"Witness to what?" I asked.

"Your stupidity," Meredith answered, though she was giddy and kept laughing.

A man sitting across from us held himself with Philip's same exacting posture, a reminder of their radio silence since that dinner weeks before, except for one day, when I'd written in their dog notebook that Alice had had a strange bowel movement, and one of them had written back, *noted*.

The train moved aboveground through two-story neighborhoods that looked more Midwest than New York. Then came the Atlantic, so vast and shimmering that I must have made a face.

"Second thoughts?" Meredith asked.

"Only first thoughts here," I said.

At the beach, blowing sand stung our ankles and gulls hovered in the wind. The opaque outline of freighters drifted on the horizon.

Janice and I undressed. I wore a Speedo she'd recently

encouraged me to buy, so small it felt obscene to wear in public, though our only company was a group of wet-suit-clad surfers. Janice had on a polka-dotted bikini, her skin pinked from the cold.

We ran toward the water. Waves flopped onto the beach with wet heft. We were in to our thighs, the cold so acute it burned. A wave gathered, and Janice dove under, but I hesitated and its muscle knocked me down anyway, pinning me to the sandy ocean floor. I was certain I was done for, but as I stumbled to my feet I saw that the water didn't even reach my waist. I paddled out to where Janice lay in a back float.

"I don't think I've ever been this cold," I said.

"You're from Minnesota," Janice answered.

"The cold there is different."

"Different how?"

"Not wet," I said.

Janice wrapped her arms around me. I imagined her as a mother one day, her affection so regular her kids would think nothing of touch or eye contact. My father now reserved his love for the Lord; my mother treated affection like a recently expired food. Janice's tattoo of a woman's face was water-flecked so that it appeared to be sweating. She moved hair off my forehead, pointed to the next breaking wave. We dove under. I opened my eyes to watch the grace with which she cut through the greenish sea, the waves above us rising and crashing and rising again. I grabbed Janice's leg, startling her, but then she saw me, bubbles boiling from her mouth, and in one seamless move yanked my Speedo down, swimming away with it in her left hand.

I was asleep when the phone rang. Staggering to answer it, I saw that it wasn't yet seven in the morning. A pause followed my grumbled hello. Then Philip said, "It seems I've woken you, young man."

Old man, I thought, peevish at his early call. But I told him it was good to hear from him.

"We have to head to London," Philip said. "A last-minute thing."

"Have a nice trip," I answered.

"Thank you. But the dogs."

"I can still walk them."

"Could you come now? We need you to stay with them, if you're able. It's no notice at all, I know. Nicola was meant to ask you."

It was a Sunday, and I'd been thrilled to sleep in. But Philip's call, the chance to be useful while staying at their house was thrilling, too, so I threw clothes into my bag and got onto the subway.

The dogs skittered from room to room. One of them—I still got them mixed up when they were in motion—circled the luggage.

"Gordon," Philip said. He wore sunglasses and a gray sweater. A watch gleamed on his wrist. "You're too good. Nicola!" he called up the stairs.

A silence settled in that I wanted to shrug off, so I said, "I'm sorry that, at your dinner a few weeks ago, I let that Marcus fellow kiss me."

"When Marcus has something in mind," Philip replied. He patted his pockets, found what he was looking for. His rising eyebrows made it clear he had more to say. "Nicola told me, too, that you'd perhaps had one too many."

"I was nervous."

As I knelt down to accept the dog's eager affection, I sensed Philip was looking at me. Part of me wanted to tell him that the sunglasses made his looking obvious, also secretive. But I wanted that attention, to pretend I was so involved with the dogs that I didn't notice my T-shirt riding up or the sunlight brightening my arms. There was a heightened quality to being noticed that I coveted. I moved my fingers down Lola's back, felt Philip follow the path of my hand. His face inched downward as I unknotted my sneaker's laces.

The doorbell rang, and Nicola rushed down the stairs, also wearing sunglasses. I wondered if this was a rich-person thing.

"The farmer here to save us," he said, kissing my cheeks before turning toward the door.

"I can get the luggage," I said.

"No need, lovely Gordon," Nicola answered.

A moment later, the driver came in, grabbed the bags, and wished me a good day.

After Philip and Nicola left, the dogs and I went on an epic walk. We left the Village and passed their gallery in Chelsea, where a series of burnt-looking sculptures was on display. The dogs drank from a clogged gutter. They stopped in the middle of the sidewalk to take endless, hissing pees. Back at the house, I stood in a front window, hoping passing people might get a glimpse of me.

I called Janice to share the luck of my last-minute gig.

"So you're not coming," she said.

"Not at the moment, no," I answered, then remembered our plan to drive upstate to an outdoor sculpture park that afternoon. We were going to bring weed and a picnic and play CDs she and I loved, though Meredith hated them.

"I'm getting paid stupid money to stay with the dogs," I said.

"That's stupid," Janice answered.

Annoyance tightened her voice. I thought of the nights she'd stayed at Meredith's rather than our apartment, trying to tally her neglect and throw it back at her.

"We can go some other time," I said.

"Something else?" she asked.

"What's that?"

"You called to say something else?"

"I just wanted to tell you I can't go today," I said, though I hadn't remembered our plan.

I waited for Janice to say more. When she didn't, I said, "So I'll see you," and hung up.

I turned on the radio, then the television, but my unease at Janice's anger held on. I watched a movie with no recollection of its plot, went on a run in Nicola's exercise clothes, going so far uptown that my knees began to throb and I had to take the subway back. I made pasta with sauce whose label had not a word of English, then wandered to a bar, where I finally found distraction in a man with a Clark Kent jawline. I looked over. He looked back, giving me the attention I always wanted then, still do, I suppose. The man introduced himself. He leaned in as we talked, our banter taking on the urgent weight of secrets.

"We should go somewhere," the man said.

"My place isn't far," I answered.

He picked up my jacket and his so I had to follow him.

Once at Philip and Nicola's, though, the man turned mean. I often liked a bit of aggression, though his carried no playful subtext. He pulled my arm. I told him it hurt, but his tight grip stayed. When he asked how I managed to own such a place, I answered that I was house-sitting and he said, with a snide expression that made him both handsomer and more terrifying, "So you're the butler" and threw his weight against me. He pinned my wrists down, fucked me roughly so that I grimaced, then looked at me like the grimacing was my fault. He came and collapsed on me with the aggressive exuberance of a football tackle, got dressed shortly after.

"Butler," he said, and slid into his shoes.

I smiled, then wondered if my smile was part of the problem, that I wanted roughness but was also afraid of it, that I needed to tell people about this man who'd been terrible to me, not mentioning that terrible was what I'd asked for.

"Make sure the door closes behind you," I said.

He left it open and walked down the sidewalk without turning around.

The next few nights, I stayed in. I tried on Nicola's expensive sweaters, ate sculptural pieces of chocolate, and found it all boring. I wondered if wealth was a kind of deadening, though when I remembered how little I had in my bank account and the heaviness that had plagued me back in Bay

Ridge, I grew angry at my easy forgetting. Once, at two in the morning, I made the dogs walk to the river with me where men used to fuck in droves, though now it was just people sleeping on benches and rats rattling through a garbage can and an old man with headphones on, his music so loud that, as he passed, I heard what sounded like a symphony.

I missed Janice. When I got back to Philip and Nicola's, I called our apartment. The machine picked up. "Just saying hello," I said. When she eventually heard the message, she'd realize it was from the middle of the night. I hoped she'd know that me calling late like that was my version of an apology.

On my last night of dog-sitting (though I didn't know it was my last night then), Janice finally called.

"How are your dogs?" she asked, in her regular, amused fashion.

"They don't let me smoke inside either," I said.

"Those bitches."

"Literally."

I teared up at the return of our easy rhythm. One of the dogs, on the couch it wasn't meant to occupy, looked at me with risen ears.

"You should leave those bitches and come to a party with us," Janice said.

"When?"

"In three hours."

"A party sounds nice," I said, and went to Nicola's closet to find something to wear.

The party was in a warehouse basement in a Brooklyn neighborhood even more abandoned-looking than Gowanus. Rusting steel beams held up the ceiling, its walls damp and cool. Colored lights warmed certain corners, the rest of the place washed in shadow. When Janice saw me, she said my name with a force that ousted the music and competing conversations.

"You came," she said.

"I said I would," I answered. Doubt flashed across her face. But she took my hand and said there were drinks. We moved through the party's swarm of bodies to find them.

A few hours later, when I told Janice I had to leave, her sharpness returned. Anyone's displeasure seemed to me a hair's breadth from injury then, so I told her another hour wouldn't hurt, and she took me to a bathroom to do coke. As two in the morning came and I told Janice I was heading out for real, she pointed to a pair of thin, weary-looking men, with cheekbones and postures that made me think they were Russian.

"Have you talked to Matthew and Dennis?" she asked.

"I've been with you, like, the entire night," I said.

"They told me you're wildly fuckable."

I told Janice to bring me over.

Matthew and Dennis and I exchanged obvious observations about the party and its people. I waited for our conversation to peter out, but each time I made a C+ joke, they laughed and touched my shoulder. As their interest tightened, my awkwardness fell away and I began to speak with audacious authority. When they whispered to each other, I said, "Deciding who's going to ask me to go home with you?" Theirs was a confidence I'd seen for so long as a foreign language. But my closeness to it now, the sense that they wanted me, made me wonder if it was less about a test to pass and rather a feeling to inhabit.

"Actually," Matthew said, "we were whispering about what we want to do to you."

The three of us found a cab from God knows where. In its back seat, one of them kissed my throat. The other squeezed my dick through my jeans. When the driver told us to knock it off, we groped one another more furiously.

Leaving their apartment a few hours later, my dog worries returned. They might be afraid, might have answered my neglect by pissing on an expensive carpet. I had money for a cab, but no cab appeared. So I walked, and the havoc the dogs had likely wreaked ballooned to destroyed cushions and curls of tart vomit, vases broken into several sharp pieces. Whenever a car passed, I hoped it was a cab, though it never was, though once the people inside a car rolled down their windows and asked me what I was staring at. I gave them a thumbs-up and turned a corner.

Back at the house, the dogs jumped and circled me, shivering as I picked up their leashes. But before I could get them outside, one, then the other, peed across the floor. I ran for paper towels, annoyed at their overactive bladders, relieved that their piss had only marred the hardwood.

I hadn't eaten dinner, so I heated up leftover Thai food. Next, I ate a pint of ice cream, then finished with a pungent wedge of cheese, its price tag so absurd that, as a bite oozed down my throat, I said to the dogs, "That was probably a four-dollar swallow."

Shortly after, I threw up, then passed out on the sofa. I woke up late the next morning to the dogs' tongues dampening my face and ankles. My outfit from the night before lay crumpled across the floor.

The dogs and I had just come back from a walk when I saw a message blinking on the machine. As I pressed play, Philip's tired baritone filled the room.

"Gordon, we've just landed," he said. "We will see you soon."

I sped through the house, collecting the plates and mugs and clothes I'd left everywhere. Each car outside I assumed was theirs. Each clicking branch the front door opening. As I stuffed sheets into the washing machine, I thought I'd throw up again, but the feeling passed. The phone rang. Hoping it was Philip with news of traffic or construction, I answered. It was my father.

"Thought you were living at that other number," he said.

"Mostly, I am," I answered.

"Gordon," he said, a dripping pity in his voice I had no interest in.

"This is where I work."

"Your girlfriend said you were staying there, with some men."

"You know she isn't my girlfriend," I said.

He sighed. I used to be expert in his sadness, his happiness, too, especially when it spun wild. But Philip and Nicola would be back any minute, and I was angry at Janice for giving Dad this number, at him for using it.

"You can't," I said. Exhaustion amplified my anger. "You can't just come and go."

"I'm not," Dad said with a self-satisfaction that allowed me to forget how I'd once felt close to him, or rather a sense of closeness that was right around a corner, a conversation in another room whose words I couldn't quite make out. "I'm just worried about you."

I answered that I'd outgrown being worried about, though I wanted exactly that, people up at night wondering about my finances and feelings. I told Dad I'd call him soon.

A cab pulled up outside. A woman from across the street—she had an ancient, foggy-eyed cocker spaniel—tottered out of it. I made coffee, and bought flowers at a nearby deli, arranging them in a vase. I was putting away glasses when the front door unlocked. The dogs let loose a series of tandem barks. Nicola saw the flowers and coffee and looked at me like I was a precious mineral. I wanted to be that. Wanted, too, not to need his look to authenticate my value.

"Young man," Philip said.

"Stay and have coffee with us," Nicola added.

Philip's brow dropped, darkening his look of tired goodwill.

"You need to settle in," I said.

I kissed each of them on the lips, wondered why I'd done it, and left.

At home, I flopped onto my air mattress and fell asleep. I woke up hours later to darkness outside and the ringing phone.

"Why am I so popular?" I mumbled, though even in jest that notion thrilled me. Philip said hello before I had the chance to.

"Did I wake you again?" he asked. "We have a good doctor. You could go to him for your sleep problem."

I assured him there was no problem. He asked if I could stop by in the morning. "Before your other dogs."

Worry wound through me. I might have broken something, missed a security camera that showed them the company I'd kept. Or my father had called again, asking what I really did for them.

"We have a proposition," Philip said. "Though I think young people use that word in a more carnal way than is my intention."

I asked him what time. He told me. On the notepad next to our phone, Janice had written: *Your Dad called 5x.*

I walked to the bar, hoping to find Janice there, to call her out for having shared Philip and Nicola's number. But when I arrived and saw her there, all my imagined chidings dropped to the floor. Janice handed me a drink.

"Queer beer," I said.

"Sometimes I think you only like me because I serve you," Janice answered.

She smiled, though I sensed its reluctance, trust's frayed edge.

"I'll happily serve *you*," I said.

"What happened?" she asked. "Last night, I mean."

I told Janice about Matthew and Dennis, amplifying the already considerable length of Dennis's dick to claim it had probed previously unexamined parts of me.

"Like a deep-sea explorer," Janice said.

"Cock Cousteau," I said.

Janice laughed and topped off my beer.

It got late, the bar about to close. Janice asked if I wanted to wait for her.

"Always," I answered, and hoped that was true.

Janice moved her finger across the scar on my forehead. "You never told me about this."

"My father," I said.

Her attention sharpened, so serious it startled me.

"He didn't like hit me or anything, but that scar, he's the reason."

"Also the reason you don't answer his messages?"

There was no single event to point to, no hinge between before and after, though when I tell people about him, it's sometimes easiest to cite the accident or his unswerving devotion to the Lord rather than what was truer, that like an artery's blockage, our end was an accumulation.

"Yes and no," I answered.

"Very specific," Janice said.

But there was no easy answer to give. I could tell her

that my father confounded me, that in moments I'd loved him with a fierceness my young self didn't know what to do with, that I'd been ashamed of him with that same wild fire, and learned early how loving someone meant to also see the ways they were pathetic and small.

As we finished cleaning the bar and Janice clicked off the lights, I hoped what she and I had would return without her anger's bitter aftertaste. In the years since, Janice is the person I've become closest to, though we live far apart now and don't have to share the stultifying slog of the day-to-day. Still there are moments when she's failed me with a force I'm undone by, and I hate to consider the ways I've surely done the same to her. Years after we'd lived together, when Janice and her wife had decided to try for kids, she mentioned casually that they were going to use the sperm of her wife's dear friend. I'd called to report on a mediocre date but cut the story short, sure Alex and Janice had ruled me out, that they saw me as too caustic and strange, too easily wooed by self-pity. I didn't call her again for weeks. When Janice reached out, she acted as if everything were normal. Perhaps that was easier, just as it seemed easier for me to nurse my hurt rather than decide whether I wanted someone with my genes out in the world, scared and mean and miserly in the way I can be, though I try and remind myself that I also experience moments, even now, of such joy that I cry or laugh or have to walk for hours to manage its electricity.

Janice double-checked the locks on the bar's front door.

"I said yes and no before, because that's the only way I can answer," I said.

"I know, Gordon," Janice said, and hailed a cab though

we only lived a few blocks away. The cabdriver asked why we didn't just walk. Janice repeated our address, then tapped on the plexiglass barrier. The driver pulled out onto Fourth Avenue, moved neck and neck with the handful of other cabs taking people home.

5

The proposition: that I quit dog walking and become their personal assistant. They'd had one before, Philip told me, thought they didn't need one again.

"We were wrong," Nicola added.

The three of us sat in their dining room. Nicola, just back from the gym, drank a smoothie. Sweat darkened his hair. Philip, stoic and straight shouldered, asked what I made walking dogs, offered me ten dollars more an hour, and put out a hand. Usually, I loved that feeling, the breathless excitement from just catching a train, but now I didn't trust it. I wanted to tell them that I hadn't even been qualified to walk dogs, that my last job in Minneapolis had been as a host at a mall restaurant with giant menus and a sad, bounteous salad bar and customers who tried to use expired coupons. But the money was good, and dogs had become tedious. I accepted Philip's hand. He beamed, telling me they were having a party that weekend at their upstate place and were hoping I could help out.

"For his birthday," Nicola interrupted. "A big one."

"Happy birthday," I said.

Nicola asked if I was curious about Philip's impending new age.

"Not really," I said.

"But this weekend," Philip asked. "You're free?"

"I can make myself free," I said, though there was a party for Meredith's birthday, and missing it would surely rekindle Janice's sharp-edged annoyance.

"A costume party," Nicola said. "Something you might not have expected. Dressing up is one of Philip's favorite things."

"So it's upstate," Philip repeated. "Did I mention that already?"

"His memory's beginning to go," Nicola said, and pointed to the blender he'd just used. "Your first task."

"Gordon's not our housekeeper," Philip insisted.

"I don't mind," I said.

Nicola went upstairs. I cleaned the blender, put away the fruit and powder he'd used.

"That's not the job," Philip said. I told him I knew, but that part of the job was being flexible. Philip answered that he was late for a meeting.

"Nicola's late, too?" I asked.

"Nicola is late as a general rule. Thinks it shows insouciance."

In the time I'd known them, they'd shown each other no outward affection. Part of that made sense to me (I found out the next day that Philip's upcoming birthday was his seventieth). But there must have been something in Philip's deep voice and wry smile that captured Nicola still, the man he'd fallen for fifteen years before just under the surface, a palimpsest. I cleaned a pair of coffee mugs. Philip's embarrassed expression stayed.

"Someday I'll tell you about the terrible jobs I've had," I said. "And you'll understand that a few dishes is nothing."

After Philip left, I used their phone to give notice at the dog-walking service.

"But this job," my supervisor said. Her name was Deb. "It was a favor to Meredith."

"I thought you were desperate for someone," I answered, adding that I could continue for the next two weeks.

"No need," Deb said, and told me she'd shadow me the next day, which she did silently, except for when the TV actress's saluki wouldn't move until I picked it up and carried it outside.

"I hope you didn't do that every day," Deb said.

"Of course not," I lied, though when I'd decided to start carrying the dog rather than drag it through the door I'd seen it as a feat of problem solving.

I got to their house after my last dog-walking day with flowers Nicola had ordered. Philip and Pavel the painter were there.

"Flowers for you," I said to Pavel. He looked confused.

"He's joking," Philip said. "But he's such a dear to get us these."

"You're a florist?" Pavel asked.

"Jack of all trades," Philip answered. "Come, Gordon. Look at the painting Pavel's brought over."

On the dining room wall hung a small portrait, the head

and shoulders of a young man painted in assertive colors, in crude strokes I assumed were intentional.

"We're debating whether or not to frame it," Philip said. "I think it's perfect as is."

"A frame marks where the painting begins and ends," Pavel answered. The accent I'd detected at dinner resurfaced.

"But the painting does that," Philip said.

"It's up to you, of course," Pavel replied, in a dismissive tone I hadn't heard anyone use with Philip before.

"What do you think, Gordon?" Philip asked.

They stared at me. Philip's clean, soft face, Pavel's taut and angled. His nose was large, his mouth small, a mismatched strangeness that worked in unlikely harmony.

"A frame could be nice," I said.

"Gordon, ever the middle child," Philip said. "You *are* a middle child, aren't you?"

"Only," I told him.

"Me too," Pavel said.

"Well," Philip said. "Gordon's a genius at many things, but even he'll tell you he isn't an artist."

"It's true," I answered. "The frame was just a vague opinion."

"The best kind," Philip said, just as Pavel added, "I'm not sure what that means."

Philip invited us for coffee. One sip in, a phone call came in that he needed to take.

"I like it," I said. "The painting. It's striking."

Nothing on Pavel's face registered my compliment.

"You grew up on a farm?" he asked.

"Minnesota," I said.

"A thousand islands there."

"Lakes."

"Geography was never my forte," Pavel said.

"Forte sounds like a word you'd use."

The stillness of Pavel's face was that of a sleeping person, but his eyes were laser focused, as if examining the smallest unmoving thing.

"A useful word," he said finally.

He walked to the windows. I followed. Pavel was a few inches taller than me, pale, blue veins mapping his jaw. He was thin, apart from his arms, which were stacked with muscle and made me wonder if he did something for work that involved heavy lifting. His astringent smell filled the space between us.

"Do you have a job?" I asked. "Besides painting, I mean."

A blip of a smile before his blankness returned.

"I just paint," Pavel said.

Outside, a squirrel scurried back and forth.

"Prague," he said. I tried to figure out what I'd just missed. "When you asked where I was from at dinner. I've been in the States since I was twelve, but once a foreigner, I suppose."

"I didn't mean to be rude," I said.

"I know," Pavel answered.

I was washing our coffee cups when Philip returned.

"Pavel," he said. "Let's keep talking, to frame or not to frame. Gordon, could I trouble you for one minute?"

Pavel left. I'd hoped to walk out with him. His strange, cricket-like demeanor left me nervous, hopeful, and I wondered if sleeping with him would be a demerit in Philip's eyes. Philip asked me to pick up pastries in the morning, also that, once I delivered them, I stay to cut up fruit.

"A major client," he said. "I could take her to Bouley or Wallsé. Still, she wants to be invited to my home and eat eggs I've scrambled for her."

Unsure if he wanted commiseration or a compliment, I said, "You're a great cook."

"Adequate."

I agreed to be there by nine.

Outside, I was thrilled to find Pavel waiting. I lit a cigarette. He asked for one. His cheekbones sharpened as he inhaled. He thanked me for the cigarette, kissed my cheek, and left. Watching his shoulders recede in a steady float, I knew Pavel would soon grow into a considerable distraction.

––––––––

At the bar that night, I told Meredith and Janice about the new job, the party my bosses needed my help with that weekend.

"Helping how?" Meredith asked.

"This and that," I said.

"Very specific."

Janice, eyes on the drink she was making, asked, "Did you just quit the job Meredith got for you?"

"I offered to stay on until she found someone else."

"Noble of you," Janice said.

"Come now," Meredith intervened. "They're paying him more."

"But you already had plans this weekend," Janice said.

The toughness I'd marveled at in her when she dealt

with difficult customers and catcalling men grew thornier when pointed in my direction.

"It's a lot more money," I said.

I reached for her hand, but she stacked glasses and poured beers, lingering at the bar's far end. When she came back her face had softened, and I saw an opening.

"When they asked me to work this weekend, after what they agreed to pay me," I said, "I didn't know how to say no."

"You need to work on that," Janice answered.

Under the bar's colored lights, she looked almost like Pavel's painting.

"I do," I said. "I need to work on that," those words a cleansing, though I also remembered the times my father told my mother he could change, how she believed him, then regretted her wasted optimism.

"Honey," Janice said. "Just don't become one of them."

"One of what?" I asked.

Her look told me to stop pretending not to know things about country houses and matching dogs and last-minute European trips. How easily Philip and Nicola's life could move from mockery to aspirational.

"I wouldn't," I said, knowing, too, that wanting often beat out promises.

"What are you two talking about?" Meredith asked, when she returned from the bathroom.

"Dogs," I said.

"Rich queens," Janice added.

Meredith took a cigarette from my pack, waved it in the air, like a baton. "Same difference," she said, then told us she was hungry. I went across the street, got a pizza for the three of us to share. I hadn't eaten all day, and as I picked up another slice with the last still in my mouth, Meredith said, "Look at him."

"Yes," I answered. "Look at me. Look at me, look at me," and Meredith laughed until her eyes watered, though when I asked her later what had made it so funny, she didn't explain.

6

The dogs and I arrived upstate first, in a rental car crammed with food and flowers, Alice and Lola in the passenger seat either nuzzling my shoulder or pawing the dashboard. I was so busy managing them and worrying I'd forget the house alarm's code that I didn't take the place in until we were safely inside.

The house was modern, ringed in floor-to-ceiling windows, with a living room that could have housed my apartment three times over. Everything, from the floors to the countertops, looked polished, and the river shimmered through the windows. Upstairs were four bedrooms with large beds and light pouring in and, of course, art. Abstract paintings filled one room, line drawings of flowers and men hung in another. I wanted to lie on each bed, leave indents on duvets as pristine and white as new paper. Instead I went into a closet, found a striped T-shirt, and put it on along with a pair of shorts Nicola wouldn't have fit into again with even the most draconian fitness regimen. I found the first-floor room where I'd stay. As I looked at its bed jammed into a corner, its only window darkened by shrubs, Nicola and Philip's generosity turned piddling. Still, I thawed beef stock and washed lettuces. And just before they were scheduled to arrive, I put the T-shirt and shorts in my room, telling myself they'd never miss them, though I wonder if I saw what I was doing then as stealing or as a perk of my employment. Or if—like Nicola and his aspirational clothes—I knew what was true, but preferred the nonsense I'd invented.

The annual costume party—Philip called it his "silly indulgence"—always took place on the weekend closest to his birthday. That year, eight people were staying over, other guests in nearby houses and hotels.

Philip and Nicola were driven up by Adam, a man who took them on any trips longer than a cab ride but shorter than a flight. Philip walked into the kitchen right away to marinate the pork roasts. I chopped what I was asked to chop. Nicola disappeared into their basement gym. For his Plato costume, he'd wear a toga that would show off much of his chest and back. I turned to Philip and said, "The unexamined abs are not worth having." Any laughter I'd heard from him before paled in comparison. As I washed parsley, I chided myself for how much his laughter lifted me. But there was a pull Philip had, a sense he deserved all that was his, that he could change his mind and suddenly deserve other things.

"What's *your* costume, young man?" Philip asked.

"I didn't realize I needed one," I said.

Philip winced, rinsed his hands, and told me to follow him.

A guest room's walk-in closet housed racks of costumes. Hangers whispered as he moved them.

"I grew up in a family of serious people," Philip said. "My father was in banking. My mother had been a debutante and a great beauty, also quite stern. She had relatives in Jamestown, if that gives you a picture."

"With the Kool-Aid?" I asked.

"That was Jonestown," he answered. "I'm talking about Virginia."

I made a comment about John Smith, and he said, "Exactly."

Philip went on about his mother who rarely drank or smiled, who he didn't realize until his adulthood had been depressed. A yearly costume party for her birthday had been her one joyful indulgence. She'd transform their house in Beacon Hill, hiring actors to dress up as royalty or monsters.

"There was one year, I was maybe fifteen, and I'd had it," Philip said. "I didn't want to play dress up with my mother. Teenagers, I find, have an unparalleled capacity for a self-involved sort of cruelty. I told her I wanted to spend that weekend with friends, maybe go to the movies."

"And it broke her heart," I posited.

Philip moved through a series of costumes that may have been Egyptian.

"She canceled the whole thing. She'd invited fifty people. Told them not to bother. 'Look what you did,' she said, on the morning of her birthday. She was smoking at breakfast, something she never did—she had all sorts of opinions about smoking and laughing and music at the table. Then she returned to bed."

I thought to put a hand on Philip's back, but doubt squelched that impulse.

Philip handed me a white suit and vest, a pair of black boots. "The shirt Nicola wore with it seems to be missing, but if you button up the vest, it'll almost be the same."

"It'll show off my cleavage," I replied.

"You *are* a funny one," he said. "Try it on."

Not wanting to seem prudish, I took off my shorts and T-shirt. I slid on the pants; the vest and jacket. After I stepped into the boots, Philip walked me over to a mirror.

"You know what movie you're in?" he asked, and I nodded.

I wished I'd known Philip as a younger man, when he might have worn revealing costumes himself, his parties frenetic and raunchy, him the hub around which things spun.

The dogs found us in the guest room and dropped onto its rug. Philip kept looking at me. Though I had no interest in sleeping with him, I didn't want him to stop looking either.

"It's amazing," he said.

"Me forgetting a costume?" I asked.

"How you and Nicola's former self are the exact same size."

Philip went downstairs. I stayed in front of the mirror, lifting my arms, shifting my hips to see how others might see this costume on me when I danced or cooked or walked into a room.

A few hours later, guests arrived. Some wore elaborate costumes, including a queen who came as a queen I'd never heard of. His wig was a spire of curls, fake birds woven into it. The few men closer to my age had on costumes that showed off their bodies—a sexy Viking, a sexy sailor. The sailor, Andrew, worked at the gallery. In my few interactions with him, he'd toggled between annoyed and indifferent. But when I opened the door, he said, "Oh, you!" kissed my cheek, then asked where to put the wine he'd brought. Most of the guests, though, lived in that nebulous haze of elite middle age. A few of them had on sexy costumes, too, including a woman named Helen who showed up as Aphrodite. She was bone thin, with narrow, muscled arms, and I wondered at the deprivation required to sustain such an austere version of herself. As I brought more ice to the poolside bar, Andrew and the Viking came over for vodka.

"Did you see Helen?" Andrew asked.

"Isn't Aphrodite the goddess of fertility?" the Viking asked back.

"Well, that ship has sailed."

Their faces pinched with callous amusement. I wanted to defend Helen, though she didn't strike me as a particularly pleasant person. But saying nothing was a complicity I'd be buried under, so I told them, "Unlike us, Helen was fertile once."

Mistaking this for another barb, the Viking said, "I bet her insides have been shriveled up since the day she was born," and slipped an olive into his mouth.

"There's a better party we're going to soon," he added.

"Better how?" I asked.

"Greg has to stay, I think," Andrew said.

"Who's Greg?" I asked.

"Your name?"

"Gordon," I answered.

"I knew it was something with a *G*," Andrew said, his

tone implying that he'd tried, his trying enough. I poured myself a drink.

"Greg does have to stay," I said. "This is his form of employment."

Shortly after the food was served, the younger guests left for the better party. Those who stayed danced on the poolside patio. The sun's last embers dimmed behind the Catskills, and a string of lights was flipped on. A few people clapped at their arrival, then laughed at themselves for clapping, the crowd looser now that the younger guests, apart from me, had gone. A gregarious, gray-haired photographer named James took on the role of DJ. The dozen dancers shouted in approval at each new track he played. I was dancing with a woman named Rebecca when a car pulled up in front of the house.

"I wonder if that's the police," I said to her.

"Wouldn't that be something," she answered, holding space between each word in hopes of passing for sober.

I went inside, opened the door, and found Pavel. Part of me had hoped he'd appear; a louder voice had tried to warn me against adolescent pipe dreams.

"I heard they'd poached you," he said, and kissed my cheek. A scratch from shaving interrupted his smooth neck, his hair damp from a shower or swim.

"The other young ones have gone already," I said.

"What other young ones?"

I said the Viking and sailor's names. Pavel shrugged.

"Where's *your* costume?" I asked.

He lifted a mask to his eyes. It was a delicate red, adorned in hand-painted feathers.

"You have a place in these parts?" I asked. "A country house?"

"A friend lets me use their house from time to time," he answered.

Nicola, toga slipping from his shoulder, embraced Pavel. Helen and a rail-thin man sat at the edge of the pool, kicking up arcs of water.

"Pavel, meet Plato," I said.

Pavel allowed Nicola to pull him onto the makeshift dance floor. He was, to my surprise, an exuberant dancer. His hips caught the song's rhythm. His shoulders and hands found quieter percussive waves to ride. One song ended. Another began. Philip raised his hands in the air, danced over to James the DJ, and kissed him on the mouth. He could dance, too, but his movements stayed careful, Philip both enjoying himself and watching each time his feet touched the ground.

Rebecca waved me over.

"Was it the police?" she asked. I nodded.

"But you charmed them," she said, insisting I dance with her again.

A minute later, as I spun Rebecca around, I saw Pavel walk back to his car. I caught his eye. He waved and left.

Rebecca called the next song "the best one ever," though seconds later she went from dancing to swaying. We stayed that way, slow dancing to a fast song, and I wondered about the friend whose place Pavel borrowed, if friend was the right word to use.

A man jumped into the pool. Nicola splashed in next. Soon, most of the guests were in the water. One woman, stripped to her underwear, stood at the pool's far edge and performed a perfect flip. People clapped as she surfaced. She gave them a small, sheepish bow. I was moved by their clapping, by people my parents' ages and beyond jumping and diving and half naked, discarded costumes drifting across the pool's surface with the elegant indifference of jellyfish.

"Come in," Rebecca called from the water. Her dress was still on—she'd come as some ancient painter—and ballooned around her.

"I think this is polyester," I said, but she shook her head.

Nicola floated in his underwear next to a woman named Veronica, who I found out later was good friends with Hillary Clinton. I stripped to my briefs and moved to the edge of the pool. James, the DJ, whistled. Nicola called out, "There he is!" Philip sat in a lounge chair (he was dressed as an explorer, in a helmet and velvet pantaloons), his face dark so I couldn't tell if he was watching.

I dove in. The water was perfect. I wished Janice was there with me so she could understand why I'd had to go, for her to float close, a relenting grin spreading across her face as she whispered, "Yes, this makes sense to me now."

⸻

After a few more hours of dancing, then beignets the guests ate as if they'd been without food for days, followed by James inviting me into the pantry to do coke, grabbing my ass as I leaned down to sniff, but in a way I understood was playful rather than sexual, the guests left. The town's one available cab picked people up, dropped them off, then came back for more. At three in the morning, there was finally quiet.

Philip and the overnight guests went to bed. Nicola and I cleaned. A small army of glasses crowded the counter.

"You're a good farmer," Nicola said. Then he kissed me. I hadn't been interested in him, but with the enthusiasm of his kiss, my interest materialized.

"Let me show you the barn," he said.

It sat behind the house, empty apart from some tools and crates of spare dishes. Toward the back, extra lawn furniture sat in a neat row. Nicola brought me to a chaise longue.

"I worry this is stupid," I said.

"Listen, Gordon," Nicola said.

"You usually call me farmer."

"A nickname, yes. But listen."

Our knees touched. Booze leaked from his mouth and pores.

"I'm with a lot of people," he said. "Philip, too. Or he used to be."

"He's lost interest?" I asked.

"He's still very interested. But finding other interested parties . . ."

Nicola tried to pass this off as humor, though I sensed he saw Philip as both a crystal ball and cautionary tale.

"But I work for you," I said, even as Nicola kissed me and I kissed him back.

I knew this was a mistake, one I'd enjoy, his single-minded attention a web I was unlikely to outwit. Nicola kissed my throat. His fingers slid under the vest he'd worn a decade before. I let out a noise, and he looked pleased at the effect he had.

"I'm not the jealous or vengeful type," he whispered. "I don't see you as that either."

"I don't think I am," I said.

"So this can be as big or small as we want it to be. Something or nothing or every once in a while."

Nicola was a great salesman. Perhaps that made him such an asset at the gallery.

"Let's keep it small for now," I said.

We made out and jerked each other off. Of course Nicola had a lovely dick. Big but not wildly so. Well groomed, perfectly straight, a delicate foreskin.

After we were done, we lay on the chaise. Its frame dug into my shoulders.

"Will you tell Philip?" I asked.

"Will I tell Philip," Nicola said, patted my thigh, and headed inside.

Walking back to the house after giving him a head start, I tried to calculate how stupid I'd just been.

I was drifting in and out of sleep, the sky shifting to the dull gray of soon-to-be morning, when I heard a noise. In the bathroom next to my room came retching, then sickness's wet rush. I left my room for the kitchen, thinking the person might need something. Even more, I was curious. The toilet flushed, water ran. I put dishes away.

The door opened and Philip stepped into the kitchen. A few hours before he'd been drunk. A boa had appeared that he'd worn, twirled. His startled expression now turned my curiosity to voyeurism.

"I didn't wake you, I hope," he said.

I shook my head, told him thoughts of cleaning had woken me. He seemed to see through my excuse, but was polite enough to pretend, and said, "To be young again," then returned to his room.

An hour later, Rebecca appeared.

"Did you even sleep, Gordon?" she asked.

"A few hours, I think."

As we drank coffee, she told me stories of the gallery's early years. She'd worked for Philip until she'd decided she needed to break up with New York and moved to Vermont, where she taught art at a hippie boarding school.

"Philip is loyal," she said. "Even though I imagine he seems distant and strange to you."

When my bosses came downstairs, I was making the guests eggs. Nicola appeared first. He kissed everyone good morning, gave me an easy smile, and went out for a swim. Perhaps what we'd done was, as he'd insisted, inconsequential. Philip showed up next. He made requisite jokes about all they'd drunk, what James had forced people into. When I told him his eggs were almost ready, he rested a hand on my shoulder and called me "the best young man."

The only hint that he was rattled came later in the day. I was packing the rental car I technically wasn't old enough to drive when he said, "Gordon, could you take the dogs back with you? I need a few days off from their demands."

He and Nicola weren't coming home until Tuesday morning, back for just a few hours before flying to an art fair that wasn't the name of an herb after all. Competing feelings swooped in: the annoyance that they thought nothing of my availability, the thrill at the additional pay. But I was becoming essential to them, being needed a drug I couldn't turn down.

Rebecca and I left at the same time. In the driveway, she turned to me and said, "You're good for them, for Philip especially."

It was a perfect early summer day, the sky a blazing blue, grass in a neighboring meadow bobbing in unison. Rebecca stood between the rental car and me.

"I don't mean to overstep," she said.

"You're not," I answered, dumb to what she was talking about.

"It's just that Nicola," she said, "can be slippery. Always finds a way to get what he wants."

"Makes him a good salesman."

I thought of the walk to the barn, the house behind us with some windows still lit.

"But you understand," she said. "I'm not mad, you know. And don't like to share people's secrets."

I tried to think of a way to make it clear that Nicola and I weren't anything, that a small thing had transpired that wouldn't happen again. But all I could come up with was the word, "Noted," then, "No worries."

Rebecca wished me a safe ride back. The dogs stared at me through the car's windows.

On the ride home, I thought of what Rebecca had seen, what Philip knew, what that meant for me. Though part of me worried about Philip's feelings, my larger concern then was self-preservation. When I talk to Janice about it now, she says that I wasn't being selfish but taking care, and I answer that both can be true, that both were true for me.

Back at Philip and Nicola's, the dogs hopped onto the sofas they weren't meant to be on. I put food away and checked the machine for messages. There was a reminder about a dentist appointment for Nicola I'd have to reschedule, a message from a woman in smoky French. The next was for me. "Since you aren't getting my messages at the other number, I thought I'd try here again," my father began. "I'm wondering if this is where you live now. Just tell me when you call back."

He called as if we talked all the time, insisting he had important things to say, when by important he meant disapproving.

I erased his message.

The next day, I waited until I thought he'd be at work to return his call. I began my message by telling him that he needed to stop contacting me at my job. As I talked, I grew livid at not being listened to, and thought of a play I'd once seen where a character lamented about the attention that had to be paid. I wrote *attention* on a scrap of paper and ended my message with this: "I don't leave random messages where you work." This was petty, also true, though I didn't know where Dad was working then, or if he even had a job.

7

My father was in his late forties when I was born, my mother a decade his junior. After so many years when she'd been convinced that she'd end up alone, the relief of his interest blinded her, and it wasn't until she was married to him and pregnant with me that she realized she didn't want him. But, like the jobs she lingered in until she turned too disgruntled to function, she stayed. She picked fights with him over trivial things. In turn he saw critique in her most bland observations, often answering with avoidance or overreaction. Recently, Mom told me it was like she ended up with two kids when she'd bargained for one, that she'd married Dad for a sturdiness she'd expected him to offer. But he'd looked to her for that same thing, and when neither of them had it, disappointment became their shared language, and they held fast to what didn't work rather than hold on to nothing at all.

Dad was also, for a brief time, my best friend. In terms of the way each of us focused our attention tight on the other, but also in our shared, petulant need. Dad got hurt when I didn't laugh at his jokes. I got hurt when he treated my sadness as comedy. But he transformed the hours after school with trips to the department stores to try on clothes we couldn't afford; his favorite albums blared at home until neighbors complained. There were dinners of sugared pop-corn. Snow days where we scavenged through drawers and coat pockets until we found enough money to go to the movies, Dad crying when things didn't work out for the main character, also when they did. But when he lost a job or when he and Mom were stuck in a barbed rut, he'd stay in bed all day or drive around until he ran out of gas or eat in front of the television with an urgency that looked more like injury.

There were a few bright pockets between him and my mother. The dinners where he told a terrifically funny story and she coughed with laughter. At Mom's sister's wedding, the two of them danced close and shared a single piece of cake with a frank interest I found thrilling and embarrass-ing. Another time, after Dad dropped a chunk of weight, I noticed them looking at each other with famished attention. Mom stood behind him when she didn't know I was in the room and pulled at the skin on the back of his neck. He pressed her against the kitchen cabinets so hard utensils rat-tled inside drawers. In those moments, I tried to disappear, what they seemed to want being just the other person, their mutual interest a hard, tight circle.

But that all ended an afternoon shortly before my thir-teenth birthday when Dad ran a stop sign he insisted wasn't there so that I ended up in the hospital with a broken arm and a shard of glass wedged into my forehead. Unscathed, he fled to his friend Daryl's in Milwaukee. And with Dad gone, my mom found a new hobby: being aggrieved. Her distress grew each week Dad stayed away, turned into her swan song when she learned that Daryl had recently found religion, and while sleeping on his couch, Dad had, too. When he finally visited us several months later, Dad talked about sinners with the same alarmed suspicion people used then when they mentioned the Soviet Union or AIDS. Mom stayed in her room the whole time, while part of me waited for Dad to admit he was kidding, *Candid Camera*–style, though he never did. Instead he brought me holy cards, the Jesus on them handsome in a 1970s-pop-star way.

At the end of my sophomore year of high school, Mom came home from work and told me I'd be staying with Dad for the summer, though I hadn't seen him in close to a year. When I pressed her on it she said, "Sometimes you're too much, Gordon." I didn't know if this was in reference to the question I'd just asked or me in general. Either way, I went to stay with him. He worked at a mattress store then, one he'd soon get fired from for talking to customers about the church too much. He used that phrase—the church— more often than he said hello.

Dad lived in a tiny, barely furnished one-bedroom. A single Bible verse was taped to the fridge next to a postcard from Montana that the former tenant had left. That postcard bothered me. Its picture was fine: blue sky, sharp mountains. But its message was to someone named Nancy, and when I asked Dad who that was, he said, "I don't know." His formerly shaggy hair had been tamed into a crew cut.

He sat at his kitchen table in just an undershirt and boxers (his apartment had no air-conditioning).

"It was there on the fridge when I moved in," Dad added. "We should change."

I asked why, though I knew we were going to church. Next, I asked if church was air-conditioned, waiting for some inanity about the Lord keeping us cool, but Dad let out a smiling sigh and said, "I forgot about the way you ask questions."

"I didn't know I had my own particular way," I said.

"I've missed you, Gordon."

I told him I needed to take a shower, and I tried to jerk off thinking of Marc Nilsen from the winter before, a boy who'd picked me up then dropped me with an ease I'd been undone by, then my friend Cheryl's dad (in most of my fantasies about him, I either asked him for help with a math problem or he asked me for help fixing his boiler, sex some sort of mutual aid), but horniness didn't stick.

As we drove to church, the car's air-conditioning blaring, Dad thanked me.

"For what?" I asked.

"For getting in a car with me after what happened. For coming this summer."

"Not like Mom gave me a choice," I said.

He laughed, though I sensed a woundedness that laugh was meant to cover, so I added, "But I was happy when she told me. I think she was hoping I'd see it as punishment."

"She does have an interest in punishment," Dad said.

Seeing his pleased relief, I added things that weren't true: how after she told me and I didn't protest, she got annoyed, how I'd half expected her to say she'd changed her mind. It was strange how little I'd thought of Dad in the two years he'd been gone. I'd never written or called, even on holidays. As we turned into the parking lot in front of his small cinder-block church, its lawn a competition between leggy azaleas and crabgrass, it hit me that I'd hurt him, that I'd woven myself so tightly in my own role as abandoned that I couldn't consider what lay beyond its knitted pattern.

People in the parking lot smiled when they saw Dad. One woman asked, "Is that Gordon?"

"Indeed," Dad said.

The woman's name was Mrs. Mueller. She had a folksy drawl and a sturdy, no-nonsense frame and asked about the bus ride from Minneapolis.

"Your father's been so excited to have you come, you know," she said.

"Me too," I answered, and, sensing Dad listening from a few paces ahead, added, "I've missed him," less interested as to whether or not it was true.

It's easy to just remember the uncomfortable couch I slept on, the endless hours of worship, especially with all that's happened since, but in those months, what had been fun and light about my father returned. There was a weekend he borrowed bikes from a friend that we rode everywhere, my large father surprisingly adept as he leaned deep into turns. Nights when neither of us could sleep (the two fans he had nothing against the humidity's gluey weight), and we sat at the kitchen table sweating in just our underwear as he taught me spades and gin rummy, some other game that involved slapping hands. When he came home each night, he asked about what I'd gotten up to with an open curiosity I found suspicious first, then kind, and I told him about a walk I'd taken or the groceries I'd gotten us, and he said that on his next day off he'd take me to the public pool, which he did, Dad doing cannonballs that rocked across the water until the lifeguards whistled and he put up his hands in apology, though when he came back to our towels his face was red from held-in laughter.

Dad asked about what brought me joy—he often posed that question. I talked about my few friends, mentioned Marc whose mom my mom had worked for, but only said that we had the kind of friendship where we didn't have to talk to understand each other. I felt ashamed of the truth I'd left out, Marc on top of me, his dick so far into my mouth I felt my uvula trembling against it, the time sex hurt badly but I wanted him to keep going even when he said, "There's blood," and I answered, without knowing what I meant, "Blood makes it better."

Dad seemed interested in everything I said and did. One night, eating ice cream sandwiches on his building's porch, an occasional car drifting past, he asked if the sofa I slept on was enough for me, and I knew he was, with a roundabout cowardice I hated but understood as one of our shared traits, asking if I might want to stay beyond the summer.

Then Brian, one of the teenagers at church, caught my attention. He played the piano during services, was cute in an awkward, earnest way. Brian was kind to me. He invited me to his young persons' Bible group where he talked with wide-eyed sincerity about passages and prayers. I began to sense something beyond Christian fellowship when Brian lent me a bike or a bathing suit, a polished presence whenever I sat next to him, so unlike Marc Nilsen who months before told me where to sit or lie down. Brian wanted my attention, seemed scared of it, too. That made me mean to him at times, dedicated at others. One day, he picked me up and I told him I wanted to drive though I didn't even have a learner's permit. His face flushed, though I waited it out and he relented, yelping when I barreled toward stop signs or veered too close to the median. When he dropped me off later, I leaned in to hug him. I felt his rabbity pulse, the damp heat from under his arms. I squeezed him hard until he pushed me away and said, "What we think we want isn't always good for us." I stood on the curb as he drove away.

At dinner that night, Dad offered his usual blessing. At its end, he added that he was glad I'd found a good friend because kind people deserve one another. But I toyed with Brian, and I knew that when I'd been the toy, the person playing had the power to make a day perfect or wretched with a gesture or a few careless words. As Dad finished his prayer, I vowed to stop messing with Brian, knew, too, that I'd probably break that vow. I ate the lasagna in front of me fast, even though it was so hot it burned as I swallowed.

Six weeks into my stay, Dad and I were invited to a barbecue at his manager's house. I'd grown tired of Brian's steady,

puritan attention, his startled look when I caught him staring, so I agreed to go. The barbecue was at a suburban split-
level. The manager punctuated most things he said with a
fluttery laugh, his guests primarily families with young kids.
A few of those kids asked me to play tag with them. I did for
a while, but felt stupid so I lied and said I had to stop because
of asthma. An hour or so into it, the host, whose name was
Arthur, said, "You should have a look-see." Dad stood. He
told me to follow him. It was a hot, still day. A trio of kids
splashed in an aboveground pool. We walked through a side
door and into a small basement apartment with carpet the
color and texture of oatmeal, and shoebox-size windows.

"I'll leave you to it," Arthur said, fluttering out a laugh,
then walking outside.

The apartment had a combination living room–kitchen,
two bedrooms down a narrow hall.

"What's this?" I asked.

"Thinking I'm ready to upgrade," Dad said. "A room
for each of us."

I tried to picture Dad's furniture in these rooms, where
in the smaller bedroom my bed might lie, and felt a hollow-
ness close to hunger, though I knew food wouldn't staunch
this feeling.

"Does Mom know?" I asked.

"Nothing for her to know as of now," Dad answered.

"You're asking me to stay?"

Above us, the muted whoosh of the sliding door
sounded and feet drummed across the ceiling. I knew I'd
tire of Dad and his church, but having him to tire of, his
hurt and sanctimony when I strayed, even that took on a
sunset's tinge. He examined cabinets before turning to me

with Brian's same doting shyness, and said, "I'm saying this is here, if you want it."

I told him I was hungry.

We went back to the barbecue. I ate fast, barely chewing. Chip shards and tight nuggets of half-chewed meat ached as I swallowed. I was about to get more food when one of the kids waved to me from the pool, telling me to come in. I took off my T-shirt and climbed into the water.

"Didn't you just eat?" a second kid asked.

"He ate a lot," a third added.

I looked at the kid's freckled face, his expression of pissy, ginger confusion, and said, "You sound like you're obsessed with me," then slipped under the water.

Dad's church was unlike the few I'd been to before. People there shouted and stood when they were taken hold of by the spirit and often cried in awed appreciation. They also spoke in tongues. Sounds spewed from mouths of women who were otherwise mousy. Men who never said more than three words in a row unfurled rivers of indecipherable language. It lifted people from chairs. Threw them onto the floor. When it went on too long, I worried they'd stay that way forever.

One day it was my father's turn. He raised his hands in the air and barked out strange sounds. Tears sped down his cheeks. His stunned focus looked almost sexual, though it was brighter, less fraught. Though I'd felt something similar in Marc Nilsen's basement the winter before when he pinned me down and stuck different parts of himself inside of me, there was something about how my father could access this feeling whenever he wanted that I wanted, too, an immediacy, a cleanness. He dropped to his knees. Parishioners swayed and touched his shoulders. Mrs. Mueller nodded in praise and Dad's voice fell into a register so deep I felt more than heard it.

The next afternoon, I asked Brian if he could teach me. He told me that speaking in tongues was something to surrender to rather than learn, and I saw hope on his face that I was moving away from my terrible impulses. We'd just finished a meeting of the young persons' Bible group he ran, wiping soda spills from a table.

"I might stay," I said. "With my father, I mean."

I told Brian about the apartment, the room I'd have, the tiny window that would show the passing shoes of the people upstairs. He looked terrified. I stepped toward him, our faces inches apart. Brian crossed his arms.

"You shouldn't confuse God's love with other things," he said.

The lights above us buzzed. A poster behind him said, *You're in God's Hands*, a pair of large hands cupped and fuzzy in the background. I smelled the soda on Brian's breath, saw his eyes glazed with worry.

"You need to fight it," he said.

"Fighting doesn't win," I answered.

He looked disgusted and terrified before he gathered himself. "Thinking that way leads you down paths you don't even see."

But I liked that not seeing. It was one of the few real, good things I could think of, like the surprise years later when men noticed me, their attention a narrowed valve, a balance between movement and pressure.

"If you don't want to be my friend," I said, surprised at my bald-faced manipulation.

"I'll always be your friend," Brian said, and asked me to shut the lights off when I left.

On the walk home, a thunderstorm unleashed itself. Rain tripled the weight of my clothes, and turned my T-shirt translucent. At home, Dad saw me and laughed with delight. "My soaking boy," he said, and pulled me in for a hug. When he let go, my wet shadow marked him.

"I think you should tell Arthur we want that apartment," I said.

"I'll talk to him in the morning," Dad answered, and told me to shower while he went to get us a pizza.

I pictured Brian in that tiny shower with me, our feet entwined as if dancing, shoulders knocking shampoo bottles to the floor, and tried to believe that once he let himself do what he wanted, he wouldn't feel wicked or afraid but surprised at having waited so long.

Arthur told Dad that there were repairs he needed to complete, that we could move in in October. Dad reported this when he got home from work.

"Poor Nancy," I said.

"What?" he asked.

I pointed to the postcard on the fridge. "She'll be left behind."

"Ha," Dad said, then told me he wanted to stop by the church. When I didn't get up, he stared at me.

"I'm going, too?" I asked.

He nodded, and we walked out to his car. I asked if the new place was near the church, too.

"When we go places," Dad said, "you should pay attention."

Boredom soon crept in. There were days where Dad talked too much about Leviticus and Corinthians, dinners with church friends who, if they weren't talking about sinners, droned on about items on sale at the grocery store. Insomniac nights when Dad read scripture out loud or insisted that, at three in the morning, we scrub the toilet or organize the refrigerator or vacuum until the people downstairs complained. I missed Mom then. She often treated me as a nuisance. She also left me alone. When Dad was at work, I walked through parks covered in brown August grass, the heat so intense the only people there were teenagers smoking on a jungle gym. I waved, but they ignored me.

One day as I walked, Brian drove past, stopped, and offered me a ride. We went for milkshakes. I drank mine fast so that the bridge of my nose ached. I appreciated the pain's distraction. When Brian asked what I'd been up to, I said, "Sinning." He looked wounded and afraid and told me he was late for something.

"Lying's a sin, too," I said.

"I *am* late for something," Brian told me, and dropped me off at Dad's. Dad had just gotten back from work. He stood in front of the whirring box fan, the skin on his face pushed back by the breeze, and I wondered if staying with him was a mistake, though Mom's was just a different version of a letdown, so I lay on the sofa and pretended to nap, listening to the fan and the traffic grinding outside, the vibrations from Dad's footsteps.

A few weeks later, in the midst of the preacher's sermon on how we were loved but unworthy, I grew restless and wanted to feel something else, so I opened my mouth and let out a noise. The sermon continued. I stood up, opened my mouth again, hoping for sounds like the others I heard, guttural and ancient-sounding and urgent. But what poured out of me was soft and nasal, packed with pauses and a repeated "Um." I closed my eyes, hoping that would help, that whatever spirit hovered just above, like a rattled insect, would land. I moved into the aisle, on my knees, and wished I could stop though it didn't feel like something to bow out of. I opened my mouth again. Different iterations of blah, blah, blah. The spirit might come, show Brian he was right, that if I let it in, I would no longer imagine his dick and ass, the way his breath might feel against my neck. But that was desperate pretending. I shifted into English. "I want the wicked thoughts to leave me," I said, my shooing motion answered by a few tentative hallelujahs. I cringed at the word *wicked*, sure I'd never think things through enough before starting them. All eyes were on me. I tried again. Words in Spanish came, followed by the few phrases of Korean an exchange student had taught me, then the nonsense sounds of a Michael Jackson song. I croaked, stopped, tried again. "I want," I said, unsure of what to say next. I started to laugh at my wild failure, the pipe dream that this might have worked if only I wanted it desperately enough. I opened my eyes.

People looked at me with embarrassed fury. The preacher put a hand on my shoulder, and said, "Thank you," his face lobstered with an anger he tried and failed to hide.

At home that night, Dad hit me for the first and only time. He slapped me across the face, raising his hand to hit me again. But when I nodded for him to do it, he put that hand down.

"You never even told your boss we were taking the apartment, did you?" I asked. It was the first mean thing that came to me, but Dad's startled recognition made me wonder if I'd stumbled on the truth, stumbling the primary way I'd moved through the world. I kept going. "And you were never going to tell Mom I was staying, because, despite God being your best friend and all, the thing about you is that you'll always be afraid."

I felt as if I'd won, though I hadn't wanted to win, a part of me still hoping for the boring distraction of Brian's prayer meetings and Sundays next to Dad teary eyed with the need to be forgiven. "You'll always be afraid," I repeated, words that bounced, returned to me.

I tried, half-heartedly, to mock-speak in tongues, but it felt too stupid. In going back to Mom's, at least I wouldn't have to pretend to put stock in goodness or joy or agree with Mrs. Mueller when she talked about how things happened for a reason, when they just happened and happened and happened and happened.

I started to cry, didn't want Dad to see it so I sat down fast, resting my head on my knees. I stayed that way until his bedroom door clicked closed, then packed my bag, pulled the Montana postcard from the fridge, and hitchhiked to the bus station. I was picked up by a middle-aged man who looked so repulsed when I put a hand on his knee that I waited to get hit again, though he just made me get out of his car.

I made it to Mom's, but she was at work. When she got back, she said, "Didn't think you'd be back so soon."

"Didn't think I'd be back at all," I answered.

"Ha," she said, and lit a cigarette.

I asked for one. She told me they were bad for me.

"I know," I said, and she handed me her pack.

As we smoked out the kitchen window, she asked how Dad's had been. I talked about the prayers he recited and the terrible couch I slept on. Mom's frowning relief grew, so I left out anything about the apartment I'd thought he and I might move into or Brian who wanted me but wanted to be saved more. Or how, when Dad had burped out strange, confident noises, I'd envied what he believed he was doing.

"I'm hungry," I said.

"You know how to feed yourself," Mom answered.

"I do," I said.

She went into her room. I found bread and cheese and figured it would do, that at least I'd feel full for a while.

8

After I'd left the message telling my father to stop calling, he vanished as quickly as he'd appeared.

Work for Philip and Nicola moved at a steady clip of mistakes and solutions (fresh currants when they wanted dry ones, pleats pressed into pants they weren't intended for). But I got to be friendly with their tailor and accountant and the clerks at the package store. I learned what a private bank was, the difference between a half dozen cheeses they had opinions about.

Janice forgave me my gaffes. I bought us new plates to replace her mismatched ones and blackout shades for her bedroom. We went to the beach on our days off, Meredith in jeans and a T-shirt the whole time so we joked she was our security detail. I briefly slept with a friend of Janice's who did drag, coming home and unwittingly infecting every surface in our apartment with glitter. For weeks, we found it in our hair, our food. When I had to stay at Philip and Nicola's while they were at an art fair or visiting a collector, Janice grew to accept those absences, especially now that I used my better salary to buy us a living room rug and good coffee, bottles of fancy, ink-dark wine.

I was smoking on the fire escape with Janice, telling her about a book Philip had lent me, when the phone rang. August's soupy heat reduced us to sloths, so we let the machine handle it. In one of the dirt-lot yards below, people were hosting a barbecue. A charcoal fire glowed. The air above it wobbled. I kept trying to convince Janice to shout down to them to *throw us up some meat.*

Back inside, Janice played the message. It was my father's wife, June. I was so thrown by her old-lady voice that I didn't take in what she was saying. But seeing Janice's face, I rewound the tape and heard June describe the heart attack my father had just had. "He's stable, but not out of the woods," June said. "We're all praying for him."

Janice pulled me in for a hug, her sweaty breasts pressed to my sweaty shoulder. I told her I wasn't sad, that he and I hadn't been close in forever. Not wanting pity or advice, I added, "Guess I should call, make sure he's not dead."

Janice went into her room.

I stared at the phone, worried I'd have to go to Milwaukee, helping Dad to the bathroom and into his clothes for days then weeks while Janice and Philip and Pavel continued on without me. I took our cordless phone onto the fire escape so I could smoke and talk to June at the same time. At the barbecue below, people sat on any available surface, plates of food balanced on their laps. The phone rang before I got around to dialing. It was Philip, his voice a salve.

"Young man," he said.

"That's me," I answered.

He asked if I had a passport. I'd gotten one a few years

before. "In case of emergencies," I'd told Alan, though really, I wanted to be the type of person who needed one.

"I do," I said.

"Excellent. Make yourself free next week," Philip said. "I'll give you the details in the morning."

I smoked and knew I should call my father, wondering if he was awake or not, if his breathing and peeing had been farmed out to machines. I took a drag, pictured his hand on his chest at the attack's start, eyes bulging with fear. Dad strapped to a gurney as he was hoisted into an ambulance. I dialed the first few numbers, stopped. The second time I made it beyond the area code, but lit another cigarette rather than finish. At the barbecue below, people talked and laughed and ate. Charcoal was added to the grill. Its flames—greedy and reaching—painted nearby walls and faces. As I waited for worry for my father to reach me, it was my life as it had recently developed that I grew scared might vanish, Janice and me losing touch, as happened with most of my friends. She might move to a commune with Meredith, or to Portland, as she talked about doing from time to time. I climbed back inside and knocked on her bedroom door, not knowing then that in a handful of years Janice would end up in Massachusetts with a wife, that they'd live near a beach and have two daughters. One of those daughters would turn out to be mean and complicated and, as a teenager, call Janice a stupid bitch, saying it louder when Janice told her, "It doesn't feel good when you say things like that to me." That daughter would be in and out of institutions, would die in a car crash before her seventeenth birthday, ruled an accident though there were no skid marks suggesting she'd tried to stop. Janice would call to tell me. We'd stayed in touch after all. When I'd answer the phone with a dumb nickname I had for her, she'd whisper, "Meredith died," and for a second I'd think she was talking about her former lover, forgetting she'd named her oldest child after her ex who no longer uses that name or gender and lives in Nashville now, regularly posting their poetry on Instagram.

I crumpled up the slip of paper I'd written June's number on.

Janice opened her door and said, "Sugar pie. Tell me what happened," and I understood that I'd use my passport however Philip asked, him a path forward, Dad a swamp to get stuck in.

"I guess the heart attack was minor," I lied.

I picked up clothes strewn across Janice's floor and began to fold them. I handed her a T-shirt and dress, a pile of crudely folded bras.

"So you're not going to see him?" she asked.

There was an answer I was meant to give, all concern and large gestures, my own wants moved aside for a while. But each time I tried to consider my father's plight, I felt as if something was being taken from me. And when I chided myself for such entrenched selfishness, I thought of the selfishness I'd grown up around and learned to see as necessary, a tool to keep intact the small corner that was my own.

I shook my head, handed Janice another folded shirt.

"You know, Gordon," Janice said. I sensed her gearing up to tell me something hard and true. But then keys jangled in our door and Meredith appeared with Chinese food.

"We're in here with your girlfriend's underwear," I said.

"Of course you are," Meredith answered.

We ate in our tiny living room, the two of them tucked on the love seat, me on the floor. From time to time, Meredith talked about the terrible TV show she was working on, or commented on how I was eating with the speed and focus of the starved. Mostly, though, the three of us looked at our food, chewing noises for company. And as I cleaned my plate and filled it again, I tried to imagine where Philip might take me.

PART TWO

9

The car was the silver of a polished mirror. Even on that cloudy early morning, light bounced off its hood in narrow, wolfish angles. In its window's reflection stood Philip and me with our similar heights, though I wore the hoodie and slouch I always did while he had on a button-down that stayed crisp despite hours of international travel. He dropped the keys into my hand.

"What's this?" I asked.

"Don't ask questions you know the answer to," Philip said.

His sunglasses were mirrored, too, and with his smile and perfect posture, the cloud white of his hair, he looked like a politician or movie villain.

On a nearby runway, planes angled into the air.

"Why are you handing them to me?" I asked.

"I asked back in New York if you were a confident driver," Philip said. "And you answered with some story about a car you'd had and sold. What color was it again?"

"You shouldn't ask questions you know the answers to either."

"Cheap-stripper blue," Philip said. "I remember the words. I just don't know what they mean."

"What do you think they mean?"

"Europe has made you assertive, young man."

"We haven't even left the airport."

"Well then," Philip said. "I suppose I'll need to gird myself for whatever new you is about to emerge. I asked because I need someone who can drive well. I haven't driven in years."

"Not Andrew? Amy? Adam? Everyone who works for you has names that begin with an *A*."

"Three people."

"So they don't drive?"

"Not well," Philip said. "Also . . ." He pursed his lips, and I sensed he was deciding how much of his hand to show. "They wouldn't have appreciated it."

"Because they've been to Europe before and I haven't?" I asked.

"We should get going," Philip said.

The car was a stick shift. My ex, Alan, had had one and taught me its basics, the two of us in a parking lot late at night, Alan telling me when to shift up and down. I pulled onto the main road. Cars buzzed past, and I switched to a higher gear.

"Garish, I imagine," Philip said.

"Bright, too," I told him. "Cheap strippers, they want to be noticed."

A sign told us that Geneva was six kilometers away. We zipped through a tunnel, emerged to a wall of dense shrubs on either side of us. The announcer on the radio spoke in quick, purring French, and Philip translated things about trade deals and a new reality show. A volcano that had been written off decades before coming back to life.

I dropped Philip off at the lakeside Four Seasons, then went to the cheaper hotel I'd found for myself a few blocks away (my last-minute addition to the trip meant many of the hotels where Philip would be staying were already at capacity). The place where I was staying sat on a busy, charmless street. At its front desk, a woman battered by fluorescent light addressed me in French. I spat out one of the few phrases I'd memorized from the dictionary Philip had lent me: "Je suis désolé." Her face dulled as she switched to my mother tongue.

The elevator was barely big enough for me and my duffel bag. It had a gate I had to pull.

My room had a single bed and a television bolted to the wall. Traffic growled through its window. Still, I was in Europe for the first time, and wanted to take advantage of that, to leave my hotel's derelict street and return to Philip's, full of storefronts shaded by colorful awnings and window boxes bursting with flowers and facades of warm, clean stone.

Philip had told me to let him nap until four, so I wandered. I passed wrought iron balconies, their railings curlicued and lacy-looking, shops that seemed to have been extracted from a quainter era. Streetcar wires clanged in the wind, and people young and old glided down the streets on bicycles. Their jackets and hair lifted behind them, faces ruddy with cardiovascular satisfaction. But this storybook quality was interrupted when a moped buzzed next to a woman on a bike and plucked her purse from its basket. The woman screamed. Other cyclists raised hands and voices in protest. I checked to make sure my wallet and passport were safely in my pocket.

A block later, I met a man walking a dog. The man had grayish eyes and dark hair, a lean fitness I liked. I knelt down. The dog trotted toward me. The man's face lit up with an amused, coy smile. Afternoon sun gilded his face.

"Cute dog," I said.

The man's smile faltered, and he shortened his pet's leash. The dog snorted in surprise.

"Chien," I added, pulling that word from God knows where, then, "Je suis désolé." The man and his dog went on their way. I pulled the dictionary from my pocket to scour its list of useful phrases, then closed it, reciting as many as I could remember.

I walked through the marble-floored lobby of Philip's hotel, a sunset mural busying its ceiling. With a coffee for him in hand, I knocked on his door.

Philip's room was large, with a balcony that overlooked the lake. Outside, the sun fought through the clouds, its light pebbling the water.

"You brought me coffee," Philip said.

"It was in the lobby," I answered, and placed it on one of his room's many tables.

I sat down, the frays and stains on my jeans magnified by the sofa's pale fabric. Philip noticed me noticing and asked, "Did you bring anything less lived-in?"

"I think so," I said, though the only good clothes I'd packed were those he'd rejected at their first party. Sensing my discomfort maybe, Philip asked me about my first

European afternoon. I talked about the robbery I'd seen, my failed flirtation without a common language.

"Not that you need that, per se," Philip said, and told me he was going to hop into the shower. I didn't know if I should stay or leave.

He came out a few minutes later in a white robe, a buffed shine to his hairless legs, and the confusion as to why I'd been invited on this trip grew. Nicola might have told him about the barn. Philip might have assumed I'd understood what agreeing to come really entailed. I tried to warm myself to the idea of sleeping with him, though as I looked more closely, I noticed his thick toenails, their edges the yellow of an old photograph, and the wiry white hair clinging to his collarbone and hoped that his admiration's steady light would carry me through a fuck or two unscathed. Philip slathered his face with moisturizer. He looked out at the houses peppering the lake's far shore. When he turned back to me, I stood, unsure if he was about to kiss me or make a comment about my clothes, unsure, too, which I would have preferred. But he just smiled and said, "The jet lag will pass," then told me about the collectors he was having dinner with that night, his description making it clear he'd be going solo. Maybe my clothes had led to a demotion.

"I can entertain myself," I said.

"I have no doubt," Philip said. "But I'd love for you to help me find my way there and back."

His cheeks were red from shaving. Water clung to his hair in crystalline beads.

"Meet me in the lobby in half an hour," Philip said.

I sat in the lobby next to a towering, fragrant floral arrangement. Guests drifted past, and the reception desk's phone trilled with quiet regularity.

"Bonjour," a woman said.

She had on a white shirt and gray pants, a hotel name tag shiny on her lapel. I looked at my ratty jeans, then back at her, angry at the question I suspected would come next.

"I'm waiting for Philip Belshaw," I said.

She nodded. "May I get you a coffee? Perhaps a glass of wine?"

"Sure," I said, though when she asked what kind of wine, I answered, "Whatever's easy." She listed several. "The first one," I said, not knowing if it was white or red. As I drank expensive wine (it was white), I grew angry at the judgment people passed when they saw me, though if I'd understood the world as they did, I wouldn't have dressed this way even when I scrubbed my toilet. Philip had probably never scrubbed a toilet. Even as a kid, he'd surely had people to drive him places and clean up his messes and iron his clothes so everything always looked perfect, even when he wasn't leaving the house.

I finished my wine in a few large swallows.

Three days before, Philip had explained to me that Nicola couldn't go with him on the European business trip they'd planned. We sat at their kitchen island. One of the dogs was just out of sight, lapping water from its bowl.

"Too much happening at the gallery," Philip said.

He picked up a stack of magazines and tapped it against the counter.

"So my passport," I said, and took it from my pocket.

"Good. You're going with me instead."

His eyebrows sloped toward each another in a sharp V.

"You're not free?" he asked.

"Of course I'm free," I answered, and his brow retreated.

That night, I called June. She told me a small part of Dad's heart had died in the attack, but there was hope for recovery. She asked if I might visit, and I told her, "I'm currently in a foreign country," though I was in Brooklyn still, deciding what to pack.

"The connection sounds like you're next door," she said.

"Progress," I told her, and asked if Dad could talk. She answered no, that she was at home. I was bothered by her attempt to lure me back, also the negligence of her being home rather than by her husband's side. Everything made me angry then, and I couldn't imagine the sliver of rightness that would have satisfied me. I had wanted to tell Dad about Europe, for his holy zeal to drop long enough so I could hear the thrill in his voice at the prospect of me in fancy hotels and driving on roads bound together by kilometers rather than miles. But when I asked June if I could call Dad directly, she said that they hadn't paid for a phone in his room. It was expensive, and everyone who wanted to talk to him was already there.

I was about to hang up when June said, "He talks about you every day."

"I'll call again," I said.

I knew I should have promised more meaningful action, or at least offered contrition. But my first trip on a plane and to Europe crowded out any better answer, wanting all

I could consider, the weight of it in my hands, its tingle in my throat as it moved close to becoming real.

"He'll look forward to hearing from you," June said, then hung up.

I shoved the clothes I'd chosen into my duffel bag.

Philip had a terrible sense of direction. On our first night in Geneva, I walked him to a restaurant five minutes from his hotel, and he was shocked by how close it was and the ease with which I got us there.

"When I first moved to the Village," he said, "all those strange, angled streets. I was lost all the time. Walking in circles, or more like rhombuses."

Philip sometimes turned himself into the butt of a joke, but carefully. Even when he remarked on his terrible sense of direction or mentioned a passing man too striking to give him even a small scrap of attention, Philip still steered things. A woman in a crosswalk spoke to him. He answered back in French that sounded baritone and feminine at the same time.

"What did she want?" I asked.

"To compliment my scarf."

It was steely gray, folded in a way that made me think of a book on knots I'd once read.

"It *is* nice," I said.

"We should get you one," he answered.

"I don't know that I can afford it," I said.

Philip didn't reply, and I felt the stifling weight of the rules I didn't know, though even as I pictured the sad, clueless version of me that I cultivated and blamed, I understood that in mentioning my slender means I was fishing for his interest or assurance or a touch on the arm.

"This is the restaurant," I said.

The place had a giant kitchen diners could peer into, tables ringed in elegantly punitive chairs. Philip adjusted his scarf and tucked his hair behind his ears. It was like watching an actor walk onstage, dropping into character just as the light hit him.

I went to a bar with soccer on the television and ate a sausage stew. When I got back to Philip's restaurant, I found him outside waiting.

"Where's our car?" he asked.

"We walked here," I said.

The street's dim lighting exaggerated his aggravation.

A cab passed. Philip raised his hand, and it pulled over.

Without thinking, I said, "I'll walk." Sensing I was being childish, bratty even, I added, "Just need a bit of fresh air before bed."

Philip got into the cab without looking back at me.

After returning to my hotel, I climbed into bed. And though my eyes ached from their hours of uninterrupted work, each time sleep crept close, annoyance at Philip's own annoyance returned, along with annoyance at the way he'd stood in his bathrobe that afternoon so I didn't know what he planned to do with me.

We moved on to Zurich, then a night in Stuttgart, Philip going to an event with someone he called the Countess, though I wasn't sure if that title was real or a joke. I spent hours waiting in the car outside grand houses or museums, saw the itch of Philip's disappointment when I drove down streets strangled by traffic or showed up at a different time than he'd wanted or when, once, he climbed into the car and I had the radio playing a pop station and he huffed before saying, "Why is this young woman moaning like she's injured?" When I answered with a joke about the particulars of her injury, his brow rose in shock that I'd thought his question had been anything other than rhetorical.

The more Philip aimed his disappointment at me, the more thoughts of my ailing father took on the warm patina of missed opportunity. Me sitting by his hospital bed while machines beeped and nurses floated in. The forgiveness he'd ask for in a pleading whisper. But each time quitting and flying back early felt like my next logical step, Philip would share a moment of kindness or express relief that I'd gotten him to some hard-to-find restaurant, and that need to flee would vanish as fast as it had appeared.

On the drive to Munich a few days later, I confessed to Philip that I hadn't been able to find a cheap hotel where I could stay; I'd been told there was a conference in town. He fiddled with a dashboard vent. On either side of us, a dense thicket of suburbs.

"You mean to tell me you've been staying in dumps?" Philip asked.

"I wouldn't call them dumps," I said.

"What would you call them then?"

"Adequate."

"For the next few nights," he said, "we'll get you a more suitable room."

I considered telling Philip how I lived back in New York but didn't want his pity. We drove past short-shorn fields and a grid of dark pines, a cluster of close-knit houses.

That night, Philip at a dinner, I wandered. I smoked several cigarettes while standing on a bridge, the dark river sliding underneath me. As people passed in duos and trios, homesickness gathered steam, for Janice, and Dad's rambling messages, for my mom who played the same songs over and over when she was in a mood. I found an internet café and paid to sit in one of its booths to make a long-distance call. I dialed Dad's, got the machine, so tried my aunt in Phoenix instead. Mom had been staying there since the end of her latest engagement.

"Gordon," my aunt asked. "What's wrong?"

"Nothing," I said. "Just haven't talked to Mom in a while."

My aunt Frances, a thin, nervous woman, was high up at the local electric company.

"I'll say," she said. "How's Minnesota?"

"Hot, I imagine. But I'm not there."

As I told her about my job, my recent days in Europe, I realized that I hadn't spoken to my mother since I'd moved to New York.

"Your mom doesn't live here anymore," my aunt said.

"What happened?" I asked.

"Nothing happened."

Outside the booth people crouched in front of computers, screens turning their faces an anemic blue.

"She has an apartment a few miles away, a job answering phones at the Y."

"She hates talking on the phone," I said, hoping we might commiserate, searching for familiarity's steady grounding. But my aunt ticked her tongue, and I knew she wouldn't help me.

"It's a job, not a pleasure cruise," she said, then gave me my mother's new number.

———

I stood outside the restaurant until Philip's guests left and felt like a mistress. Felt sick, too, of worrying about his frustration, so I asked him, "What's the male version of mistress?"

"Lucky, I suppose," Philip answered, then told me he could smell cigarette smoke on me.

"I'll walk farther away," I said.

I wanted him to tell me that taking me on this trip was a mistake, for me to fly home early in one of the smaller seats I'd spied behind us on the trip over. To then visit Dad and tell him and June and the nurses about the whims of the rich, their impossibility.

Philip hooked his arm in mine.

"I actually love the smell," he said. "It reminds me of when I smoked, which I did for decades, like a fiend. When I smell it, young man, I miss it terribly."

We paused at a store with purses in its windows. Philip's white hair, my dark, messy mop showed in reflection.

"You can smell me whenever you want," I said.

"The things you say," Philip answered.

"I shouldn't say things?"

"You should always say things. That's why I like you so much."

Philip kept his arm hooked in mine, any urge for an early exit collapsing as fast as it was constructed. Back at the hotel, Philip squeezed my shoulder then walked to the shining bank of elevators.

But the next morning, his sourness returned.

"I thought you were buying other clothes," Philip said.

"I couldn't find any," I said, though I hadn't looked.

People streamed in and out of the lobby.

"I find that hard to believe."

"I don't know where to look," I said, my words close enough to the truth to hold water. This tendency to lean on almost truths still lives in me, though decades later I'm better able to resist it, to understand the holes I'm digging, the bullshit I'm trying to pass off as a clean bill of sale, even to myself.

I wanted Philip to say he'd take me to a store with personal shoppers, music thrumming so each outfit I tried on felt part of a montage. But he answered, "You should look harder," and told me about a lunch he'd need to be driven to at the house of someone who was once royalty, who would be royalty still had the tides of history washed up on a more dictatorial shore.

While Philip went to his room to make phone calls, I asked the concierge about clothing stores. I told him how my boss didn't like my wardrobe, inventing insults Philip hadn't said about it. The concierge kept his eyes on the list he was writing for me.

At the first store he'd suggested, mannequins in all black and clothes in precise piles, I spent too much on pants and button-downs, more on a scarf and small rectangular sun-glasses, then black boots that made my feet ache. After I'd paid, I walked past a rack of belts and dropped one into my bag. But an alarm went off as I walked out. I felt dumb and done for, though I mimicked Philip's impatience and said, "I forgot to pay for this." The clerk rang up the belt without looking at me.

The next day, waiting for the elevator after running errands, I found Pavel there, too, armed with his usual blank expression. My heart was a thumping tail.

"I thought you were in New York," I said.

"Collectors of great importance I need to meet," he answered, his impression of Philip correct and unkind.

With his shorn hair and pale skin, Pavel looked almost infirm. Still, there was a beauty to him I wanted to lay claim to, odd features that came together in strange harmony. A bag of face creams crinkled between my fingers.

"I'm starving," Pavel said.

"You should eat."

"Meet me back here in a half an hour. I'll take you to lunch."

"I could eat some lunch," I said, trying to mask the electric thrill of his invitation.

At an internet café that afternoon, I read an email from June telling me she'd heard my message and appreciated my prayers (I hadn't offered any). There was also an email from my mom. *It seems that you called*, it began. She went on about her job answering phones and tidying locker rooms, about the relief she'd felt since leaving her fiancé George. She ended her message with this: *Are you really in Europe, or is this one of your jokes?* I started to write back, but didn't feel like it. Thought to write to June, too, but was frustrated by her mention of prayers I hadn't offered. I opened an email from Janice instead. *Sugar*, it began. *M. and I decided to take a break from work and drive cross country. We'll be gone for a month or two.* She added that she had left rent checks, asked that I water her plant. Instead of writing back that I wanted to quit my job and join them, I told her about lunch with Pavel in a place with pale floors and striped wallpaper, the two of us eating a fish I'd never heard of.

I was about to log out, when a new message appeared from the email address truebeliever31. *There's a computer here I can use*, my dad began. He wrote about the rehab center where he was staying, the walks they made him take, and the device they had him breathe into to measure his strength. *I hear you have a fancy job and are traveling*, he continued. *I always knew you would do bigger things. Even when you were young the world we lived in was small for you. I admire that about you Gordon. The way you push.* There was none of June's veiled disappointment. No sense he expected me there while I was tangled up with the wider world. Even his blessing at the email's end didn't bother me. I wanted to write back that I'd forgiven him, though he hadn't asked for any. Instead I wrote that it was so good to hear from him, that as I read his message, I could hear his voice saying those words. *I hope June told you about the messages I've been leaving. How I've been thinking about you.*

Driving Philip to a dinner that night, he asked what I'd done with my day.

"Pavel's here," I said.

He was quiet for several minutes. Then, as if we'd been in one continuous conversation, Philip talked about the two collectors who'd bought Pavel's work in as many days.

"He might just be a star," he said.

"A reluctant one," I answered.

"That's just a performance."

"Seems genuine to me."

"That's what makes it so compelling."

Philip cracked open his window, and cool air barreled in. I wondered if he noticed the new clothes I had on.

Just before we turned into the driveway of the place he was having dinner—he'd called it a house, though it seemed more in palace territory to me—Philip asked me to stop the car. He got out and moved to the back seat.

"Keeping up appearances," he said. "You don't mind, do you?"

As I looked down the pin-straight driveway, trees on either side made more regal with lighting, Dad's words about my larger destiny soured on my tongue.

"Of course I don't mind," I said, though I pictured the clenched thrill of saying the opposite just to see how he'd answer.

Later that night, Pavel called my room. "I'm at the hotel bar and think you should come."

"A long way down," I said.

"Come soon," he told me, and hung up.

I changed into a shirt I'd recently bought, the most I'd ever spent on a single item of clothes. It was black and carried the slightest shimmer. "He's probably just bored," I mumbled, though those words skidded across the surface rather than sinking in.

The hotel's bar was walled in dark wood, with assertive, muscular moldings, the music that played whispery and clean. I sat down next to Pavel and ordered a beer.

"My treat," he said. "In case there's something else you want. Tobi here makes fantastic cocktails."

"I didn't order a beer because I'm poor," I said.

"I wasn't suggesting." The ice cubes in his drink glittered. His pale eyes stayed on me.

"I might want to paint you," Pavel said.

An older couple sat at the bar's far end, her hair shiny and round, his tie so tight it appeared to be choking him.

"You weren't at dinner tonight," Pavel said.

"Was waiting outside though. The things we do for love."

"I find it hard to tell when you're joking."

"I usually am."

I looked back at him as if in a childhood staring contest, a game I'd loved for its mix of aggression and intimacy.

"I suppose I spend most of my time around serious people," Pavel said.

"That's your problem right there."

I was thinking of ordering another beer when Pavel leaned close and said, "Walk me to my room."

We got into the elevator. It pinged as we passed each floor. Pavel's pale hands were crossed just above his groin, and breath filled his chest.

Once at his door, Pavel kissed me. His tongue pressed mine into submission, a suction to his kissing that was surprisingly, desperately hapless. I moved my hand down his back, felt its collection of thin, taut muscles. Just as my fingers found his belt, Pavel stopped them. He closed his mouth, kissed me a final time, and said good night.

"There's a word for this," I said.

"You mean teasing? That isn't what I'm trying to do," he answered. "But I'll see you in the morning."

I went downstairs. The concierge from before stood at his post.

"You clean up well, I think is the expression," he said, with sibilant precision.

"I do," I said. He looked surprised at my frank confidence. "But I have a question. Where are places to go for people like us?"

"You are meaning?" he asked.

"For fun," I said.

He nodded as if we were in the midst of a more professional conversation, then whispered, "If you wait a block away, in front of the bank, in half an hour. I am done then and can take you somewhere."

I wasn't particularly interested in the concierge. But I needed to move beyond the ache of Pavel dangling his attention in front of me only to yank it away, so I said, "At the bank, great." A man I assumed was his manager walked past, and the concierge handed me a brochure about a castle turned museum, saying in a loud, community theater tone, "This should answer all your questions."

The next night I went to pick up Philip after a dinner and found Pavel with him. They dropped into the back seat, Philip's expression softened by booze.

"We should have a nightcap," he said.

To turn right, Pavel tapped the back of my seat once, for left, twice. Munich's storefronts glowed like museum dioramas.

Inside the bar dance music thrummed and men clustered close together and porn played on monitors. Though it wasn't the place the concierge and I had gone to, it had the same overloud debauchery.

"What would you like?" I asked.

"Something with an umbrella in it," Philip said.

"Wine has been had," Pavel added.

"We sold more of Pavel's work at dinner," Philip said. "Best thousand dollars I ever spent."

"Dinner cost a thousand dollars?" I asked.

"A little umbrella," Philip said.

The bartender made him a pineapple-flavored drink. On a nearby monitor, a man swallowed an entire cock as if it were some small morsel.

I returned with drinks for them, a club soda for me. A man passed and eyed Pavel. Territoriality tightened my gut.

Philip took a sip of his drink. "What *is* this?"

"What you asked for," I said.

A nearby group of men started to dance, and Philip

cooed with appreciation. I'd only seen him giddy like this at his birthday. Even after several glasses of wine, Philip usually stayed stoic and clear. I wasn't sure what had changed, but he seemed to be having fun, and Pavel touched my knee under the table. One of the dancing men tried to take Philip's hand, but my boss shook his head. "Aber Gordon will mit dir tanzen," he said, telling me to join in his place.

Philip stared at me, a reminder that I was on the clock, I supposed. On the monitor above us, the cock swallower was now being pummeled from behind. Philip's brow ticked downward, water emptying from a tub. I didn't want to be told to dance, though days before I'd considered sleeping with him had it come to that. But the possibility of sex had felt kind, an attempt at closeness, Philip telling me to dance a way for him to stand over me with his heels on my back. The man I was meant to dance with began to lose interest. But Philip's remained. I wanted to meet his power play with refusal. But Pavel looked worried. And even before I gave in, I knew I would.

The dancing men invited me into their circle with polite indifference. I engaged in a minute of perfunctory grinding before I said, "Danke," and sat back down. Philip looked overjoyed, perhaps because he'd pressed and I'd caved, maybe because it was fun to watch me dance. My meanness lost out to embarrassment, as it sometimes did. Philip had taken me to Europe after all. And I was at the receiving end of Pavel's sharpening attention. So I sipped my club soda and crossed my legs and asked if I was allowed to smoke in this place.

Umbrella drink finished, Philip announced that he needed to sleep. We climbed into the car, the two of them in the back seat. Two blocks in came Philip's soft snores.

"When you were watching me dance, were you thinking about painting me?" I asked.

"You're not a bad dancer," Pavel said.

We were stopped at a red light. Philip's snores rose and fell.

"Should I meet you?" I asked. "After I drop him off, I mean."

I wanted to spend the night with Pavel, for the sex, of course, but also his arms around me as we slept, eyes pinning me in place first thing in the morning.

"I think it's sleep for me," Pavel said.

Back at the hotel, Philip's nap seemed to have sobered him up, so when I hit the elevator button for his floor and not mine, he answered, "I'm not as bad as all that" and kissed my cheek. His lips were damp plastic. In my room, I listened to the occasional click of doors.

As I lay there, riled up and let down, why I wanted Pavel coalesced: He was extraordinary. Men I'd dated before had been clever or cute, also earthbound. But being in his orbit felt like a drug both expensive and hard to find. I chided myself for thinking I could have him, afraid, too, that I was close to something I wanted a great deal, and might not get.

Sleep wouldn't come. Each time it seemed close I'd think about Pavel saying, "It's just sleep for me."

I didn't see him again for the rest of the trip.

10

The next night Philip invited me to drinks with a wealthy couple. I wanted to ask why. Even more, I wanted to go, so I kept quiet. My new boots clomped as we walked through the building's tiled lobby.

The hosts, Marcel and Stefan, opened the door and, seeing me next to Philip, said, "You're not Nicola," and handed us martinis.

"How did you snag this one?" Marcel asked.

"I scooped him up, as it were," Philip told him.

"Scoop," Marcel said, and the three of them laughed.

Their apartment had high ceilings and low, square furniture. Views of a cathedral crowded its windows.

Philip examined a painting, commenting on depth and aesthetic, then asked, "Did you get the photos I sent over?"

"Pavel Brozik," Stefan said. I wondered why Pavel hadn't come.

As the hosts drank more, they made comments about my eyes and my shyness. I was thrilled to be noticed, even by men I had no interest in. Stefan handed me a glass of wine. I told him he was trying to get me drunk.

"Succeeding, it seems," he answered, and listed places in Europe I needed to see.

"Maybe Majorca," Marcel said.

"That beach where it's all men and no clothes," Stefan added.

"Sign me up," I said, the heat of the hosts' shoulders warm against my own.

Philip stood up. "We've abused your kindness staying so long."

"Hardly," Marcel said.

He was the handsomer of the two, his eyes the color of a winter river. But Philip insisted we had to leave and Stefan looked chastened as he went to get our jackets. I tried to understand what had just happened.

Philip and I walked next to a tree-lined canal. Birds darted between trees, their wings hollow breaths. The drinks I'd had numbed the back of my head.

"There are many ways to flirt," Philip said.

"Meaning?" I asked.

"Meaning you don't need to lie down for every man who gives you his attention."

At an intersection, Philip turned right. "We go left," I said, sure that he'd wanted me to flirt, also to pretend I wasn't doing so, my failure at pretending what he found distasteful. At the next intersection, Philip waited for me to tell him which way to go.

"I assumed," I said, "that I was invited to these drinks and not others, to be flirted with."

I was young, figured that Stefan and Marcel wanted some of that as theirs. Watching a tram packed with passengers whip past, I thought to burn it all down. But Philip's hard expression gave way, with it a chance to swallow my anger and embarrassment, at least for a while.

"I don't always know how to be," I said to fill the silence. "When people flirt and it's clear we're going to sleep together, then I'm fine. When it's just flirtation, I don't know. When to start and stop."

"You can say no to things," Philip said. "With what you do as much as your words. A *thanks but no thanks*."

"How do I do that?"

"There isn't a formula," he said, though I imagined there was.

Philip put his hand on my back. I picked up my pace and the hand fell away.

"That's a good start," he said.

At the hotel's entrance, the doorman looked lost in thought. When he saw us he snapped to it, opened the door, and wished us a good evening.

"Thank you," I said, and tried on a smile that was polite but guarded, realizing the doorman did that same thing all the time.

In Philip's room the next morning, running through the day's schedule, he stopped mid-sentence and told me he'd made a dinner reservation for the two of us that night.

"It's our last night here after all," Philip said.

"Pavel, too?" I asked.

"That isn't possible," he said. "Seeing that he's stateside again."

Rain rattled the windows.

"Let me guess," Philip said. "He didn't tell you."

"Doesn't get an A for communication."

"Young man," Philip said.

"This young man is fine," I told him, hoping to stave off a falling feeling. "But," I went on, "I don't know why I'm thinking of this now, but Andrew at the gallery." Philip raised an eyebrow, perhaps expecting me to confess my love for Andrew instead. "He sent me an email yesterday. He thinks my name is Gregg. Though I've corrected him several times. Even spells it with two *g*'s at the end."

"Who spells Gregg with two *g*'s at the end?" Philip asked.

"Who spells Gordon like it's a different name?" I asked back.

"I'll talk to Andrew," Philip said, and told me he'd meet me in the lobby in an hour.

I went up to my room to change. As I picked out clothes, I got snagged on Pavel's silent exit. "Maybe he doesn't want you," I mumbled. But as I slipped into the outfit I'd chosen, I rejected that idea. He hoped to paint me after all. I pulled out a package of Band-Aids, covered the delegation of blisters on my heels and toes, and put my new boots on.

The restaurant had thick stone walls and crisp tablecloths, and a waitstaff that moved through it with noiseless elegance. Men were required to wear jackets, so Philip lent me one of his. It fell wide across my shoulders.

After we ordered, I turned shy, and Philip took on the bulk of the conversation. He told me about his first time in this restaurant, then listed places I should travel to someday. The little travel I'd done had been to forgettable places—a mosquito-rich campsite in Wisconsin. A motel at the dusty foot of South Dakota's Black Hills.

The food appeared. I considered telling Philip about Alan, but sensed he'd find it boring, then about the professor I'd fallen for in college who'd rejected me bluntly and given me a C. The waiter placed rolls onto our plates with silver tongs.

"The food's so good we aren't even talking," I said, and chewed a mouthful of potato for longer than necessary. I asked if he was eager to head home, embarrassed at the stock question I'd leaned on.

"Sometimes I prefer life in a hotel," he answered.

He cut his fish and smiled as if I were sweet, also lacking. I ate the rest of my dinner in silence then loitered in the bathroom until he'd had time to pay the bill.

———

It was a relief to get back to my room, though embarrassment at my failed conversation tainted it. At a dinner where I was meant to be charming, all I could come up with was clichéd observations about the food and the dogs and the lingering rain. As I lay on my bed, still in Philip's blazer, I closed my eyes, knowing I'd likely wake up fully dressed the next morning, and remembered an email from June I hadn't answered, in which she asked again when I might come visit.

I put a pillow over my face and closed my eyes.

———————

A knock woke me up. My heart raced at the possibility of Pavel, until I remembered.

It was Philip. He slouched against the doorframe. Glancing at the clock, I saw it was three in the morning.

"I think I've been poisoned," he said. "Food poisoning, I mean," and threw up in his hand.

I breathed in the rotten, vinegar smell of his puke and brought him into my bathroom. Philip threw up again, this time in the sink. His face fell as he pulled down his pants and sat on the toilet.

"I'll give you some space," I said. But he took my hand, squeezed it. Breathing through my mouth, I rubbed his back, felt its cool, loose skin.

"I'm sorry, young man," he whispered.

After an hour the worst seemed behind him. Philip sat on the bathroom floor, his thighs bone-white and hairless.

"You should take a shower," I said.

I turned on the water, testing its temperature with my hand. All the while, I did my best not to look at the traffic of varicose veins lining his legs or the white thatch of hair above his penis. He stepped into the shower, slipped. I held out a hand to steady him. When that seemed insufficient, I stripped and joined him.

"I'm sorry," he croaked.

"Shh," I whispered.

Seeing him in this state erased my lackluster perfor-mance from dinner, so I washed his face and lathered up his midsection, picked up the removable showerhead to rinse his hair.

I dried Philip off and dressed him in one of my T-shirts and a pair of my underwear before helping him into bed. His clothes drooped over a chair. His watch ticked loudly.

"They should have given you a bigger bed," he said.

"I'm just one person."

"But what they're charging," he said, then shrugged, his indignation in the rearview mirror. "It wasn't all some ruse to see you naked, you know," Philip added.

"Would have been some ruse."

"Not that it was unpleasant to see."

I tried on a look that said *thanks but no thanks*, but gave up, kissing his forehead and lying next to him.

"Nicola worries," Philip said. "And it's annoying the way he worries."

"So we shouldn't worry him about this."

Philip lay with his back toward me. A door in the hall outside creaked closed.

"Nicola didn't stay in New York because of the gallery," he said.

"I figured," I said, though I hadn't, then pictured the man Nicola stayed for, Nicola's dick in my hand.

"He and I have never had an interest in a certain kind of exclusivity."

On the street outside, the plaintive two-note wail of a siren sounded. Dampness from Philip's hair shadowed his pillow.

"But things seem to be changing," Philip said. "He says no when he used to say yes. Vanishes for days then returns without saying where he was. That leaves me waiting. And I'm not good at waiting, as this week has probably made clear to you."

I wanted to offer a signal that I had, that it didn't matter, so I rested a hand on his warm back.

"I guess I'm waiting for him to leave me," Philip said.

He turned to face me, his blinking sped up. In the dim of the room, I couldn't tell if he was crying.

"He's always known how old you were," I said.

"Knowing and experiencing aren't the same."

"I have a dumb question."

"Is there any other kind?"

Minty heat huffed from his mouth.

"If you think he's going to leave you, why don't you leave him instead?" I asked.

Philip's breath quickened and I worried he'd get sick again. But he put a hand on my forehead and answered, "Because maybe I'm wrong."

Then he fell asleep.

I lay there wondering if this was what it was like to be a parent, with your child during a moment of abject fear or illness, disgusted by them, grateful, too, to have been with them at their most miserable.

Philip's hand sat next to mine. I held it. Light from outside leaked in through the window.

―――――

I pushed our flights back a day to give Philip time to recover and got our rooms for another night, saying "Entschuldi-

gung" more times than I could remember. The day we were
scheduled to leave, I went for a run, then treated myself to
an expensive lunch, showing up at Philip's room after, my
duffel bag in tow. His suitcase lay open and unpacked, and
the television blared.

"We'll be late," I said, and began tossing clothes into
his bag.

"Stop with that," he said with his earlier irritation.
"Something's happened."

I first mistook what was unfolding on TV for a Bruce
Willis movie. But with its shaky cameras and shrieking too
primal to be performed, I soon understood it was real.

"A second plane just hit," Philip said.

Smoke billowed from the Trade Center. A German
newscaster spoke with non-newscaster agitation.

"Look," Philip said.

Leaning close to the screen, we watched people jump
from the building's windows, holding each other's hands
as they barreled toward the ground. When the first tower
collapsed, Philip let out a noise whose only match was that
of the wounded deer I'd heard when I'd gone hunting with
a childhood friend, its wet, mournful cry shivering through
me for days after. Philip rested his head on my lap. He sput-
tered out incomplete phrases, "This can't" being the most
common. I rubbed his back, told him we were safe in this
hotel.

"But Nicola," he said.

"He has no business being down there," I answered.
"Even if he did, he can never get out of the house before ten."

Philip winced. I apologized for my ill-timed joke. Dust
darkened the TV camera.

For hours, we watched the towers fall on repeat. Also people running, a deluge of dust and smoke closing in on them. Later shots showed the Brooklyn Bridge, pedestrians in place of cars, their hair whitened by dust, as if cast as old people in a school play. I said that we should turn it off, and Philip agreed, but the silence allowed us to imagine more planes as bombs, more buildings falling in on themselves, so we turned the TV back on then ordered room service that neither of us ate.

The hotel informed us that our rooms were now booked by others, so we found a different place with one room free for the night.

"I hope you don't mind sharing," Philip said, as we checked in.

"I'm not worried you'll try to seduce me, if that's what you're asking."

"I hope, really, that you don't think of me as some old man who just wants you along as eye candy."

"I don't think of you that way," I said, the thrill of being considered eye candy one I kept to myself.

Philip told me he'd try to reach Nicola again.

In the middle of the night, Philip and I had gone to the hotel's business center. When he logged in and saw an email from Nicola (*I wasn't anywhere near all that*), he began to weep. His weeping was strange, beautiful, too, in its unvarnished way.

A man came into the business center, saw Philip crying,

and did a terrible job of masking his annoyance. I looked up at him and said, "Do you not know what's happening?" and the man left. I held Philip closer, felt lucky to be there with him, though I knew better than to say that out loud.

"He's fine," Philip repeated, then asked if I could email Nicola back for him. I wrote as Philip, telling Nicola I was so relieved to know he was safe. At the end I added, "Gordon is taking good care of me," then hit send and told Philip we should try to sleep for a while.

Philip and I became known as "the Americans." People he barely knew invited us to dinner. One wealthy collector insisted we stay at her house, though Philip politely refused. The new hotel I found for us was the fanciest so far, and though my room was small and faced a back alley, the place had a spa and a garden with architectural shrubs, a staff that seemed to be everywhere, asking if I wanted sparkling water or coffee.

On our second night, at a dinner at a large house, we were stars. But Philip's smooth benevolence had left him, replaced by long pauses and short sentences. He was asked what it was like being away from New York just then and said only, "Difficult." A question came next as to whether he knew anyone who'd been killed, and he answered, "Who can say?" When he continued in that same monosyllabic vein, guests turned to me. I answered elaborately about the strangeness of watching office workers run for their lives, how, had my life taken a slightly different turn, I might have been one of them.

"You're not an aspiring artist?" someone asked.

"I'm not an aspiring anything," I said.

A few people chuckled. I let them think it was a joke.

They asked about my family. I answered truthfully about my mom's piecemeal jobs, adding stories of Dad and Jesus. I thought to talk about him as a joke, but terror turned everyone serious. So I mentioned his fellow parishioners writhing on the floor. The time my father, essentially a stranger to me now, spoke in tongues and how, despite the jadedness I wanted to feel, it was like listening to an unexpected, heartbreaking song. A refilled wineglass was a call for me to keep talking. I told them of the cold I'd grown up in, the college I hadn't managed to finish, my ex I knew would end up a dentist like his parents, though he was trying to rebel by working at a bank. They laughed at that, made dentist jokes. All of them had perfect teeth.

Toward the end of dinner, I realized Philip had left to use the bathroom a long time before. I excused myself and found him lying on a sofa fortified with pillows.

"I can't believe we came," he said.

"They're being nice," I said.

"Wanting us to perform at a time like this."

"I'll tell them you have a headache."

"That sounds like an excuse," Philip said.

"What should I say then?"

"Let's just go."

Walking back to our hotel, Philip's stunned gloom lifted. "I didn't know all that about you," he said.

At the elevator, he kissed my forehead, pulled gently on my ear, and said, "Sleep tight." And though I thought I would, in my luxurious room, excitement kept me awake. I performed push-ups in hopes of exercising feeling out of myself, moved on to stretches I'd learned in fifth grade. In the middle of a series of squats, I heard noise outside and saw a trio of hotel staff members smoking. I waved. They waved back. I belonged down there with them, listening to stories about guests' outlandish demands, but their expressions asked me one question: How may we help you? I smiled, shook my head, and closed the curtains.

Flights to the States were grounded. I called Philip's travel agent every few hours, but got the same answer.

After two days of lunches and dinners, Philip began to decline invitations, making a thoughtless barb about us refusing to be their hired hands. He took me to museums. In front of certain paintings, Philip asked me what I saw.

"It's good," I said of one of a woman next to a window.

"That's not what I asked."

He told me to look closely, talked about color and gesture. Philip was trying to instruct me. What he offered didn't take. And though I often clung hard to the imagined, at that moment I didn't want to. So I told him the truth, that I saw black marks I hadn't noticed before, the frame coming undone at one corner, but none of it felt revelatory.

"Not like your father and Jesus," Philip said.

"I hadn't been thinking about that," I told him.

"I just don't want you to be reluctant."

Reluctant wasn't what I felt, so I said as much.

"What are you feeling then?" he asked.

"Like I want a coffee. To go to one of those outdoor cafés where we can people-watch."

We found a café. I tried to look at a woman and her dog,

a pair of sullen, squinting teens, but Philip's company was a distraction. Our coffees done, clouds piling up above the skyline, I told him we should go back to the hotel to rest for a while.

That night, at a pub with tall ceilings and medieval-looking chandeliers and waiters who placed beers at our table before we ordered them, Philip asked me what was next.

"I don't know," I said, unsure of his question's specific meaning.

"I mean after you've worked for us," Philip clarified.

"I like working for you," I said, and talked about other jobs I'd had, and my parents who treated work like a chronic condition to manage.

"There's more, you know," he said.

"I know," I answered.

He arched his eyebrows, out of pity, I thought first. But it was potential he wanted to convey, a sense that I could want and actually get things.

"That will have to be our project," he said. "A map, of sorts."

A waiter whizzed past, dropping new beers in front of us on his way.

"When we get back," I said, "what will *you* do?"

He talked about the shows they'd have to postpone because of the attack. I wanted to know about Nicola, who, when Philip finally reached him on the phone that afternoon, said that the connection was too bad for any sort of conversation. "Young man," Philip said, then waved the waiter over for the bill.

We walked down a narrow street, buildings pressed close so we could barely see the sky. People glided past on bicycles, a few of them rang their bells. Philip hooked his arm in mine.

"Why didn't Nicola come?" I asked.

"Let's talk about pleasant things," he said.

"Is there someone else?"

"I don't want to think about that now, while we're having such a nice time."

Philip told me instead about the first man he'd been with, how it had blown his marriage apart. His wild years after that, "Taking amphetamines so I barely slept." He described his first orgy, saying I should try one if I hadn't already.

"So many dicks and asses," I said.

"That's the point," Philip said. "Gluttony."

He talked about a fling he'd had with Rock Hudson in his L.A. days. "I was a muscle boy for a time, if you can believe it," Philip said. "Going to Venice Beach, doing pull-ups until my arms were on fire. I was at a party and there he was."

Philip told me about a maid he'd had growing up who'd taught him the ins and outs of sewing. "I don't remember how it came up, but shortly after I met Rock, we were at another party and I was telling a story about our maid Lola, the hours of sewing she and I did. He made a joke about the sweatshop she was running. Later, though, he asked if I still knew how. Told me he wanted some pants made to show off some gifts he had in the back and front. I went to his place the next day to measure. Turns out those gifts were considerable."

"And after you measured, did you?"

"Sleep together?" he asked.

I nodded. He nodded back.

"I borrowed a friend's sewing machine, worked all night—thanks to some stalwart pills—then brought the pants over to his place. He put them on. They were perfect. But do you know what he said, the two of us standing in front of the mirror looking at those perfect pants on that perfect man?" A church chimed midnight, the street we were on empty apart from parked cars. "Make them tighter."

I asked what happened with the two of them next.

"We just slept together that one time," he said.

From his distant expression I sensed he was thinking about those pants. Also that man.

I would come to remember the private bounty of those days, Philip recoiling from everyone but me, the drive we took to a castle on an island framed by sawtooth mountains, the shops we went to where Philip saw a sweater he thought would look nice on me, a leather satchel to replace my beat-up messenger bag, and bought both. A night we lay on his bed watching a Julia Roberts movie and when he kept forgetting her name, he told me he sometimes worried he was touched by the beginnings of dementia.

"You're the most undemented person I know," I said.

He fell asleep midway through the movie. I joined shortly after. When I woke up in the morning, Philip was gone. He came back with a bag bursting with pastries. We ate them on the unmade bed, kept going when we were full, crumbs and powdered sugar dusting our chins.

We went to dinner in a place with flower arrangements so precariously centered on tables we had to lean to see each other. Our waiter answered us with deadpan amusement when Philip asked if he could take the flowers away. And just before Philip handed him the signed check, he asked, "Is there a nearby bar for a nightcap?"

"I know a few," the waiter said in crisp English.

"Another question," Philip said. "My friend is hoping you'd have that nightcap with us."

The waiter didn't look over at me as he told Philip the name of a bar where he'd meet us in an hour. He took our signed check and went to a different table.

"What are you doing?" I asked.

"He's been looking at you all night," Philip said.

"So?"

"And you've been looking back. Two sharks circling one another." Philip's brow flattened with annoyance. "So I'm helping you out," he said. "Is your concern that I want to be a part of the action? I don't, so you can rid yourself of that fear."

"That wasn't my fear."

"What then?"

The hardness I'd had to contend with in the last ten days grew.

"I didn't realize he was looking at me," I said.

I hadn't realized I'd been looking either, any more than a person normally looked at a waiter. A busboy stacked several plates on his arm.

"Young man," Philip said. "We need to do something about your eyes."

———

After the drink, the waiter walked back with us to the hotel. Once in my room, he undressed and kissed me with an urgency so unlike his earlier poise, and I wished for more time with him, in this city, Pavel demoted to a mild ache. As the waiter slipped a condom onto my dick, I thought to thank Philip, who'd noticed the waiter and me watching each other. Then I moved into the waiter and could only think about that. And when my hands crept toward his throat, he nodded, and I put them there.

The waiter was asleep when the phone rang. A web of early-morning light covered the comforter. It was Philip's travel agent. I'd become well acquainted with her in the last few days.

"Did I wake you, Gordon?" she asked.

"Pretty early here," I said.

"That's a yes, I take it. I'm sorry for that. But I got flights."

The waiter let out a sighing exhale. A blanket sat at his hips, showing off his stomach's delicate dappling of hair.

"Great," I whispered.

"You can leave later today," she said.

The waiter's T-shirt and brightly colored underwear lay on the floor. I picked the underwear up, moved it to my face, and breathed in.

"Anything for tomorrow instead?" I asked.

The travel agent—her name was Valerie Esposito; Philip and I had taken to using that full name whenever we said it—answered, "I thought Philip was eager to get back."

"Something came up here," I said.

"Okay. Give me ten minutes."

I hung up and kissed the waiter's stomach. He woke up laughing, telling me my mouth tickled. He said "tickled" in such a delicious way that I asked him to say it again.

"Why again?" he asked, sitting up so the blankets fell and I saw he was already partly hard.

"Because I want you to," I said.

"Tickled," the waiter repeated.

I didn't answer the phone when Valerie called back but waited until the waiter and I had secured a date for that evening to hear about the new flights she'd gotten us.

I found Philip at the hotel's restaurant. The headline of his newspaper, written in large font and all caps, discussed armed force and prayers.

"We're saved," I told him. "We can leave tomorrow."

"Oh," Philip said.

Another night was punitive for him. But another night was all I wanted, so I told him, "It was the best Valerie Esposito could do."

"She's a miracle worker, for sure."

"Speaking of miracle workers," I said, and began to tell him about the waiter's skill and particular gifts. But Philip looked at me with pained embarrassment, and I realized that I'd been talking loudly enough for nearby guests to hear the details I'd begun to share about the waiter's ass and the noises he made, how, when I was on top of him, he leaned his head back so I could only see the whites of his eyes.

II

Pavel's studio was so warm it was almost a relief to take off my shirt. He placed couch cushions on the floor, a sheet on top to give a bed's appearance.

"Lie here," he said, and I did.

The day after I'd gotten back to our stunned, jittery city, flyers everywhere with photos of missing people we all knew weren't missing, Pavel called to ask if I was free to sit for a painting.

"For your show?' I'd asked.

"That opens in a month," he'd answered. I wasn't sure if that was a yes or a no.

The show should have opened that week, but the attack's aftermath put elections and sporting events and concerts on hold. Pavel's opening was postponed until October.

"You could have painted me in an actual bed," I said.

"No bed in my studio," Pavel said.

He lifted my chin. A spare brush sat behind one of his large, pale ears.

I told him I wanted to see the painting's progress; he told me that he didn't work that way and asked me to stop talking. Outside, a woman yelled at a child or boyfriend or dog, and sirens rose in harried repetition. I closed my eyes.

"Open, please," he said.

Pavel snapped a photo of me. He adjusted my hips, shifted my chin. The brush in his hand dripped paint onto my back, though he didn't notice or apologize. I wanted him to press that brush against me until I felt the metal beyond the bristles. I asked what that part on the brush was called and he didn't answer.

The cell phone Philip had given me on our return home rang. I ignored it. When it rang again right away, Pavel looked over to it and said, "Nicola."

"Could you pass it to me, please?" I asked.

As soon as Nicola started talking, I knew I had to leave.

"We aren't finished," Pavel said, as I put on my shirt and shoes.

"I'll come back later."

"There won't be light later."

"Tomorrow, then," I said, and tried to look at the painting, but he shooed me away.

"You know how Nicola is," I added.

Pavel's mouth squeezed into a scowl, and I remembered Philip talking about his gifts as a performer. He could have been an actor in period pieces playing a Nazi or a man whittled down by consumption.

"You told me you were free," Pavel said, helping himself to one of my cigarettes.

"With this job, I'm free, then I'm not."

"Maybe you should get a better job."

I walked down his building's stairs, knowing no other job would allow me to lie shirtless in Pavel's studio, its only requirements to stay still and look at him. From two floors above, he called my name, his alien handsomeness amplified at that angle.

"Come tomorrow morning early," he said.

"Like five?" I asked.

"Always joking. Eight."

I said I'd be there. He answered with a smile so large I didn't even mind getting up early the next day, or think to tell him that this would've been easier had he invited me to sleep over.

———————

Nicola stood in the vestibule, newly, deeply tanned. I waited for his flirty smile, but his face stayed sour. He walked me to the downstairs half bathroom.

"Did you miss us?" I asked.

"Do you hear that?" Nicola asked back. The room was quiet. Then came a plink. "It's been doing that for days. Please call the plumber."

"Who's your plumber?"

In his squint I sensed he didn't know. The sink plinked again.

"It's awful," Nicola said.

Without the warmth of his flirtation, standing so close to him took on an uncomfortable intimacy.

"I heard you charmed everyone on the continent, as it were," Nicola said, in a spot-on Philip impression.

"I tried to charm," I said, wanting to amplify that myth, though I'd spent most of my time there waiting until Philip needed to be taken places.

Another plink. I smiled, hoping to resuscitate what had once been playful between us.

"Philip talks about you now like you're his best friend or something," Nicola said.

I wanted to know the specifics of what he'd said, if Philip had overstated our closeness to turn Nicola jealous or afraid.

"We did get close," I said. "But then again we were together during a tragedy."

"The tragedy was here, not there," Nicola answered in a voice too loud for the small space we stood in.

One plink, another.

"That sound might drive me mad," Nicola said.

"I'll take care of it."

"Yes, Gordon," he said, then told me he had things to do.

Pavel took photos of me. He had on the same shirt and shorts from the day before, the same splotches lined his shins.

"You look like you slept here," I said.

"I did," he said. "No talking."

His first significant show was weeks away. There would be reviews in major publications, Pavel a wunderkind or a flop.

He finished the photos, told me I could go. But before I did, he lifted up a canvas. It was the painting from the day before, unfinished, he kept saying, though it looked done to me. Painted-me looked as if he were deciding whether to share a delicious secret.

"I know you're busy," he said.

"I can come back later," I told him.

I hoped these paintings might end up in fancy houses or museums, people making eye contact with painted-me because they felt they had to, though maybe they wanted to as well.

"Good," Pavel said. "I have other ideas."

As October began and people emerged from their terrified cocoons and the flyers of missing people began to bleach in the sun or fall off walls and telephone poles, plans for Pavel's opening were finalized. The gallery rented out the back room of a restaurant for a post-opening dinner. There was a menu to confirm, seating arrangements to be agreed on, a florist to rein in. After each marathon day, I got back to our apartment, saw the machine blinking, and hoped it was Janice, still on her road trip. I checked the mail for flashes of her handwriting, slept in the bed still inhabited by her smell, and tried on her tank tops, loose without her hips and chest to anchor them. I talked out loud to an imaginary her about the thrill of Pavel painting me, also how I didn't trust that feeling.

One night, Pavel and I worked late. We slurped down Thai food, then continued. At three in the morning, he said we should pause. I was getting ready to leave when he said, "Pausing is not stopping."

"Sometimes you speak in riddles," I said, with performed exasperation.

"We nap, then continue." He paused. "Is that clear?"

We lay on his studio's sofa. He pressed his back against me. I started to get hard and tried to turn, to hide my interest, but Pavel said, "Glad you enjoy being here," then went to sleep.

An alarm went off three hours later. Tiredness stung my eyes. "I have an idea," Pavel said, and painted me lying on the sofa. In his T-shirt and underwear, the pale hair on his legs fuzzy in the sunlight, Pavel told me I didn't even need to open my eyes.

Afterward, I went straight to the gallery, where Philip wanted to review the dinner's seating chart. I waited for him in a room they called the library. A shelf of art books rose to the ceiling, and skylights warmed the large table. I worried I might smell.

Nicola and Andrew moved through the room. For a moment, I wondered if it was Andrew who Nicola had stayed home for, though his rulebound nervousness made that unlikely.

"Are you wearing what you wore yesterday?" Nicola asked me.

"Yup," I answered, and looked at the seating chart where, next to two adjacent names, Philip had written an emphatic *No!* A nearby phone trilled; Andrew left to answer it.

"Pavel showed us a new painting," Nicola said. "Well now I know what you've been up to, keeping him distracted before his opening. Did Philip ask you to babysit him?"

"I'm not babysitting," I said.

"The painting isn't half bad," Nicola said.

"Thank you."

"You didn't paint it!" Nicola smiled, reconsidered,

then told me Lola needed to be taken to the vet for her indigestion.

"Wait," I said. "Didn't Philip have a maid growing up named Lola?"

In his annoyance, Nicola looked older.

"I wouldn't know," he said. "I wasn't alive then."

The gallery was packed. People clustered in front of paintings, though none were of me. I grew embarrassed at how much of the day I'd spent imagining versions of myself on these walls.

Competing conversations swarmed the room. Old women moved between the art and one another, while younger guests gathered in opposite corners, Sharks and Jets with innuendo rather than switchblades. A woman walked in. People gave her space. It was a famous former model I remember seeing on the cover of women's magazines as a child.

I was in the middle of an invented scenario in which the former model bought a painting of me when Andrew came over and whispered, "What the fuck is he doing here?" into my ear. He must have been scolded by Philip about my name; earlier that evening he'd called me Gordon several times.

He pointed to a tall young man, his face on the precipice between handsome and haggard.

"I don't know who that is," I said.

"What do they pay you to do anyway?" Andrew asked.

Andrew was cute enough, though such a killjoy that any possible interest I had in him dried up long ago.

"If you could let me know who that is and what I'm supposed to do about him, that would be helpful," I said.

"That's Eric," Andrew said. He let the name linger, but realized it meant nothing to me. "You really don't know."

Andrew walked me to the gallery's office. He asked for a cigarette, which I begrudgingly gave him, and explained that Eric had been Philip and Nicola's assistant until his romance with Nicola had become so egregious that Philip had fired Eric and kicked Nicola out. After half a year of traveling, Eric had returned to New York, wooing Nicola with such flirty intensity that they'd picked up where they left off, and then some. "Who do you think Nicola was with when you were in Europe? Eric's parents have a place on the Cape. Apparently, it was some gross, sandy fuckfest."

"That doesn't sound gross," I said.

"You've clearly never had sex on the beach."

"Just the drink. So this Eric. What am I meant to do about him?"

When I interrupted Nicola's conversation, he shot me a look of vaudevillian bother.

"Did you invite Eric?" I asked.

"How do you know about—"

"Because he's over there pretending to look at the painting of the man with a chessboard."

Nicola's face was shattered glass. I wished meanness didn't taste so good to me.

"I told him not to come," Nicola said. "Fuck."

"So you want me to get rid of him?"

"How?"

"I'm not calling the cops, if that's your concern."

I thought of Philip waiting for Nicola to leave him, and wanted this whole situation to blow up in Nicola's face.

"If you could make it clear that I'm not asking him to leave," Nicola said.

He was a coward. Understanding this made things simpler between us, wobblier, too, as there'd be no limit to the maneuvers he might resort to.

I passed the famous former model, also a man who called out the name Natasha, before stopping at Eric's side. Close up, his haggard qualities took center stage. Protruding eyes. A nose and chin in a drawn-out, narrow set. I looked around to see if Philip had noticed his arrival but couldn't spot him.

"Hi there," I said. "I'm Gordon."

"I've heard about you," Eric answered, with a smugness that annoyed me.

"So we've heard about each other."

Eric examined a painting of one man's hand resting on another man's knee.

"I can be here," he said.

"Technically," I replied.

He moved to the next painting. I walked with him.

"Pavel's good," I said.

Eric shrugged. A waiter zigzagged through the crowd. I leaned in to take in the same detail Eric pretended to be so invested in.

"This is harassment," he said.

"I'm just looking at the art," I said.

"No, you're not."

"Technically I am."

He moved to another painting. I mirrored him. His work not to pay me any attention, his consternation of a spoiled child finally told no; I found all of it thrilling and worried it might be the same coldhearted excitement newbie cops felt when they first walked around in their uniforms. Eric sighed, his expression toggling between flustered and meanly pleased.

"Nicola told me you're an asshole," Eric said, and left.

Andrew came over shortly after, thanked me for dealing with him. I thanked him back for finally learning my name.

"I didn't take you for such a bitch," he said.

You didn't take me for anything, I wanted to answer. But I grabbed a flute of champagne from a waiter, then walked around in hopes that the famous former model was still there.

Pavel found me, told me he wished we could hide and have a cigarette together. But someone called his name, and his worn-out face switched to delighted.

Nicola's laugh echoed, Philip and the model huddled in conversation. I moved close, hoping for an introduction. But they kept on talking, and I pictured Eric and Nicola in that barn, Nicola saying to him the same words he'd said to me. *It can be a big thing or a small thing or nothing at all.*

Then Audrey from their first dinner party arrived. She saw me, smiled, and said, "Good thing they didn't paint the walls an army green."

"Good thing they didn't paint them pea-soup green, either," I replied, surprised that she'd remembered me.

At the dinner, people flocked around Pavel. The famous former model insisted she sit next to him, though she hadn't been on our seating chart at all.

In the middle of dinner, as I checked with the restaurant's manager about dietary restrictions, Pavel came, took my hand, and said he needed me. We went to the restaurant's garden, empty on that damp night.

"You want a cigarette?" I asked.

He wrapped his arms around me, kissed me, told me he had nothing left.

"I've heard many of them have already sold," I said.

I felt him shrug. I took off the glasses he had on, asked if they were real.

"Aren't you going to say something?" he asked.

"I am saying something."

"I mean, a pep talk. Some comfort at least."

Pavel was wound up. It was nice, in a way, to get a glimpse underneath his unruffled exterior. I kissed him.

"The glasses are real," he said. "For reading usually, but . . ."

"There's an effect you're going for," I said.

"Do they not look right?"

"They look perfect," I answered.

We returned to the dinner. Philip came to double-check that the dessert didn't have walnuts. I wanted to say that crème brûlée never has walnuts, as the restaurant's manager had just told me, but told him, "Walnut free," then, "Seems like tonight's going really well."

"Exceeding expectations," Philip said. He leaned close to me.

"What are you doing?" I asked.

"Seeing if you'd had a cigarette."

"Am I not allowed?"

"Maybe you don't remember," he said. "In Munich, I think, what you'd said to me. That I could smell you anytime. I was trying for levity."

Andrew called Philip over.

At the far end of the table, Pavel removed his glasses. Nicola found me to ask about the crème brûlée, too. "Crème brûlée never has walnuts," I told him, though a few months before I hadn't known what it was.

The evening wound down, and Philip grew exhausted. Nicola sat in busy conversation with a handful of guests, wooed by their attention.

"Let's get you a cab," I said to Philip.

A month before, I'd lifted him into the shower, let him rest his head on my lap as we watched the towers collapse in a loop.

"Nicola hates being alone," Philip said, once we got outside. I was unsure what brought this comment on, but I wanted to hear more, so I nodded. "The dogs were his idea, so there'd always be some other creature in the house."

At the dinner, Nicola had barely spoken to him. Only when Philip made a toast did Nicola move next to him to rest a presentational hand on Philip's back.

"The dogs feel more like yours," I said.

"Because I remember to feed them."

A cab passed, already occupied. Headlights struck Philip's face, and tires hissed across the wet pavement.

"Nicola isn't a planner unless he's trying to avoid being alone," Philip said. "Then he plans like mad."

"But you're okay? You and Nicola settled things?"

"Who can say," Philip answered, and raised a hand. A cab coasted over to us.

Inside, most of the guests were gone. I walked over to Nicola and said, "Philip went home."

"There's a surprise," he said.

The woman next to him guffawed. I decided then that I hated him, also Pavel, who seemed to have left without telling me.

As my cab home bounced over potholes, the driver honking for no obvious reason, Pavel's aloof charm started to sour. Alan back in Minneapolis was more obviously good-looking. And the redhead I'd slept with a few months before had recently left a message on our machine, just saying hi. The defeat I'd been saddled by in my first days in Europe came back to me, and as we stopped at a red light, I felt ready to end this job.

The cab approached the bridge. Other cars jockeyed to get there first. Taillights stuttered off and on in a glowing row.

My phone vibrated. It was a text from Pavel, showing his apartment's address, the phrase *c u thr*? after it. *Mom*? I wrote back. *Ha* he responded, then, *Y/N*? The cab's radio crackled. The air freshener dangling from the mirror spun.

Y, I answered, and told the driver there was a change of plans. As he grumbled about the illegal U-turn he had to make and I told him it would be worth his while, I felt like I might lift off the ground.

Pavel lived in a narrow building on a narrow street. He buzzed me in. I walked up one flight, another, elated and surprised that this was about to happen, surprised, too, that Pavel lived only a few blocks away from Nicola and Philip.

12

Pavel's apartment was sparsely decorated: white furniture and bare walls, a mattress centered on the floor of its largest room.

"You survived," I said.

Pavel kissed me hard, his jaw scraping against mine, and pulled off my shirt. His teeth traced my chest, my stomach, and he took me into his mouth until he gagged. As he undressed, his pale body glowed, the look of wanting on his face so thrilling to see that I let out a noise. He slid a condom onto my dick and whispered, "I've thought about this." Though I'd thought about it, too, with worrying frequency, I answered, "I know." When Pavel came, he gasped as if being flogged, croaked out, "Keep going," when I asked if I should stop. After, he patted my chest. I worried I was being dismissed, but he didn't ask me to leave.

"You fascinate me," Pavel said.

"I'm just unfamiliar," I said. I knew I was right, though I wanted to be wrong, for his fascination to hold as I moved from novel to ordinary. Pavel rolled me onto my stomach, told me it was his turn. I stopped caring about anything beyond his body moving on top of mine.

The next morning, after the two of us lay in bed reading reviews of his show, one calling him "a bit of a rock star," Pavel asked what I was doing later.

"No firm plans," I said.

"I'll see you tonight then?" he asked.

I stared at the ceiling, the answer he wanted hovering in my throat.

"Okay, rock star," I said finally.

Pavel held the hair at the back of my head, pulling it as he kissed me.

Each day, Pavel wanted to squeeze more painting in. Sometimes in the evening, or at morning's earliest edge. For one, I posed in my underwear. In another, I leaned on my forearms. He got annoyed whenever I needed to take a break.

A week later, he asked to paint me naked. I undressed and worried I'd get hard, my greatest fear after middle school gym class when all the boys were forced to shower in one mildewed room.

Pavel took out his camera.

"You're taking pictures?" I asked.

He'd done the same for the other paintings. But Pavel having photos of my dick to evaluate or share left me nervous. I didn't trust this would last, could picture a future moment when he referred to me as a guy he used to paint, while I stayed stuck in the slog of pining for him. In his studio, with me naked and the radiator's scolding hiss, it felt like he and I had already ended.

"I destroy the photos when a painting is done," Pavel said. "Try to keep still."

I took the camera from his hands. When I first snapped a picture of him, he looked annoyed. I took two more. Annoyance turned to interest, and he peeled off his clothes. I took another picture. I put a finger inside him, took a picture of that, too, told him these pictures would get destroyed. He nodded. And just when I was about to move on top of him, he grabbed his sketch pad and began to draw, his hard-on brushing up against the paper.

I'd come to drop off packages when I heard raised voices upstairs. It was noon, a time Philip and Nicola were rarely home.

"You can't make new rules," Nicola said, voice punching down the stairs.

"There aren't new rules," Philip said back. "But you've reinterpreted, as it were."

"As it were *not*, old man!" Nicola shouted.

There was quiet for a time. Dust lazed in the sun angling through the windows. Then Philip said, "You've always known how old I am."

I was about to leave when the dogs emerged from the kitchen, barking excitedly in my direction.

"Anybody home?" I called out.

Philip moved halfway down the stairs.

"Thought you'd be at the gallery," I said.

"Is my presence an inconvenience?" he asked.

"Of course not. I've brought packages."

Nicola appeared behind him, all smiles as he said my name, like some soft-boned sea creature, able to move into seemingly impossible spaces. He asked if I wanted coffee. I lied and said I had a dentist appointment.

Philip looked tired. I wanted him to tell Nicola to leave, me there to witness Nicola's stunned fear as he understood what he'd pushed to an ending.

"Call if you need anything," I said.

I went to Pavel's studio and found him waiting for me. Rather than get right to painting, he pushed me against a wall, yanked my pants down, and began to fuck me. His teeth pinched my shoulder. Fingers dug into my hips. He finished with his usual choking noises, then told me not to move. A condom drooped at my heel, the aching relief of just being fucked all I could consider. I heard the soft flip of his sketch pad being opened, a pencil scratching across one of its pages. I told him I needed to go to the bathroom. He asked if I really needed to or could wait.

"I'll try," I said.

"Try hard," he answered, and went to find his camera.

At home I played the latest message from my father. He talked about a time our pipes burst and the walls looked like they were weeping, how Mom had gotten fed up and gone to her sister's while Dad and I cut holes into the wall. "We kept peeling back more wall, looking for the busted pipe," Dad said, pausing to take a breath. "And you stood behind me the whole time, in your winter coat. Kept telling me how you could see your breath, how it reminded you of

Mom's smoking. You stayed with me as I opened up walls, saying, 'maybe this one,' when I wanted to give up. I remember wanting to give up, also you behind me."

I remembered, too, how startled I was each time Dad's sledgehammer had sounded, my words as much encouragement as a hope he'd stop. We went out for Chinese after and ate wonton soup so hot I felt it snaking down my chest. And when we got back to our apartment's half dozen cavernous holes, I said, "Maybe we shouldn't have done this," and Dad looked at me like I was hurting him.

I erased his message.

Janice's last postcard had just come in from the Rockies (its entire message was the words *I MISS YOU SO MUCH* in all caps; I'd cried when it arrived), so I broke her rule and smoked in the apartment. I didn't want to stay home alone. But when I called Pavel, he didn't pick up. So I got on the subway, took it to my former Bay Ridge stop. I walked past my old apartment (I saw lights on, felt for whomever had ended up there) and stopped outside Food Land. Inside was a cashier I recognized, another I didn't. The sign's demise continued, mostly vowels remained. I thought I heard my phone ring, but when I pulled it out, there was nothing. It wasn't until I got home that it rang for real. I felt a flood of relief, sure Pavel was calling me back. It was Philip.

"You okay?" I said, in lieu of a hello.

"You sound winded," he said. "Out for a run?"

"Yes," I answered, lying my shorthand.

He told me that he and Nicola were going upstate for a few days and wanted to leave the dogs with me.

"When are you leaving?" I asked.

"We're already in the car."

I wanted to be angry at how they considered my avail-ability only in afterthought, though I did the same thing.

I called Pavel again, got his voice mail, and left him a message to let him know I'd be staying a few blocks away. I didn't hear back from him until the next day. As I posed for him then, I noticed that in the finished paintings he'd exag-gerated my scrawniness so that I looked angry and infirm.

Things sped up after that. Pavel and I were together most nights, meeting his artist friends, listening to their confident opinions.

At one party, a woman named Gretchen asked me what I did. I told her.

"So you're an art dealer?" she asked.

The apartment we were in was large, a grand piano in a corner buried in guests' coats.

"No. I, like, pick up their dry cleaning and give their dogs worm pills."

"That's hilarious," Gretchen said.

A few minutes later, she asked if I had a spare cigarette.

"I'm all out," I said, despite the pack's outline bulging in my shirt pocket.

I went to a different room, tried and failed to engage in conversation with a man and a woman who first asked me if I knew Dagmar, second if I'd gone to school with them.

"Who's Gretchen?" I asked Pavel in the cab home.

"A rich girl who thinks she's a painter," he answered.

"She's not?"

"I mean, she paints," Pavel said.

He described her work, talking about how most of it featured open windows. He told me next that several were set on dark streets, how some included a river, details meant to convey how bad it was.

"Got it," I said, though I didn't, and wondered how Pavel described me to other people.

"I used to work at a grocery store," I said one night as I posed. He had me slouched in a chair.

Pavel shushed me, but I kept going. I talked about Thor/Vince, Marcy's crush on me.

"I had a job one summer in high school, in the typing pool at my mom's bank," he said.

"This wasn't in high school," I said, and realized Pavel rarely asked me questions.

An hour later, the painting as far as he could take it then, Pavel told me he needed to walk. We left the apartment at three in the morning, holding hands even when someone in a passing car shouted obvious, awful things at us. Getting to Gramercy Park, he moved his hand between the narrow, iron railings and pulled a key from under a rock.

"Trespassing," I said.

He kissed the back of my neck.

We went into the empty park. A statue of a man stood in its center, head bowed in proud submission.

"Was this a soldier?" I asked.

"Actor," he said.

I climbed the statue's pedestal, sat in the carved chair he held on to. I leaned back so that the actor's hand touched my cheek. Pavel lifted up his camera. It clicked as he took one shot, another, as he moved close to get a detail of the actor's hand on my cheek. It would turn out to be the only well-known painting in this series, this one called *G. and the Actor*. I looked it up recently and read that it's in a private collection.

We went back to Pavel's, slept for a few hours. Then I left to walk and feed the dogs. I called after to see if he was doing more painting. He didn't answer. When I finally saw him two days later, he told me he'd been in that part of the process where he needed to be alone.

"You understand," Pavel said.

We were at a bar in the East Village, new candles pressed on top of old ones to make waxy mountains, everyone in the room candlelit and beautiful.

"I don't understand," I said. "But I'm not an artist. I don't have particular times I need to be alone. Unless, you know, I'm doing something in the bathroom."

Pavel smiled at my dumb joke, and the bartender refilled our glasses. I didn't tell Pavel that for the two days I thought he'd been done with me I'd flipped between the shock of being dropped and the surprise that he'd ever been interested. He stayed quiet for several minutes. When he finally did talk, he played with the wax on the candle in front of him.

"I have to tell you something," he said.

"Do you have it?" I asked.

"What?" he asked back.

"Is this the 'I'm sick' talk?"

"What?" he said again, then, "No," surprised that I'd even considered that possibility.

He told me we should go outside, for cigarettes and privacy, and turned to the bartender to say we'd be back. I felt reassured by the "we" in his statement, though I also sensed that the we was ending.

13

Once we'd lit our cigarettes, Pavel told me he was going to Mexico City. And though I asked, "For vacation?" I understood he meant something more substantial.

"Going to live there for a while," he said.

A car passed in a smear of music, and my stomach hollowed with surprise. I had no right to be surprised though. I'd long put my money on a world I imagined rather than the one that existed.

"Your apartment is here," I said.

"It's my friend Whitney's. She's been letting me borrow it while she's been in Sydney, but she's coming back. I thought I told you."

"What's in Mexico City?" I asked.

"A cheap apartment. New things to see."

I couldn't imagine going someplace else for newness, knew if I'd had an opportunity to leave, I'd consider Pavel as a reason not to. I hardly knew him but already he'd turned into a country for me to claim.

As Pavel stepped closer to me lust took over, though I wanted anger's sour purpose, or at least enough pride to compel me to walk away. He kissed my forehead, my mouth.

"Now you know why I was being weird," he said, some great burden unknotted.

"I still think you're weird."

"Always joking."

"We should finish our drinks."

"Oh," Pavel said with surprise.

"You want me to cry?" I asked, the anger I'd hoped for breaking through, more so when his eyes softened with what looked like boredom.

"Let's go back to my place," he said, then told me he wasn't leaving for two weeks.

Back at his apartment, he pressed a hand against my stomach. I felt its resistance when I breathed in. He put his free hand on my cheek, leaned close so I could smell his wine breath.

"I'll probably be back in a year," he said, with whispery sincerity.

I was angry still, so I turned him around and went at him fast. He closed his eyes though I wanted them open. He came with his strangulating sounds and muttered, "Thank you" as if I'd gotten him a coffee or reminded him to bring an umbrella on a day it was forecast to rain.

"You could always come visit for a bit," Pavel said.

"I'll let you know when my schedule opens up."

Pavel was asleep two minutes later. "Mexico," I whispered. He didn't stir. "Pavel lives in a hovel," I added. "He sometimes grovels and talks about Václav Havel. If not, he reads a novel." I laughed at my stupidity, remembering then that I was still dog-sitting. I left. When the dogs were done, I rang Pavel's buzzer, but he didn't answer.

He called the next morning to ask if I'd left because of his news.

"The dogs," I said.

He told me I should come over, that we should use his last weeks in the city. Though part of me wanted to shift to the sad solidity of remembrance, those next weeks brought a snow day's elated surprise, everything whittled down to hours with him in bed and at restaurants and in his studio where for several hours, stillness was my one goal. Though each time I sat for him the same worry returned: that he'd started things up with me because he knew he wasn't sticking around.

For Thanksgiving, Pavel went to visit his aunt in Philadelphia. Philip and Nicola celebrated with a dinner at their place in the city, where I was the helpful friend. Rebecca from the summer was there. I pulled her aside and said, "I haven't forgotten what you said." She looked embarrassed and again I felt as if I didn't know the rules.

Nicola was pleasant to me for a change, talking about the godsend I'd been. "Before him, we barely managed," he told the group. When someone suggested we all say what we were thankful for, Nicola said that he was thankful for me. My face heated up. I didn't trust him. But it was nice to have a break from his overcaffeinated annoyance. When my turn came, I blurted out that I was thankful for Philip taking me to Europe. From Nicola's tapering smile, I understood that I should have included him in my message. I added something to that effect, Nicola's annoyed expression unmoved. A man whose name I kept forgetting declared that he was thankful for his dermatologist, pointing to places where wrinkles had once been. "Voilà," he said.

"Voilà," we repeated, in lieu of cheers.

Pavel left at the start of December, the blow of his departure softened by Janice's return. I was so thrilled at her homecoming that I found it hard to talk to her, answering her questions about Pavel and my job in short, declarative sentences. But in a few days I became reaccustomed to her steady attention. She made dinners for us to share, invited me to sleep in her bed with her, the two of us tucked under a duvet I'd recently bought, where she admitted she'd been afraid to come back to the city after the attack. Janice told me stories, too, of Meredith singing along to cheesy songs on the radio, also how, when they moved through the lunar landscape of southern Utah, she'd wished I'd been with them. "I told Meredith, if we just had Gordon with us, it would have been perfect," Janice said. Her face glowed under the Christmas lights strung across her ceiling. She brought me back a *Don't Mess with Texas* T-shirt and chocolates from San Francisco, a jar of pickled pigs' feet from Alabama she kept insisting were delicious.

A week into her return, her stories shifted to those of Meredith's moodiness, the states they drove through where Meredith didn't say a word. But each time I asked if they were breaking up, Janice's brow tightened and she said, "Sometimes things are hard," in a tone that seemed meant to convince her and me at the same time.

Janice got a job at a dive bar with a beamed ceiling and large maps on its walls and a back room where bands played and burlesque was performed. Burlesque became her obsession. She talked about one of the performers with an excitement I translated as lust. A few weeks into the job, Janice started performing, too, showing me the pasties and tiny thong she'd bought. She stood in our living room, a corset pushing her breasts almost to the latitude of her shoulders.

"What does Meredith think about all this?" I asked.

"I haven't told her," Janice answered.

I'd just gotten out of the shower, the apartment steamy and shampoo-smelling.

"When we were in Tucson," Janice said, "at a barbecue of a friend of a friend, one of the guests, an older dyke—hot in a weathered sort of way—she and I struck up a conversation. Within minutes, Meredith told me we had to leave. She didn't talk to me for almost a day."

"Because of the old lady?"

"A hot old lady," Janice added.

"So you're not telling her."

"For now," Janice said, then asked if I thought less of her.

"Never," I said.

I kissed her forehead. My damp hair brushed against hers.

For Christmas—Philip and Nicola off to a Caribbean island—I stayed with the dogs. As they were leaving, Philip handed me an envelope. There was a tasteful card inside, also fifteen hundred dollars. I was so flustered I forced the dogs to take a walk in the rain. As we meandered through the neighborhood, I smoked and passed expensive stores, glad the wet dogs kept me from going inside.

Janice and Meredith came over the next day, guffawing as they explored each room. As Janice and I lay on Philip and Nicola's bed, Meredith told us how much each piece of art on the walls might go for.

"You suggesting we rob them?" I asked.

"Just informational," Meredith said, and we went onto the back patio to smoke.

We scoured the city for a place still selling trees and found Philip and Nicola's decorations in a closet. Janice made us bitter cocktails as we trimmed the tree while Meredith told us about the job she'd just gotten for the broadcast of the Times Square New Year's Eve show, with its combination of long hours and ludicrously good money.

"I still don't know what a gaffer does," I said.

"Because you don't listen," Meredith told me.

The dogs' tails shook the tree's branches.

———

Janice and Meredith slept in Philip and Nicola's room. In the morning, we made eggs with lox, drank mimosas with their champagne. I took out the cash Philip had given me and spread it out on the counter one large bill at a time. "Our job is to spend this," I said.

"Jesus, sugar," Janice said. Meredith counted it once, again.

I called a French restaurant Nicola raved about, asked if they could squeeze us in for lunch. When I mentioned the gallery, the man on the phone paused, answered that he could seat us at two.

In Philip and Nicola's closet, we cobbled together outfits. Over her dress, Janice put on one of Philip's cashmere sweaters. She lined one arm with the beaded bracelets Nicola had from his brief dalliance with Buddhism. Meredith chose a black blazer. I went back to Nicola's aspirational stash and picked a pair of gray pants, a white shirt with heavy cuff links. When the three of us were ready, we stood in front of the closet's large mirror. I wished for a camera, then changed my mind, as it would miss exactly what was alive between the three of us then, showing instead our blemished skin and half-closed eyes, the woozy look on my face when I'm happy.

In a cab after lunch we passed a store I'd admired while walking the dogs, regal-looking coats in its window. I asked the driver to stop, told Janice and Meredith I needed help picking out a present.

"For who?" Janice asked.

"For me," I said.

The salesperson greeted us coolly, though soon she decided we were worth her while, and swaddled us in her attention.

"This one needs a new coat," Meredith said.

I tried on coats that were simultaneously soft and sturdy. One had square shoulders, another a repetition of delicate buttons. As the salesperson helped me into a fourth one, the idea of spending several hundred dollars grew vulgar and dumb. But each time I eyed the door, I asked to try on another and reminded myself that I had money now.

The coat I settled on was dark and plaid. I paid, peeling bills from their bundle as if it were a delicate piece of fruit.

That night we smoked weed and went to a Broadway show. Its songs were cheesy, the dialogue stilted, but the tap dancing brought us to our feet. We took a cab to a club after and danced in sweaty celebration until I remembered the dogs and returned home to walk them.

New Year's Eve was coming. Along with it, rumors about the next terrorist attack: subway cars exploding just as one year switched to the next, Times Square—where Meredith would be—an ideal target. Janice began a campaign to get Meredith to quit her job, though after their cross-country trek, neither of them had any money. There were other jobs, Janice kept saying. Meredith's annoyance accumulated in tandem with Janice's worry. I wanted our easiness back, to smooth out this sudden patch of rough air, so I told them we should have a New Year's Eve dinner. Janice paused at the mention of a party, her ragtag friends at the house drinking expensive booze and sitting on luxurious furniture. She put a hand on my cheek, said, "That could be just the thing." Meredith mouthed *thank you* in my direction.

Janice invited ten friends. Many of them had friends they wanted to bring. Our guest list ballooned to seventeen.

We bought steaks and champagne and oysters, the money from Philip whittled down to scraps. Janice wore one of her corsets along with a pair of Philip's dress pants. I put on one of Nicola's suits, forgoing a shirt under the blazer.

With unannounced friends in tow, soon more than two dozen people crowded the house's main floor. They ate canapés, drank martinis. The dogs wound through the crowd, scavenging for food scraps and attention.

People smoked in the backyard, bringing bursts of cold back in with them. While I was out there, Janice's friend Aisha dropped a cigarette. Its tip singed a small hole into the blazer I had on. I convinced myself that Nicola wouldn't notice and went to check on Janice. She kept the New Year's Eve broadcast on, but muted. The screen toggled between Dick Clark and bands playing with manic glee and the crowd caged together, red-faced from cold or booze or both.

Someone spilled a drink, though it landed on the kitchen's hardwood. A different guest broke a glass and an impulse to end the party right then flooded me. But Janice walked through the crowd with childlike exuberance, her joy so strong that it infected me and her two friends arranging lines of coke on the kitchen counter and the trio of women making out on the sofa where Philip often sat reading the paper.

At midnight we gathered around the still-muted television. The ball fell, slow and cumbersome and underwhelming, and confetti covered the crowd. Janice squeezed my hand. Muted, the cheering on TV passed for wild panic. But a minute passed with no explosion. Five more and Janice's grip loosened.

"We did it," she said, and gave me a belated New Year's kiss.

Giddy with relief, Janice announced that she'd perform

the burlesque she'd been learning. Chair legs scraped as we dragged furniture out of the way. Someone lit a cigarette. I swallowed the impulse to scold them. As a bottle of champagne was opened and foam fountained to the floor, catastrophe loomed closer. But then Janice's friend Jeffrey, whom I'd briefly slept with, arrived. He moved his cold hands under my blazer and across my bare torso. I kissed him, lying as I said, "I was hoping you'd show."

Janice closed the pocket doors separating the living and dining rooms. When we reopened them, old-time jazz music played, and Janice stood wearing a corset and bottoms that barely covered her ass. She walked to the beat, turned a bentwood chair backward and sat on it, legs splayed. She pressed the balls of her feet on the downbeat, her heels next. With the tiniest pulse of her hips, Janice inched the chair forward.

The song's brassy intro gave way to a woman singing about a man who didn't know what he had, wouldn't have it much longer. Janice yanked off her corset, revealing a small sequined bra. She slammed her heels down, dropping with a grunt as the singer sang, "Gone."

"Gone," Janice repeated in a snorted whisper.

"Gone," the singer sang again, this time holding the note, her voice a deep-timbred bell. Janice rose to her feet. Never before had going from sitting to standing felt to me like a reckoning. Her hips tipped. She spun around and her bra was gone, her tasseled pasties spinning to the rhythm. A friend snapped Polaroids of Janice as she shimmied, as she climbed onto the chair.

The performance's end was met with a standing ovation from the humans, yips from the dogs, tears from me at how

Janice could transform a room's weather. We went outside for cigarettes, came in and made pitchers of margaritas and Moscow mules. Janice stayed in her costume until she got too cold.

When Meredith arrived a few hours later, Janice kept saying, "She's here!" until Meredith told her that we all knew, that she could stop saying it now. And when Jeffrey lingered, I said to him, "Why don't I show you to my room," so we went there and I remembered why I'd liked sleeping with him, also how shockingly loud he got during sex (he told me once how his neighbors had complained about his sex noise so much that his lease hadn't been renewed).

The next morning, Janice, Meredith, and I cleaned the house and disassembled the tree. When Meredith was in the shower, Janice asked me not to mention her performance the night before. I hooked my pinkie in hers. Then they left. I missed them right away, the quiet so disconcerting that I was glad for the distraction of the dogs and the relatively warm weather.

New Year's Day dragged by. I called my mom in Arizona. She asked if I was one of the people she'd seen crowded in the cold the night before just for a moment on television. When I told her I'd never do such a thing, she said, "When did you turn into such a snob?" and I felt like I couldn't win. I tried my father, too, but got his machine. He and June were likely at church, swaying in holy thanks for having made it through the year, unlike the people Philip and I had watched on television a few months before, deciding to jump because at least they'd make quick work of it, or at least, for their last moments, they'd breathe cleaner air.

Philip returned the next night, not looking tanned or rested. On his knees, he accepted the dogs' frenetic attention.

"Where's your other half?" I asked.

"Happy New Year," Philip said. Dog tongues flagged toward him. "I told Nicola I needed to be alone for a while."

The dogs examined Philip's suitcase with a series of quick, audible sniffs. I wasn't sure whether to offer congratulations or condolences.

"In Germany, you asked why I stayed with him," Philip said. "No one's asked me that before."

"That's just because I don't know any better."

I showed him the mail I'd collected, the list of phone messages, and told him I'd get out of his hair.

"Have a drink with me," Philip said. "A toast to a new year."

In the kitchen, Philip watched me make martinis. It felt good to be watched by him.

"So it's over?" I asked.

Philip shrugged, the windows of neighboring buildings a checkerboard of light.

"I heard how Pavel treated you," he said.

"Pavel was fine."

Philip's eyebrows rose.

"The paintings he did of you are quite good," he said.

"Nicola said the same thing. When I thanked him for the compliment, he reminded me that I hadn't painted them."

"Such a catty one, that man."

I asked how they'd met. He answered with the story of a lover who'd died in the early years of the plague, Philip certain he had it, too, getting tested constantly, enforcing celibacy until desire's pull grew too strong and he met Nicola.

"I have a strange favor to ask," Philip said.

"The stranger the better."

"Would you stay in the guest room tonight? I think I'll sleep better that way."

Philip reddened for the first time since I'd known him, his question now somehow more delicate than me in the bathroom as he got sick, or holding him up in the shower. He hooked a finger into his drink to exhume an olive.

"Happy to," I said. "Your sheets are nicer than mine anyway."

Philip nodded, as if in vehement agreement, then walked upstairs. I stayed up late, reading magazines, scrolling through the television, in case he came back down.

A few days later, Philip asked that I stop by the gallery. On his office wall hung a half dozen me's. Some stared. Some looked away, the dick in the naked one more substantial than its inspiration.

"Look at you," Philip said, his delight so large he looked infirm.

"I just had to lie there, or stand very still."

"Shut up," Philip said, then laughed and asked Andrew to move them around so one of me standing was next to another where I was lying down. Andrew handled the paintings with pregnant care; he told me how much he liked them.

"I didn't paint them!" I reminded him.

"Which one should we bring home?" Philip asked.

We settled on one of me in an old T-shirt. Andrew said he'd have one of the art handlers bring it to the house, though it was small enough to fit under my arm, then left.

"I'm taking us out to celebrate," Philip said, again with an expression of geriatric joy. For a moment I worried that he'd been right back in Germany: Dementia was coming to claim him. But then his face shifted, and everything wise and discerning reasserted itself.

We went to a place on the water in Brooklyn where we ate scallops and delicate chicken livers, Manhattan our starry backdrop.

I stayed at Philip's that night, too. The next night I went home, but when I got to Philip's the next morning I could tell he'd slept badly, so I returned to my apartment to gather a larger bag of clothes.

Philip got me to watch movies with subtitles. I got him to watch *Unsolved Mysteries*. He claimed to hate it, though for days he'd ask me about a particular cold case, making speculations as to who might have done what to whom. We didn't talk about Nicola at all.

We went to a gay dive bar, its wall-length mirror cloudy from decades of cigarette smoke. With its low ceiling and small windows, it felt like a basement. Foam spilled from gashes in the vinyl stools. After a few martinis, Philip pointed to a man at the far end of the bar.

"I think you have an admirer," he said.

I looked up and saw the man turn away, pleased that he'd been caught. He had an impish smile, dark scruff.

A minute later, Philip kissed my cheek, wished me a good night, and whispered, "You should have him over."

I caught his eye to see if he was joking, but his expression stayed serious, a reminder in it about seeing things and taking them.

"I was worried that old man was your boyfriend," the man said, moving to the stool Philip had just left. The bartender shook a cocktail shaker. Tina Turner rasped on the jukebox.

"A friend without the boy," I said.

I asked what he was drinking and bought us a round. His sweet smile widened, his hand rested on and warmed my back.

When we left an hour later, I took him to Philip's.

"You live here?" he asked.

"At the moment," I said, walking him up the stairs. Philip's room was dark. On the third floor, a wrinkle of light showed under the office door across from my room. The man and I stumbled out of our clothes. I left the door partly open.

When the man paused, I worried he'd changed his mind. But he was looking at the wall.

"What's that?" he asked.

"A painting."

"But it's you, yes?"

"I guess it is," I said, then dropped to my knees, felt his excitement gather as I pressed my mouth against his zipper.

The man left. I went to the kitchen in just boxer shorts to chug a glass of water, saw my compact arms in the window's reflection, the hair between my nipples that Pavel made more substantial in one painting, removed altogether in another. A gentle creaking sounded on the stairs.

"He's gone," I said.

Philip appeared in pajamas and a robe, like a TV grandpa.

"You're half naked," he said.

"Was all naked five minutes ago. Anyway, you've seen the whole shebang before."

"A lovely shebang," he said, then looked embarrassed. "God, I've become one of those old men."

"I don't mind."

Philip's shoulders and brow fell in defeated choreography. I put the kettle on. He seemed to be moving farther away from me when I wanted the opposite, so I said, "That guy from your first dinner party. *He* was the lecherous one."

"Marcus," Philip said.

"You're different."

"How?"

Though I often lied or chose vagueness, I wanted the opposite then, so I said, "I like it when you look at me. Like how Pavel did when he was painting. Trying to catch every delicate detail." I turned back to my reflection, saw pride in how I'd begun to hold my shoulders. The floor was cool against my feet. Philip smiled, relieved, and said, "Catching every detail, yes."

We made tea and drank it in the living room with the television on. It was the middle of the night, so we settled on an old sitcom Philip claimed he'd never seen, though he recognized one of the actresses from when she'd once come into the gallery to haggle over a painting. As the show went on, with its puns and pratfalls, Philip kept saying, "I don't know why this is funny," though his laugh slipped out in percussive darts that woke up the dogs.

"You had fun?" Philip asked, looking at the television rather than me.

"That man knew what he was doing," I said. "With his mouth and dick alike."

"Nice when they have expertise."

"He was loud toward the end. Couldn't seem to get enough of my nipples either."

"I heard that," Philip said. "Not that I was listening."

Characters on TV argued. A laugh track rose in chortling waves.

"I mean," I went on, "they kind of hurt now."

I was shirtless still and turned my chest toward Philip. He looked quickly, agreed the man had done a number on them, then got up and came back with two whiskeys.

We clinked glasses. Antics unspooled on television, and I grew tired in the way I did as a child, knowing sleep would soon overwhelm me.

I woke up on the sofa in the morning, wrapped in a blanket. Philip lay asleep on the other sofa, his breath deep and rattling.

I was making coffee and feeding the dogs, the blanket caping my shoulders, when Philip found me in the kitchen. I waited for his shyness or reserve, but he asked if I'd gotten that man's number the night before.

"You want to call him?" I asked.

He shook his head.

"But it sounded as if you had fun," he said. "That's all I was asking about. More fun."

I got dressed and walked the dogs and hoped Nicola wouldn't come back, though of course he would, if only to get more of his clothes.

14

I returned from walking the dogs one night and heard Philip talking to someone. As I stepped into the kitchen, I found him and Janice at the counter, her face assertive with makeup. She'd left me several messages I'd meant to answer.

"Here he is. Alive and well as you can see," Philip said.

"Hi," I said, and kissed her cheek. Her perfume was a brassy, floral approximation. Her T-shirt's slogan—*I'm Not a Lesbian but My Girlfriend Is*—stretched across her chest.

"Your dear roommate has been trying to reach you," Philip said. "You, like our friend Pavel, don't get an A for communication."

"I've been meaning to call you back," I told her, knowing any more elaborate excuse would wither under even basic cross-examination. My face heated with embarrassment, also annoyance at Janice's unannounced visit.

"You should stay for dinner," Philip said. "Gordon, what are we having?"

"I thought we could order."

I waited for Janice to decline, for discomfort to make quick work of things, but she nodded. We chose Thai from the pastiche of menus Philip spread across the counter. As we waited for the food to arrive, Philip poured each of us a beer.

"I'd say that I've heard all about you," Philip said, "but dear Gordon holds his cards close."

Janice made a face, of surprise or hurt, and took a large sip.

"That's funny," she said. "I was going to say that he holds his cards so you can see them, even when he thinks you can't."

Philip let out an interested hum, one that asked for more information. Janice told him about the sex stories I came home with and then shared in cinematic detail, how she could often tell from my face when I was embarrassed or afraid, even when I said I was fine. I gathered up the menus, put them away.

"I wonder what he's feeling now?" Philip asked.

They turned to me, and I experienced a startled panic, as if caught eavesdropping.

"Maybe Gordon wants you to stop talking about him like he isn't in the room with you," I answered.

My anger slipped out, a stereo's volume turned accidentally, momentarily to max. But Philip covered any unease by asking Janice to tell him all about herself.

She talked about the Ohio town she'd grown up in, her parents who both taught high school and somehow stayed sweetly, earnestly in love. How when her brother first returned home after joining the Marines, Janice locked her bedroom door at night because of a menace that seemed newly essential to him.

Janice asked Philip about how he'd wound up in the art world, and the doorbell rang. I was relieved to leave the room. As I paid the delivery person and stood in the vestibule with the warm bag of noodles, I thought of the things Janice had just shared, many of which were news to me, a reminder that, even in our most intimate conversations, what I wanted most was an understanding of how she saw me.

"Dinner," I said, and unpacked the food.

Finishing her noodles and beer, Janice put her jacket on, gave Philip a long hug, then told me she was glad I was okay.

"I'm sorry about all that," I said, after she'd left.

Philip rinsed the bowls we'd used.

"I hope you hold on to her," Philip said.

"Why wouldn't I?"

He opened the dishwasher, nested the bowls on its rack. One of the dogs trotted over to lick its basket of soiled utensils.

"You should really call people back, your roommate especially," Philip said.

"I often do."

Wet whispers of the dog's tongue on a spoon, a spatula.

"Turn that 'often' to 'always' is my advice," he said.

"Should we watch something?" I asked.

"Think I'll go upstairs and read."

"It's not even nine."

"I'm not allowed?" Philip asked.

A feeling arrived that often accompanied wanting, for me at least: a sweetness turned bitter when what I'd wanted and gotten started to retreat from me.

"It's your house, Philip," I said.

He kissed my forehead. It didn't feel sweet or kind but analgesic, like when my mom's second husband, who had chickens, would hold them from their feet to calm them just before slitting their throats. My next thought: Get over yourself. I wanted to do that, but wasn't sure I ever would.

Philip went upstairs. I took the dogs for a walk. Whenever I thought to turn back toward his house, the dogs and I wandered down another street or lingered outside a restaurant. Each time the door opened, we heard the whir of conversation, saw walls of windows curtained in steam.

When I was young, an overeager student teacher once gave us an assignment to discuss a superpower we wished we had. I wrote about being invisible. For days after, boys in my class bumped into me then said, with phlegmy bravado, "Didn't see you there," and I wished I'd been able to explain that to be invisible didn't mean to disappear, but to have control over who might see me, and when and how.

For the next few days, Philip kept his distance. He came home late, gave a brief report of where he'd been, and went upstairs. I understood that I should leave. I stayed. I read magazines about fancy houses and vacations I couldn't afford late into the night, falling asleep on the sofa. When I woke up one morning to coffee already on, Philip back upstairs with the newspaper and the dogs, again I knew I should go back to Janice. But I knocked on his door and told him I was ready for the dogs, heard the thump of a spaniel jumping from bed to floor.

"Already walked them," Philip said.

But then Philip came home early one night to me making food, his look of pleased relief mirroring my own, and sticking it out felt right, a reward. While we ate, we watched one of his favorite black-and-white movies.

I gathered up the plates from dinner, knew to come back with a whiskey for each of us.

A few nights later we went to the same gay dive bar from before and struck up a conversation with a man named Lee. He was somewhere in his forties or fifties, with a wide, kind face and delicate hands. He worked in IT. Philip made a joke. Lee laughed hard. When our drinks were empty, he insisted on buying the next round. In this man I saw a chance for Philip to move Nicola into the past tense, so, when Lee excused himself to use the bathroom, I told my boss he was being flirted with.

"I don't know," Philip said, folding his cocktail napkin into a smaller square.

Lee returned, all smiles. He picked up the napkin Philip had folded and undid it, moved his fingers across its creased grid. Philip's chatty warmth from minutes before was gone. Lee looked at his watch, and I pointed out Philip's watch, one he wore all the time.

"It's nice," Lee said.

"Thank you," Philip replied, and stirred the ice in his glass.

When Lee looked at his watch again, I said, "Philip was hoping you'd come back to our place for a nightcap."

"Oh," Lee answered. His face fell, as if deciding how

to offer his regrets. But then he said, "A nightcap could be nice."

I waved the bartender over and used all my cash to pay our tab.

Inside Philip's house, the dogs greeted us. Lee crouched down to pet them. Philip kept his coat on. I went into the kitchen to make martinis. Coming back into the living room, I found each of them sitting on their own sofa.

"This drink is good," Lee said.

"Not my first rodeo," I told him, then realized it sounded like flirtation, so I added, "No big deal."

"How long have you two lived here?" Lee asked.

"Oh," I said. "To be determined, I think."

There was no change in Philip's expression, no reaction when Lola jumped onto the couch she wasn't supposed to be on.

"Cute dogs," Lee said.

"That's how this all started," I said. "I used to be the dog walker."

Most of the lights in the living room were off, so I turned a few on. Philip's untouched drink sat sweating on the coffee table.

"I'll be right back," I said, walked up to my room, and closed the door.

Shortly after, I heard the front door close, Philip's footsteps hollow on the stairs.

I knocked on his bedroom door. When he didn't answer, I knocked again and walked in. He lay on top of his blankets, coat and shoes still on.

"What happened?" I asked.

"Lee had to get back to Washington Heights," Philip said.

"You're cuter than him anyway."

"Don't do that," he said.

"I don't know what I'm doing."

I walked to the foot of the bed, pulled off one of his shoes.

"Jesus, I'm not some toddler," Philip said.

"I don't think of you as a toddl—"

"He didn't want me. I didn't particularly want him, though had he been amenable, I suppose."

"You're too good for him anyway," I said.

Philip's glare sharpened. I wondered if he was about to hit me, wondered, too, why I often waited to be hit when I could count the times it had really happened on a single hand. I hoped his face might soften, that he'd pat the bed and tell me to sit. Philip blinked at the ceiling.

I leaned down and kissed him on the mouth. His lips tightened. He pressed his hands against my chest and pushed me away.

"I'm not your charity case," he said.

"I wasn't offering charity."

"What were you offering then?" he asked.

One of his shoes was still on, the other foot in a thin, dark sock. On the mantel of a once-working fireplace sat photos of Philip and Nicola from their early years together, at an art fair in Switzerland, shirtless on a Greek beach. Philip's eyes stayed glued to the ceiling, his hands crossed at his stomach. The shoe of his I'd taken off was still in my hand.

"I'm sorry," I said.

Through the window came the soft shush of passing cars, shoes echoing on the pavement. Heat rose through the vents in a steady sigh.

"I'll let you sleep," I added, and hoped for a smattering of kind words from him, at least an acceptance of my apology, but the only indication he'd heard me came from the wiggling of his exposed foot's toes.

I put the shoe on the floor and left his room.

When I woke up the next morning, Philip was gone. I returned to my apartment for a change of clothes. Dishes in the drainer were water flecked, and the moist, floral heat of a recent shower filled the place. I thought to call Janice, to tell her I'd just missed her, though I understood that all I'd wanted was her comfort, also that I had no right to ask for it.

My cell phone rang, Philip's name on its screen a worry and a relief.

"Gordon," he said.

"I'm sorry," I answered, "that things got weird last night."

"Oh," he said. "I've decided to head upstate with the dogs for a while. I need a break from the city's noise, et cetera."

"You won't be lonely?" I asked, hearing the bleeding need in my inflection.

Philip answered with a noncommittal noise.

"Well, call me if you need anything," I said, and he hung up.

Our apartment's small size stifling, I left and got onto the subway. After a handful of transfers, I ended up in northern Brooklyn, trying to find a place Pavel had taken me on his last night in New York. It had snowed a good deal the day before he left, a surprise that early in the season. Pavel told me we were going out, that I needed to dress for the weather. Just before we left his apartment, he wrapped a folded bandanna over my eyes.

"No cheating," he said.

"What *is* this?" I asked. He didn't answer.

We walked, me blindfolded, Pavel's hand in mine. Snow crunched underfoot, pelting my neck and chin. We moved down stairs. Even blindfolded I could feel the bright lights, hear the dampening sound. A subway turnstile rocked against my hip.

Once on the train, we sat down. The conductor's muffled voice announced First Avenue, then Brooklyn. A passenger asked Pavel what was going on. "I'm surprising him," Pavel said.

We got off the subway. Snow on the unshoveled sidewalks spilled into my high tops, turning my socks wet and cold.

"Pavel," I said. He didn't answer.

"Are you even Pavel?" I asked. "Or did he hand me off to some stranger? If you're a stranger, squeeze my hand, so at least I know I don't know you."

Pavel shushed me, told me to put out my hands.

I felt chain link, heard a fence's rattle as Pavel climbed. I groped my way over the fence, too. We moved down a narrow set of steps. Then he laid me on the ground, removed the blindfold. Snow batted my face with the eager persistence of gnats.

"I'm impressed you didn't take this off earlier," he said.

We were in an empty, abandoned pool, its walls a gallery of stains and holes. Peeling paint showed a change in depth from four feet to six. To one side, a crumbling municipal building. On the other, fencing and weedy trees. Lying there, snow past our shoulders, Pavel said, "Sometimes I think about where I'm going to die."

"Being with me makes you think of death?"

"This isn't about you, Gordon," he answered.

He stood up, pulled his camera from his backpack, and took pictures of snowbound me. He told me to look away, then to move fast, my limbs reduced to smears. Pavel opened my jacket. He lifted up my shirt. My breath shivered as snow hit, melted. I waited for more pictures, but he just watched me. I hoped the snow would continue, his flight the next morning canceled, though there were always more flights. Snow kept landing on me.

"Is this some future painting?" I asked. "So memorable you don't even need to photograph it? Burned in your brain, et cetera?"

"Why do you always say such nonsense?"

I wanted to ask more questions—though they'd break whatever wobbly spell held us—about how he'd found this place, how he'd known, too, that I'd be amenable to the blindfolded subway ride, though *amenable* could have been carved onto my tombstone rather than my name.

Pavel pulled me close. He moved his mouth across my face. "You taste cold," he said.

Sometimes I think he took me to that place to confuse me or make sure I'd miss him. Or maybe he'd been bored and decided to take me blindfolded through the city, have me feel my way over a fence, just to see if I'd let him.

I walked for an hour but didn't find the abandoned pool, ended up at an all-night diner that looked so much like Minneapolis inside that for a moment I pretended to be there.

Janice and Meredith had gone to visit friends in Massachusetts, so I was home solo. I smoked cigarettes I didn't want, lay on Janice's bed unable to sleep, and tried to understand the itch that invaded me whenever I was alone. Early the next morning, I gave up on sleep and went to the internet café. There was an email from Alan asking if I'd taken money from him so many months before, another from my mom, describing a man she worked with so it was clear she had feelings for him. A message from Dad about how, in that summer I'd stayed with him, he loved when we'd gone to church together. *When people fell to their knees in praise, I saw that you were afraid. I kept telling you what was happening, but still you looked fearful. I hope you don't feel afraid like that anymore. That you see new things and look at them with wonder.* I began to write back that what I remembered was his disgust directed at me. That acting like fear could no longer reach him was his own brand of magic bullshit. My fingers whapped against the dirty keyboard. A man next to me looked at images of women with balloon-shaped breasts. But as quickly as anger had taken hold, it dissolved into boredom. I closed the message without sending it.

Leaving the internet café, I hoped walking would steady me, but my churned-up feeling grew. Though I knew Philip wanted a break, from the city but even more from me, I dialed his upstate number. It rang. I pulled out a cigarette. Nicola answered with a brusque hello.

"It's Gordon," I said.

"Hello Gordon," Nicola answered.

"I didn't know you'd be up there."

"Where do you think I've been?"

I almost crossed a street until I noticed an oncoming car.

"What can I do for you, Gordon?"

"I was hoping to talk to Philip."

"He's not here at the moment," he said. "Would you like to leave a message?"

I wondered if Nicola had started out as Philip's assistant, this job a path for men of lesser means to follow.

"No thanks," I said. Nicola hung up.

Philip had gone to see Nicola, might have told him about my needy, puppyish attention, the lackluster man I'd hoped to pin on him, the shoes I'd tried to pry off his feet.

I went to the park's woods but at this time of day there was no one around. I sat on a log softened by rot, ready to accept whatever came down the path. But what came was a man and woman walking a dog. The dog wagged toward me, though the woman held the leash to keep it at bay. After they passed, I heard their squelched laughter. I wanted to be mad, though I understood what was ridiculous about me then, eyes wide with need, ants from the log darting across my jeans and sneakers.

———————

The next night, I fought the impulse to head back to the park's woods and went to Janice's bar instead. Even with her in Massachusetts, I hoped its noise and familiarity might pull me out of the skid I was in the midst of. But inside, I found her there pouring a trio of beers.

"Didn't expect you to be here," I said.

"Massachusetts didn't agree with me," Janice replied.

"Philip and Nicola might be back together."

"Good," she said. "You can finally stop babysitting that rich old thing."

Janice floated up and down the length of the bar, laughing with strangers, her face all business when a man looked at her with porno interest. Whenever I tried to catch her eye, she held up a finger to tell me to give her a minute, though that minute didn't come.

At the end of the night, Janice came to my corner of the bar and said, "You never asked me about Massachusetts."

"I can never spell Massachusetts," I said.

Her eyes fell to the glasses she was washing. Massachusetts hadn't agreed with her, which meant Meredith. I'd been too busy gorging on the possibility of Philip and Nicola's reunion to consider what lay beyond its border.

"What happened?" I asked.

"I'm tired," Janice said.

"I'll help you clean up," I offered, but she told me it wasn't my job.

I walked home alone. When I woke up in the morning, Janice wasn't there.

15

There are times I lull myself with hope even when the evidence points in failure's direction. That feeling carried me after Nicola called and said, "We're back, please come over," and I convinced myself that they had some task for me, hoping it was to serve as a guiding hand for Nicola as he decided what to take and what to leave behind.

At the house, the dogs ran toward me. One of them whimpered. The other kept licking my shoes. My bosses sat at the kitchen island.

I kissed each of them on the cheek and tried to catch Philip's eye.

"We wanted to thank you," Philip said.

The dogs sat at my feet, probably thinking I'd walk them. As I poured myself a coffee, Nicola said, "What he means by 'thank you' is that it doesn't make sense for you to work for us anymore."

"Did I do something?" I asked.

Philip started to speak, but Nicola's voice overcrowded his. "This, for starters," he said.

Nicola pulled out a Polaroid from New Year's Eve: Janice

on a chair in her corset and heels, a sea of cheering hands in front of her. She looked beautiful. We must have missed it while cleaning up.

"A few friends," I said.

"More than a few," Nicola corrected. "Not that a few were allowed."

"I'm sorry," I said. "A moment of bad judgment."

Philip's thumb traced the edge of his mug.

"It turns out," Nicola went on, "Lucy from across the way saw things and told me." Nicola hated Lucy. She had an ancient cocker spaniel, its single hobby rubbing its hemorrhoidal ass on the sidewalk. "I ran into her recently and she told me that when we were in London months before, there were all sorts of men here."

"One," I said.

"So it's true," Nicola replied.

"Not all sorts."

"Tomato tomahto."

"Not all sorts," I repeated.

"Still," Philip added.

Sensing I wasn't there for them, the dogs retreated to their beds.

"What about a few weeks ago, with that man at the bar?" I said to Philip. "You insisted I bring him home."

Anger arrived to fill in for what had been sad and frightening a moment before.

Nicola went on about Lucy watching a striptease, the cheering, terrifying-looking horde.

"Burlesque," I said.

"We trusted you," Nicola said.

He kept talking, stopping halfway through sentences to

rearrange his ideas. He spat out the phrase "Loyalty, you know?" three different times.

"Loyalty," he said for the fourth time, and added that they were keeping my last check as collateral.

"You're a great expert on loyalty," I said.

"What is wrong with you?" Nicola asked.

"What's wrong with both of you?" Philip interrupted. His baritone filled the room. Across Nicola's face, a sharp smirk of victory.

"So this has nothing to do with the barn?" I asked.

Nicola's feline attention tightened. Part of me thought to stop, but I kept going.

"At your birthday party, Nicola took me to the barn so we could fool around," I said.

"You were hardly an unwilling partner," Nicola added.

"But I wasn't willing again."

Nicola guffawed. "If you think I've been pining for you, or Pavel is pining for you now, that every man you meet just can't get enough of you," he said, "you might want to disabuse yourself of that notion. Our friend Audrey, when you helped us at that first dinner—"

"Nicola," Philip said.

"She told us, when you were in the bathroom, that you looked like a gas station attendant."

Tears gathered. I didn't fight them, my small hope then that their appearance would make the two of them uncomfortable.

"She's not wrong," I said. "Though it was a convenience store that also sold gas. I worked at a grocery store, too. Also security at a mall where I drove around in a golf cart, which I did too fast after hours sometimes."

"Your résumé, yes," Nicola said.

I should have left then, but wanted to break more things and survey the damage.

"He's terrible to you, Philip. I see it. People at the gallery see it." I talked about the jokes Nicola made at Pavel's opening about Philip out past his bedtime. How no one could find Nicola the day of the attack because he and Eric were at a place on the beach without cell service.

"Please stop," Philip said.

He and I had been in this kitchen a week before, drinking whiskey and laughing about something Andrew had said. He'd seemed thrilled to have me stay and stay. Now he'd changed his mind. People were always changing their minds.

I added more about Rebecca's warning after the barn. "She told me," I said, in a phlegmy rasp. "She told me to watch out for Nicola."

Nicola called what I was doing "a performance," then said I should go. I asked if I could use the bathroom first. Nicola scoffed. Philip said, "Of course."

When I got out of the bathroom, Nicola was gone. Philip stood at the sink washing dishes.

"I'm sorry," I said.

"I know," he answered, and filled a glass with soapy water.

"About the barn, I mean. The other stuff, too."

"He *is* persuasive," Philip said. But his refusal to turn around told a different story. "You would have gotten tired of this anyway. Watching over me, et cetera."

"You don't know that," I said.

"You don't know either."

He placed a coffee cup in the drainer, began washing the next. He looked small at the sink, though we were the same size. I hoped he'd level with me now that we were alone, tell me that Nicola's return was temporary and I could come back soon. But Philip squirted soap onto the sponge. I sensed he'd stay at the sink until I was gone.

"Thank you," I said.

Philip nodded into the mug he was cleaning.

I left and walked to the apartment Pavel had stayed in, one I'd mistaken as his own, and rang the buzzer. After a few moments, a woman's voice said, "Hello?"

"Pavel?" I asked.

There was a pause. A shock of static sounded before she answered, "He doesn't live here anymore." There was annoyance in her voice that now I think I might have invented, though at the time it felt real, and I'd imagined she wasn't annoyed at me but that so many men had been ringing the buzzer, too, hoping they might see him.

16

I got a job temping. I wasn't a fast enough typist for the plum gigs, so I was only called in when they needed a receptionist. My first job was at a law office. I answered the phone and tried to look alertly competent (or at least like I wasn't falling asleep) and was tasked with ordering partners' lunches, taking it out of the containers it came in, and serving it to them on china and with ice water. They didn't talk to me, except one who said, "You're not Denise," and I answered that Denise had a head cold.

Janice spent most nights at Meredith's by then. I visited her at the bar from time to time, but she rarely had more than a minute to talk. I sometimes went to gay bars, but, like in my first New York months, banter escaped me, so I returned to the woods, the wordless interactions there a relief. One night, leaving after a man had wanted to have sex without a condom and I'd refused, the two of us jerking each other off instead, his rough, squeezing hand making difficult work of it, I remembered my mother telling me that she also didn't know how to be with people. She'd be sincere and they'd think she was joking. They told her she was angry when she didn't feel angry at all. I lit a cigarette, thought of the times she and I used to smoke leaning on a windowsill, or in a backyard filled with mismatched lawn furniture.

Winter wound down. The money I'd saved from working for Nicola and Philip dwindled fast with rent and the credit card bills that came back to haunt me. I got another receptionist temp job at a place with a tank of tropical fish in the lobby and a kitchen filled with snacks and drinks I took liberally from until the office manager told me I was taking too much. I was surprised he noticed me at all.

On days I wasn't temping, I took long runs or opened all the windows and cleaned, hoping that running and scrubbing would bring about some sea change. Emails and voice mails from my dad continued from time to time. He mentioned how he'd gone back to his job at an office building in Milwaukee, making people sign in and show IDs. More about the endless snow, his slow recovery. His messages wandered into recollections: him and Mom and me at some park with a river to swim in, though I never went in past my knees. *You stood so still I had to say your name from time to time just to watch you turn around, to make sure you were still with us.*

One night, I visited the bar. Since I'd been fired, Janice and I had reconciled, though we never talked about the way I'd hurt her. She kissed my cheek, told me she was glad to see me. I missed the two of us before Philip and Nicola, our apartment the only place I slept, how each time she came home and found me there, neither of us could hide our excitement. I peeled the label off my beer bottle. Janice leaned close and said she had something to tell me.

"You're pregnant," I guessed.

"Wouldn't that be the thing," she said, then asked if I wanted another drink.

I shook my head, sensing a jolt I wasn't prepared for.

"Meredith got a fancy new job in L.A. Some show where nobodies try to become singers."

"Meredith wants to be a singer?" I asked.

"Hush," Janice said. She put her hand on mine, kept it there as she talked about the ridiculous money Meredith would get, enough to rent a small house, maybe get chickens. A customer appeared. Janice served him, returned.

"You're going with her," I said.

Her expression said that she was, even though going might be a terrible idea. She loved Meredith, doubted it would last, wanted to push past that doubt to see what was on the other side. I squeezed her hand. She'd mostly been at Meredith's for the last month. When I saw her, she often talked about being tired of New York. None of this should have been surprising. But I was surprised. I waited for my tears. Instead I felt tired.

"That's great, honey," I said, and kissed her.

"I thought you'd be mad."

"Why would I be mad?"

"Don't be dumb, sugar. Mad because I'm leaving you."

"But you can always come back," I said.

I went to the bathroom, sat in a stall where people had written phone numbers of exes or friends turned to enemies. Janice wouldn't come back. Or if she did, the world would have shifted so that, even if we ended up in the same place again, this heat between us would have dissolved, too diffuse to warm anything.

"I'll miss you terribly," I said back at my stool, wondering if, had I remembered to ask her more questions, had I noticed when she was struggling and told her as much, had I chosen her over Philip and Nicola, she might have stayed. Or if at least it would have felt less like she was leaving me.

That night, lying next to her in bed, sharing a joint and listening to the call and response of sirens outside, Janice asked, "What will you do?"

Alan had asked me the same thing a year before. I hadn't known then either.

I shrugged, the question of where I might go next a dark, unfamiliar room. Part of me wanted to join them in L.A., but I hadn't been invited. I pinched the joint between my fingers, then my lips, "what next" too squirmy to hold. Bay Ridge would bring back more of my sadness. Minnesota wasn't an option either, as I'd lost touch with most friends there. One had emailed recently, called me selfish, told me I was someone who took what I needed then moved on. *You always treated me like I was important to you, now it seems I was just convenient*, the friend had written, and I wondered if there was a way out of selfishness, or if turning that idea over and over was just another way to keep staring at my own reflection.

"I don't want to be those people who were only friends for a time," I said.

"Never, hot ass," Janice answered.

I wanted to become a person who wrote long emails and made time to call, hoped I'd be able to rearrange the way I moved through my days to make that happen. As we lay there, not knowing what came next pressing against me, I said, "Pavel told me I could visit him for a bit."

"What does 'a bit' mean?" Janice asked.

"Great question," I said.

I knew I'd go, probably outstay my welcome, though the excitement of seeing Pavel, the smells of flowers I'd never heard of floating through open windows, sitting in his studio while he painted more versions of me made whatever would come after too negligible to matter. Janice fell asleep. As traffic sounded through the window, I tried to remind myself that Pavel wasn't a solution.

"Pavel who lives in a hovel," I whispered.

Janice rolled to her side; her breasts pressed to my shoulder. I let them stay there, thinking of the violent pleasure of being smothered.

When I emailed Pavel the next morning and he answered right away that I was more than welcome, possibility solidified in my hand. I raced to one of the student travel offices that polluted the city then and booked a one-way ticket.

"Return date?" the agent asked.

Other agents sat close, keyboards clicking. Posters showed beaches and ancient cities, what I guessed was a temple.

"To be determined," I answered, and handed her my credit card.

PART THREE

17

Mexico City had more going on than I'd ever experienced in a single place. Traffic blared. Construction and cars and people crowded intersections, and birds lined branches like commuters waiting for a train. But Pavel's neighborhood—La Condesa—was quiet and elegant, packed with old buildings and arched windows, a repetition of wrought iron balconies.

In the months since I'd seen him, Pavel's hair had grown. He gave me a hug and invited me inside. I wanted a kiss, a sense of his eager interest, but he welcomed me with his usual remove. I sat at his kitchen table. A ceiling fan hummed. Pavel poured me a glass of water.

"I wasn't sure you were really coming," he said.

"I said I was. Nice place, by the way."

The apartment had high ceilings and a dark-tiled floor, appliances with the round corners of a distant decade. A balcony sat at the far end of his living room, branches so close I could touch their leaves. Pavel tucked his hair behind his ears. Sunlight stretched across the floor.

"It's big," I said. "The apartment."

"Compared to New York, yes."

Paint patterned his knuckles, perhaps from some picture of me he was still working on.

We talked about my flight and the city's traffic, the two of us stuck in a stultifying politeness. I tried to dig my way out by talking about a bad date I'd recently gone on but realized halfway through that telling this story implied that I'd moved on from him, that idea both frightening and false.

"That does sound bad," he said. "Let me show you your room."

A bed and chair were its only furniture. Thin curtains over the windows rose and fell with the breeze. I sat on the bed in hopes he'd join me.

"You no longer work for Philip and Nicola, I hear," he said.

"Gossip from the gallery," I said.

"Exploring new opportunities, is what I was told."

"I was fired."

Pavel looked at the bobbing curtains.

"I can't tell if this is one of your jokes," he said.

"Me neither," I answered, then mentioned I was tired. "Jet lag, you know."

"There's hardly a time difference."

"The lag from being thrown in the air and moving very fast."

Pavel let out a small, high laugh. One of his arms hung at his side, the other bent to hold it. This awkwardness was new. I patted the bed in invitation.

"You should take a nap," he said. "Get used to being back on the ground."

He walked out, closing the double doors. I wanted to summon him back, sensed he wouldn't come, or would, only to stay at the doorway's safe distance. Despite the worry that thrummed through me, I fell asleep, waking up to the smell of coffee. A pot sat waiting on the stove, along with a note from Pavel telling me he'd gone to his studio and would stop by later.

I walked around the neighborhood. Though it had been warm when I'd landed, the evening turned cool. I found a small park tunneled in trees, a fountain in its center painted swimming-pool blue. A woman walked through it with a dog that looked like Philip and Nicola's. I hoped Pavel had told them about my visit, though he probably hadn't. I went into a small grocery store and bought a bottle of water, handing the cashier the first bill I pulled out. He smiled, imitated me shoving my money toward him.

"That is too much," he said in English.

"How'd you know I'm American?"

The man again mimicked the clumsy way I'd handed him my money. He was thin, with a thick mustache.

"Show me what you have," he said. I laid the bills I'd gotten at the ATM on the counter along with the handful of coins. He took two of the latter.

"You trust me?" he asked.

"I know where you work," I answered. His mustache fell.

"A bad joke," I said. "Yes, I trust you."

"Gabriel," he said, pointing to himself.

"Gordon," I told him, pointing to me.

He repeated my name. It sounded harsh and froggy. My parents never considered its sound in foreign mouths. Neither of them had been to Europe, not Mexico either, unless Mom, in Phoenix, had taken a day trip here. I wanted bigger things, wanted them to want bigger things, too, rather than the smallness each of us treated like a map to dutifully follow.

"Gordon isn't the prettiest name," I said.

"Gordon is fine," Gabriel replied, and handed me my change.

I left, drank the water, wanting to be more than fine.

Back at the apartment, I found Pavel waiting. On the wall behind him, the shadow of a tree shimmied.

"Where'd you go?" he asked.

I lifted up my bottle of water.

"I have water here," he said.

"I wanted to see what there was to see."

"And?"

"I found a grocery store."

"Come," he said. "I want to show you something."

As we walked, I noted the church we turned left in front of, the gas station we passed, a used bookstore with stacks of dusty merchandise crowding its window. The medians on larger streets brimmed with plants and trees. Pavel unlocked a gate and walked me through a bird shit–splattered court-yard, then up a narrow flight of stairs.

His studio was large. Drop cloths blanketed the tables and floors. He showed me a new series of paintings. I'd hoped for more of me, but these showed strangers in kitch-ens and restaurants. Some had food in front of them, others cups of coffee or glasses of wine.

"You're done painting me?" I asked.

"The gallery has those paintings now."

"How am I selling?"

"Look at these," he said.

People never answered my questions.

"I am," I said.

"Not carefully."

In one, I noticed the wallpaper from a restaurant we'd gone to in Munich. In another, seeds scattered on a plate.

"They're good," I said.

"You don't see it." Pavel pointed to a painting of a bearded man in a restaurant, wine in hand. At a table in the background, so small I could have covered it with my fist, was me.

"Special guest star," Pavel said.

"What's that?"

"What I thought you'd say. That or some comment on how I'd painted your hair."

"What's wrong with my hair?"

Impatience widened his eyes before they retreated to their customary indifference. I wanted to turn him around, to do things to him to wipe that blankness away.

"What are we doing tonight?" I asked.

"There's food in the fridge you can warm up."

"What about you?"

"I was surprised to hear from you," Pavel said. "Pleased of course."

I looked more carefully at tiny me in the background, with hair longer than I wore it. He'd also made the teeth perfect, unlike mine, unruly without the stern early guidance of braces.

"I'm saying this," he said, "because there's someone. I probably should have told you before you got here."

"Like you're dating?"

"A boyfriend," he said.

Pavel picked up a rag, folded it, and told me the boy-friend was an anthropology professor he'd met through his Spanish tutor, Araceli. Foolishness flooded me. I thought to return to the airport and see about a ticket home. But I'd traveled all this way, leaving so soon a waste, so I said, "Your Spanish tutor and the boyfriend are serious people then."

"Nothing wrong with serious," Pavel said.

My tiredness vanished. I pinched my arm so that pain beat out any possible tears at the idea of Pavel's boyfriend, or the Spanish tutor, whom he told me had quickly become one of his dearest friends.

"Thanks for leaving me food," I said.

Pavel picked a scab of paint off his forearm.

"He's in love with the paintings," Pavel said. "The ones of you. They helped woo him, he likes to say."

"We wooed him together?"

"The paintings and I," Pavel clarified.

"How does your boyfriend feel about me being here?"

A quick smile rose before Pavel told me that Francisco was a bit jealous, that maybe a bit of jealousy was good for them.

"Do you ever call him San Francisco?" I asked, then wished I hadn't. The two of them probably had serious conversations about aesthetics and anthropology, the con-jugation of a verb.

"I don't call him that," Pavel said. "But he has a nick-name for you."

I thought of the nicknames Janice had given me, she

and Meredith now driving a U-Haul through rectangular-shaped states. I took out a cigarette, asked if Pavel wanted one. He answered that he'd quit. This felt like an indictment, though I couldn't parse out why.

"What's the nickname?" I asked.

"The muse."

Pavel stayed at Francisco's. He left me a list of places to visit and maps to use. I visited the anthropology museum, Frida Kahlo's house, several churches. It was the week before Easter, churches packed with flowers and people. Outdoor markets sold every new and used thing imaginable, and pictures of Jesus hung everywhere. Some days, I got to a church and, rather than head inside, I'd find a tree and sit under it. Or I'd go into a museum, find its quietest room and stare at a painting, willing myself to see more. Sometimes I did and wished I could tell Philip. Other times I didn't but sat so still that a security guard came up, about to shake my shoulder until he realized I wasn't sleeping. Stillness became a game of sorts, the closest thing I had then to an occupation.

In my wandering one afternoon, I stumbled upon a religious performance. People packed the streets to watch. Someone played Jesus. He was good-looking, though he had on a terrible, shiny wig. I watched his mouth as he talked, his beard shining in the sun. They acted out the miracle of loaves and fishes. The performance was overblown, full of large gestures and shouted dialogue. I lingered afterward, hoping to see Jesus in street clothes, but he didn't appear. I returned to the apartment, took a nap that went so long it

was dark by the time I woke up. Realizing how late it was,
I went right back to sleep.

One night, Pavel took me to dinner. He ate quickly, looked
at his hands or out the window as I took time between each
bite. He went back to Francisco's after, said he'd stop by
the next day, though when he did, I was out trying to find
the Palacio de Bellas Artes, finally giving up and flagging
a young woman with the phrase "Lo siento." On the map
she showed me where we were, where I was trying to get to.
Though there was a subway station right there, I walked to
pass the time.

I went to the grocery store I'd found on my first night.
Gabriel saw me, beamed, and said my name. I bought a can
of soup and some tortillas, cooking them in Pavel's kitchen,
a room almost the size of the apartment I'd lived in until
a week before when Janice packed her things and I'd left
the furniture she didn't take on the street for strangers to
claim. I smoked on Pavel's balcony, watched people through
the skein of leaves, thrilled when a woman looked up at me,
though when I waved, she kept walking.

The next day, I went to Pavel's studio without being invited.
When he opened the door, he smiled deeply, resting a hand
on my back as he walked me inside.

"I'm glad you're here," he said. Pavel dropped a brush
into a jar of water. Paint's disinfectant stink singed the air
around us. "Tomorrow night it's Araceli's birthday."

"Your Spanish tutor?"

"She is that, too, yes. But for her birthday there'll be a dinner."

He repeated the story of how Araceli had quickly become a dear friend. "Like you and that woman, with the tattoos and the boobs."

"I can't believe you'd talk about your mom that way," I said.

He shook his head. "You're invited."

I wanted him to kiss the space behind my ears, grab my hair as he sometimes had, telling me that what he was doing was for my own good. To fuck me and say afterward that I couldn't tell Francisco about it, for me to ask after how to say *secret* in Spanish and Czech and any of the other languages he knew.

"Araceli doesn't know me," I said.

"She knows your paintings," Pavel said, then asked if I needed help walking back to the apartment. He wanted me to leave, but I leaned down instead, lingered in front of one of his new paintings before I answered, "Two rights and a left."

"Good boy," he said.

"I'm not a boy," I told him, but Pavel had already gone back to the painting he was working on.

I found an internet café so similar to the ones I'd used in Geneva and Munich and Brooklyn that they felt less like particular places, more like their own sad dimension. I wrote Janice a long, chatty email about La Condesa and the dinner I was invited to. I added a line on how Mexico City and Los Angeles weren't that far apart, how easy it would be for me to swing by (though that wasn't actually true), but our reconciliation was newborn, fragile. So I deleted that and wrote instead how when I asked Pavel if he'd nicknamed his boyfriend San Francisco, he hadn't found it funny. There was an email from Dad, too, with a story I had no recollection of, where the two of us planted zinnias in a garden he claimed we once had. *You were so happy when they started to grow*, he wrote. *So sad when fungus browned their leaves and petals.*

The next evening, I showered until the hot water ran out and tried on three different outfits, settling on one of Nicola's former button-downs that sat perfectly across my shoulders. I felt powerful wearing it, though that power stalled without its former owner's money or know-how. I tried to think of how I should talk to Francisco and their friends, whose English, Pavel told me, was good, though not perfect. "They won't understand your jokes," he'd added, which felt like a scolding.

I got there early, so I went to a bar across the street and nursed a beer. Through the bar's window, I saw Pavel arrive at the restaurant with a man identically narrow and tall, though his hair and beard were dark. It was the man from the painting I sat in the background of. The man said something. Pavel smiled and looked around before giving him a quick kiss.

When I arrived at the restaurant, I found Pavel and Francisco and a half dozen other people at a table by the door.

"I keep getting lost in this city," I lied, to explain my lateness.

"A maze," Francisco said.

He stood to shake my hand. He had hollow cheeks and a muted smile, seemed older than me by a good bit. "So nice to finally meet you," he said.

Araceli, short with thick hair and in large jewelry, said something in Spanish to the rest of the table, then translated: *The one from the paintings.*

Someone, in nearly accentless English, asked if I was a painter, too.

"Just a warm body," I answered.

I'd been the last to show up, so I sat at the end of the table. A woman with the sour seriousness of some of the paintings I'd recently seen at the contemporary art museum spoke to the group in fast Spanish. Pavel answered in what sounded like competent Spanish, though he'd told me his grasp of that language was too basic to even count. But he'd been fluent in three languages before the age of five, a new one an easy addition to his roster. I poured myself wine.

During a pause, Pavel translated. The rest of the guests sipped their drinks or folded their napkins as he went on about some article that had caused a fuss, one researcher refuting the work of another. "A bit of a scandal," Pavel said. With nothing to add, I nodded.

We ordered food. Every once in a while, Pavel or Araceli translated. Even in English, there was little in their stories for me to hold on to, so I poured myself more wine and noticed Francisco watching me. Candles bobbed on the table.

I wanted to brand these people as selfish and mean,

though they talked about what they knew, just as Janice and I chatted about sex and music and the dares we said yes to so we might feel something. As conversation heated up, translation fell away. When guests remembered me, they translated what had just been said, while everyone else waited, politely bored, for them to finish. "Yes," I said, or "I see," like a foreign exchange student, or an aging grandparent, their hearing diminished so what comes to them is murmuring more than words.

"How do you know Pavel again?" one of the guests asked me.

"He painted me for a time," I said.

"A hired model?"

"I worked for his gallery sort of, its owners anyway."

"You're not the one who was fired? For having wild parties and things," the friend added, a look on her face suggesting she knew I was.

"Bingo," I said. "Though it was one party. I guess it ended up being a little wild. In any case, wild hadn't been the plan."

"But it was at the house of Philip and Nicola?" This came from Francisco. "Why were you staying there?"

"I watched their dogs for a while," I said.

"Why?" he asked.

Francisco's earlier politeness fell away, replaced by an expression that asked *Why are you here?* I wanted to answer with the story of Pavel taking me blindfolded on the subway, the snow and the abandoned pool, but it would sound childish, a grasping at straws. To say that being painted by Pavel had come with a larger promise, though no promise had been made. Pavel put his hand on Francisco's forearm, in warning or appreciation. I was at a dinner with people I had nothing to say to, even when they spoke my language. Defeat's familiar weight returned to me, and I welcomed it, almost, like the sweaty relief of giving in to a fever.

"Because I was their dog walker," I replied.

Guests talked about how dog walker was such an American job, then switched to other jobs that existed only in the States, like life coaches and traffic reporters. I sat at the table's end, sometimes smiling, sometimes sipping, more often as still as the paintings of me, with as much to contribute to the conversation.

I understood then what Philip meant about Pavel's affect as a performance, felt foolish for not seeing it before, for not realizing he must have heard the story of my firing and shared it liberally. The goodwill I felt for this group sank to self-pity, a sense that this was done, that what I wanted now was another finale, a burned bridge a relief and a fuel, at least for a time.

Two people at the end of the table whispered, eyes darting in my direction, perhaps filling each other in on my delinquency, or gossiping about how Pavel had only said yes to my visit because two paintings of me had just sold. In the silence as waiters took plates away, I said, "Philip thinks Pavel's a great painter."

Nothing on Pavel's face registered the compliment, though someone at the far end of the table agreed. I looked at Pavel. He didn't return the favor.

"Thinks, too, that his false modesty, the way he acts like he hates attention, that it's as pretend as the painting of me in bed," I went on. "I was lying on the floor. Even had pants on. He made it look entirely different."

People stared at their plates. A woman at the far end of the table laughed. Pavel opened his mouth, reconsidered, and closed it again.

"Could someone pass the wine?" I asked.

Ice clattered as a waitress refilled water glasses. Pavel's face soured. In the lines etched across his brow, I could sense what he might look like as an old man. "Maybe your friends need translation," I said. "About me needing more wine. Also about the act of yours. Maybe you've even fooled yourself. That would be something, right? You fooling even you?" Wine was passed, but I changed my mind and drank water instead.

From the restaurant's far corner, the halo of a lit birthday cake floated toward our table. People sat straighter, relieved at the cake's distraction. But Araceli looked pained. At her party, I'd wrestled the attention toward me. I leaned forward to apologize, but she crossed her arms, her hard look deepening. Soon the cake was in front of her. Soon people were singing.

Back at the apartment, I smoked on the balcony. When morning began to break, I went to bed, but couldn't fall asleep. I flipped through images of Francisco in that bed with me, dark beard and serious eye contact, the efficient flick of his hips. Pavel moved in and out of those imaginings, too, also one of my mom's ex-boyfriends, skinny and mean, a man who walked with his hips leading the rest of him as if his dick were some national treasure.

I slept until the sun baked the room, then went to the grocery store where Gabriel always seemed to be. Getting

back to the apartment, I found Pavel waiting for me. My
jeans from the night before hung over a chair, my socks and
underwear puddled on the floor.

"Wild night?" he asked.

"A giant party," I said. "Invited all my neighborhood
friends."

"Have you had people here?"

"I haven't," I said, and picked up a sock.

He looked around the apartment, sighed, and said,
"You were a lot last night."

I folded the sock. Pavel waited for my answer. When it
didn't arrive, he said, "For the Easter weekend, we're going
to Araceli's family's place. A few hours outside the city, in
the mountains. Leaving early tomorrow morning."

"That sounds fun."

"So," Pavel said. "I probably won't see you."

"Why not?"

"A week will have passed."

I must have looked at him stupidly, because he said, "I
thought you said you were staying a week. Or I'm misre-
membering. A week is standard for this sort of visit."

"Right," I said. "Well, thank you for having me."

Pavel picked at paint under one of his nails.

"Would you have started anything up with me if you
weren't moving here?" I asked.

Surprise overtook his face. Maybe boldness was what
he'd wanted from me all along.

"I'm not good with hypotheticals," he said.

"That's a no, I take it."

"This feels like a question with no good answer."

"Why did you tell all of your friends I'd been fired?"

"You *were* fired," Pavel said.

I dropped the sock onto the table.

"I'd told them before I knew you'd be visiting," he said. "The parties you had. How you'd finagled an extra night in Munich to spend more time with some waiter you'd picked up. The things of Nicola's you took. Quite a story."

"I only took what no longer fit him," I said, and tried to organize my thoughts into a point about wealth redistribution, but they stayed scattered, so I added, "But you knew I might come. You'd invited me."

"A thing people say."

"That's nice."

"I suppose not," he said. A sliver of paint from under his nails came free. He flicked it into the sink.

"When I heard about why you'd been fired," Pavel said. "The party you'd had. The men you'd brought to their house and the things you'd taken. When I heard about all that, you know what I thought?"

"Why would I know?" I asked.

"I wasn't surprised," he said.

I shook my head, hoping to ward off the sense that he was right, that despite hardly knowing me he'd been able to spot the thoughtlessness I brandished like a polished diamond.

"That's not very nice either," I said.

"No," he answered. "I'm not a nice person, per se."

"Truer words have never been spoken."

He stared at me. I couldn't tell if he'd kiss me or hit me or tell me to leave right away. I had no money for a hotel, wasn't sure where to look for one.

"But Gordon," Pavel said. "I don't pretend to be."

He told me to slide the keys through the mail slot when I left.

I walked through the apartment, with its empty walls, sparse furnishings, and wondered if Pavel had removed paintings and valuables before I'd come, sure I'd take whatever wasn't bolted down. I picked up and folded my clothes, washed the sink's derelict dishes.

I wandered outside, kept going as darkness fell and I turned hungry but didn't eat. A single chime from a church I passed told me it was one in the morning. I moved into the middle of the street and lit a cigarette. Two men walked toward me, stepping into the middle of the street, too. Being mugged felt sad and correct, so I kept going. As their heads bobbed with equine ease, I wondered if I was about to get my ass kicked or worse. Their eyes were hollowed out by shadow. I didn't run, though. Years before, at a barbecue with my mom, for a reason I can't remember, the grill tipped over. Burning coals hissed onto the ground; a patch of grass began to burn. Someone ran over with ice, spread it across the fire so that it sizzled and died. On our way home, Mom said to me, "You were the closest." I'd assumed she was blaming me, so I told her I had nothing to do with it. "But you didn't do anything after," she said, adding, "You would never have survived as a pioneer." "I've never wanted to be a pioneer," I answered back. Her expression suggested that I'd missed her point completely.

The men were twenty feet away. I thought of the pain they might inflict, and realized only Janice and Pavel knew I was in Mexico City. At fifteen feet came the terror of being injured and in a foreign hospital, doctors telling me what they were doing in a language I knew only a few words of, the treatment I had no money for. "Pioneers," I whispered, waiting for fists or weapons.

The men said hello. "Lo siento," I answered, trying to relax into whatever was about to happen.

"Oh," one of them said. "Cigarette?"

"This is a cigarette."

"Yes. Can we have, too?"

"You want one?" I asked.

He held up two fingers.

I handed a cigarette to each of them, lit the first man's, the second's. I hoped they were lovers, though their offhand ease suggested they weren't. Still, I was glad for their lovely, manly faces, that they'd wanted some small thing from me rather than to rough me up.

"Hippy Easter," one of them said.

"Happy smoking," I answered, then moved out of the way of an approaching car.

The next day, I returned to watch another passion play. The crowd stood several rows thick. At its far edges, vendors sold snacks and holy trinkets, the pavement damp from overnight rain. A man playing Pontius Pilate shouted at the same Jesus from a few days before, still in his terrible wig. He stood proud and calm and on trial for blasphemy. I hoped to spy an amused face in the crowd, but the audience watched the proceedings with identical, pained worry. Then came a procession, donkeys included. A few of them shit as they clomped down the street, its smell so acute it burned my eyes. A woman next to me prayed. I closed my eyes, too, hoping to feel something other than a camera's detachment.

I stopped by a student travel office to ask about the cheapest flights back to the States. The salesperson told me about one to Houston.

"Who wants to go to Houston?" I said, and thanked her for her time.

I visited the internet café, logged in to check my bank balance, what credit I could still squeeze from my cards, and became so overwhelmed that I went outside to smoke with the other café regulars. I nodded to one. He either didn't notice or chose not to respond. I couldn't blame him.

Back at Pavel's apartment, I smoked more cigarettes on the balcony, my stomach riled up with hunger and nicotine, and tried to remind myself that this corseting loneliness was temporary, that I'd look back at me on this balcony from some future place and remember it as terrible, beautiful, too, the trees outside with their round, hard leaves and the men who stood close when I lit their cigarettes so I could see the flame reflected in their eyes. But as I looked around the apartment I'd have to leave soon, with no plan as to where I'd go next, the idea of some future ease kept losing out to the times I'd gotten through difficult days by imagining a warmer tomorrow that hadn't appeared, moments I managed loneliness by pretending it would pass like some short, acute infection.

I found pasta in a cabinet. I cooked then ate it until I moved past full to discomfort and had to lie down.

On Easter Sunday, still with no ticket back, I watched well-dressed people fill the streets. Pavel and his friends were in the mountains, maybe talking about the mess I'd made of Araceli's birthday dinner, though even the thought of that didn't get a rise out of me. A crowd funneled into a church. I followed, hoping Easter mass might rouse me from my days of wandering and smoking and skipping meals. An intricate mural crowded the church's domed ceiling. Statues of saints and virgins lined the walls. Bells tolled, and a choir of guitarists played and sang, sometimes in harmony. I found a seat next to a family several generations thick, small children squirming on old people's laps, women pulling cough drops and Bibles from their purses. I tried to find something in this family to admire, but noticed only their garish clothes and overly strong perfume, the giant wads of gum their brooding teens chewed. The service proceeded in a routine of standing and sitting. I tried to will myself to appreciate these people and this place, the priest's deep-voiced Spanish. But even with the music, the people packed close, what I felt most was a separateness, a sense I was barely there. I'd felt the same thing at that dinner a few nights before when I'd said what I'd said in an attempt to return to earth. It had grown stronger on Pavel's tiny balcony as I watched morning light creep across walls and tree trunks, as people headed to work or to church on some planet I observed through a million-dollar telescope. The man next to me sang loudly, saw I wasn't singing, and handed me a hymnal opened to a particular page. I tried to sing, my throat dry from smoking and not talking. I wished I'd never left Food Land. Thor/Vince might have warmed up to me, Marcy settling into her role as a reliable friend. As the song ended,

I let that Bay Ridge fantasy drift out to sea and wondered
what people would do if I moved into the aisle then and lay
down. My neighbor cleared his throat, and shoes shuffled
as people moved into the aisles, parishioners greeting one
another with the Spanish equivalent of "Peace be with you."
The priest shook hands, put his wrinkled palm on the head
of a baby. The man who'd given me the hymnal shook my
hand, then pointed to others waiting to shake hands as well.
I held the hands of a dozen strangers, nodded to the few
who offered hugs. I tried to appreciate this human contact,
but felt the dread of returning to Pavel's apartment, the
worry that, though I was meant to be out by tomorrow, I
wouldn't find the will to pack my bags. An old man came up
to me. "La paz sea contigo," he said, and opened his arms. I
leaned against his shoulder. And though I don't know that
anything shifted, when I opened my eyes and saw the man's
warm smile, I decided to pretend I felt better, pretend, too,
that what was difficult would pass, that I wouldn't always
be in this place or someplace like it, Bay Ridge and Mexico
City and Minneapolis's gridded suburbs all rooms in a single house I mistook for different places. I would pretend,
I thought, and moved back to where I'd been sitting. The
congregation started to sing again.

After mass, I went back to the internet café, those crouched
over computers my people more than Pavel or Philip or
most others. I checked my email, found one from Janice
with news about her Los Angeles life. Next came a new
message from my father. Unlike the meandering nostalgia
of his previous emails, this one talked about the heart

bypass he was scheduled for in a week. *Quadruple*, he wrote. *Maybe more once they see how bad it is inside your old father.* He explained that though he knew he wasn't meant to be afraid, fear stayed with him. *I'm sometimes mad that it's such a holdout. Though I'm not afraid of what's after all this, but what I'll leave behind.*

The student travel office was closed for the holiday, but there was a number I could call. Back at Pavel's, I dialed. When a representative answered in Spanish, I said, "Lo siento," and she switched to English without pause.

"I need a ticket to Houston," I said.

The representative worked quickly, wished me a good trip, then hung up before I could thank her.

18

In the two years since I'd seen him, my father had aged five times as many. His once-thick hair was reduced to wisps, and liver spots stained his hands. And though he was still taller than me, he didn't tower over me anymore.

"It's good that you came," he said, the timbre of his voice old, too.

Arriving in Houston a few days before, I got on one bus heading north, then another, trying to convince myself that I didn't know where I was going. I waited until I was hours away to call Dad and tell him I'd be staying for a while.

He and June lived on a busy street, in a house with low ceilings and small windows, wall-to-wall carpet bleached by the sun in strange geometry. But there was a guest room for me to stay in, food I could eat. My first night, I slept for twelve hours. When I woke up late the next day, I found Dad in an easy chair with golf on, though I'd never known him to play or have any interest. His wheeze competed with the television.

"June's worried about my surgery," Dad said. "It's good she'll have you for company."

"I got your email," I said.

"I sent you a lot of emails."

"You're afraid?" I asked.

Dad kept his eyes on the golf course's ripple of green hills.

"If it's my time, it's my time," he said, and told me June had left food. I was hoping for a more confessional insight, but Dad only talked about a particular player's swing, the many buses I had to take to get to him.

Dad's surgery was two days later. June and I drove him to the hospital so early it was still dark out, most streets lifeless, some traffic lights blinking rather than toggling between red and green.

While he was in surgery, June and I laid claim to a waiting room. She shook her head with polite unease when I offered her one of my celebrity magazines, held her purse in her lap like some docile pet. An intercom paged a doctor.

June and I had only met a handful of times. She wore her gray hair short and a turtleneck dotted in flowers. I asked, after morning had come and gone, if she was bored. June answered that she was never bored, then took a notebook from her purse and began to write things down.

Members of their church showed up. Some brought sandwiches. Others came with coffee and desserts. Soon, food filled the table, and June handed it out to other waiting people.

Dad's pastor, the man who several years earlier had told me to get up off the floor, kindly acted as if he had no memory of me. And then, with a wife in tow, a drooling baby strapped to his chest, came Brian.

June introduced us. Brian said we knew each other.

"You have a baby now," I said.

Brian kept his eyes on the floor. One hand cradled his baby's head. The intercom paged a different doctor's name.

"I hear you're a world traveler," he said.

"I've been some places."

I picked up a piece of the coffee cake his wife had made and bit into it. It was dry, overly sweet. As Brian watched me eat it, the pregnant attention he'd looked at me with years before resurfacing, I understood that I could still upend him.

A few hours later, after we heard from the doctor that the surgery had gone without incident, June cried and whispered heavenly thanks. She let me hug her, though it was awkward and uneasy, so I quickly let go. The doctor asked if we wanted to see Dad. June said yes. I declined, so she went without me, came back a half hour later in distress. "He just seems in such pain," she said, then wrote down more in the notebook she carried.

"Sounds like you need a drink," I said.

"We don't drink," June said, in a loud, startled voice.

In the guest room that night, rather than linger in my recent Pavel/Francisco fantasy (it had to do with being painted—there were drop cloths and brushes, admonishments to stay still), I imagined taking a slice of the coffee cake from earlier in the day, Brian eating it out of my hand.

After Dad returned home, I had to help him out of bed and get him to the bathroom. Soon we added short walks around the house to our repertoire. He told stories of my childhood until he got winded.

"That tree behind our place on Rolf Avenue," he said one day, the two of us walking down the hall that led to the bedrooms. "You'd climb all the way to the top. You'd rest yourself between branches that seemed too tiny to hold anyone human, but it held you." He stopped to take several breaths. Traffic whirred outside. The sun spread across the carpet in narrow bands. "And sometimes when you were in that tree, I'd take out a lawn chair and sit at its base. Climbing was a thing I could never do, Gordon. I'd sit there when you were in that tree for hours, and I'd say to you, do you remember? I'd say to you, 'My boy still in a tree?' Sometimes you'd answer." I remembered that tree, him sitting underneath it, how I sometimes loved his company, other times wanted to throw twigs at him until he left me alone.

A late spring snowstorm knocked the power out. We walked around the house draped in blankets. I used their grill to make us toast and eggs for breakfast, chicken for dinner. I was reading a celebrity magazine by flashlight when the power returned. The overhead light blazed, the whole house humming with electrical activity. Walking into the hall, I found June and Dad there, blinking at the brightness.

"I guess we don't need to wear blankets for clothes anymore," I said.

"You didn't tell me he was funny," June said to Dad, and took the blanket he'd been wearing from his shoulders.

The next morning Dad got a call, asking if I'd be able to help shovel the church's sidewalk. I agreed and walked there. It had turned warm. Icicles shattered and leaking snowmelt trickled from gutters. Slush slipped into my sneakers.

I found Brian and another man waiting at the church. Brian saw my feet and went inside to get me a pair of boots. They were too large, but dry. I relished each step in them.

It got warmer as we shoveled, so I took off my coat. Brian kept his on. His face grew slick, and sweat darkened his collar. I suggested he take his coat off, but he didn't, and the thrill that came from torturing him returned. I recommended again that he take it off, that he'd be more comfortable. Brian didn't even unzip it.

With my credit cards maxed out, my checking account balance the answer to a third-grade math problem, I got a job at a downtown Starbucks. I biked there using an old ten-speed Dad said was mine, though I had no memory of it. Some mornings I had to get up at four in the morning for work, and though tiredness ached across my eyes and shoulders, the busy immediacy of it brought me a comfort I hadn't expected. I made cappuccinos and placated customers whose orders I'd messed up, also those whose orders I'd gotten right, though they claimed to have asked for something else. After each shift, I biked home. On cold days, my fingers and face burned. When it rained, the weight the water added to my clothes slowed me down. But spring was beginning to win out, biking home mostly lovely, the air just cool enough to count as refreshing. In front of houses, fists of daffodils and other early flowers started to appear.

Each day when I got home, Dad made the same joke: "Your smell is a latte." June, usually in the kitchen, would poke her head out and answer, "The two of you are funny together." Though Dad wasn't funny and some part of me wanted to scoff at his pedestrian wordplay, it was nice to hear him say silly things, to notice sometimes, when I glanced up from whatever magazine I was flipping through, that Dad was watching me.

He hated the smell of cigarette smoke, so I limited smoking to my breaks at work. And with no booze in the house, I went sober for weeks. That, along with the biking each day and the steadying influence of proper sleep, left me feeling better. And though boredom resurfaced alongside it, it was nice to reacquaint myself with that feeling for a while, to see if I could outlast it or let it overtake me until it felt good, or at least comfortable.

One night I went out for drinks with coworkers. I biked home tipsy. Arriving home after nine, I waited for Dad to say something, but he just asked if I'd worked an extra shift then told me there was lasagna to heat up. As I watched television with Dad and June, an ad came on for the singing competition Meredith was working on. I threw most of my lasagna in the trash, and wished they had a computer besides the one in their bedroom, saying so out loud.

"Computers cost money," Dad said.

"Don't I know it," I said. He turned the TV volume down.

"June and I have been talking," Dad said.

The next ad was for chewing gum. Its actors had large white teeth. Dad leaned forward, elbows on knees. I waited for him to tell me I'd overstayed my welcome and wished I'd relished the easy boredom of my weeks there more. When he asked that I start paying rent instead, I was relieved.

"How much?" I asked.

"Seventy-five," he said.

"A month?"

"A week, we were thinking," he said, and turned the television volume up again.

After they'd gone to bed, I went to the backyard and smoked and decided that his asking for rent hadn't been wrong, though neither was my annoyance.

The rent talk was a prelude to other conversations. They asked that I not stay out late, as June was a light sleeper. Said next that they'd rather I not bring home friends. "We can't have *wildness* with your father's heart," June explained. With each talk there was a falling feeling, a settling as I reluctantly adjusted. I had a job, a place to stay. It was enough. Though when coworkers invited me to smoke weed in their cars during our breaks, I missed the lightness of that action, missed other things, too.

I got home from work and found Dad on the couch, breathing strangely. "I think you need to take me to the hospital," he said.

June had taken their car to work, so he gave me a number to call. Brian answered.

"My father," I said. "We need a ride to the emergency room."

Brian was there in minutes. He and I sat in front, Dad lay in the back seat. "We're almost there," Brian repeated. I kept looking back to make sure Dad was still with us.

After Dad was admitted, Brian and I sat in a waiting room. *Jerry Springer* played on TV. People in tight clothes and thick makeup sat on the dais, arms folded.

"How long have you been married?" I asked.

"Just over a year," he said.

Brian had on a tie and shiny shoes from his job as a guidance counselor.

"You met your wife at church?"

"I did."

"Did she go there when I did?"

"You didn't really go there," he said.

A woman on TV stood, pointed to a man whose mouth pulled down at the corners like a bulldog's.

"Can I ask you something? As a guidance counselor, I mean?"

Brian nodded. He had the pale, pleasant face of a missionary.

"What do you say to your students when they don't know what to do?" I asked.

"About what?"

"Anything."

Brian leaned forward. The tip of his tie dangled. I squelched the urge to pick it up, to pull.

"Sometimes I tell them to make a list. If they're the praying sort, I offer that. Or we talk about what's difficult for them. Break it down into obstacles and solutions."

"Your students must find you comforting," I said.

His expression suggested he thought I was poking fun, so I told him I meant it. "To know someone good is talking to them. I bet they leave your office and feel relieved."

"Your father worries about you," Brian said.

He went out of his way not to look at me. Years before, when he'd played piano at the church, I'd noticed his fingers delicately pressing on each key and understood the desire he felt and fought. Now he had a baby. When making that baby, he might have thought of men. I wanted to be one of those men, my greed growing as I looked at the thin band on his finger.

"Are you afraid for your father?" Brian asked.

I shook my head. My ten-speed and job, the small-windowed guest room, all of it felt like a joke I'd just realized was being played on me.

"Here's what I don't understand about you people," I said, wincing at my use of that phrase. "Why, if you're so jazzed about heaven. Why aren't you all throwing yourselves into lakes or jumping off buildings together, hand in hand and all that?"

"We don't hate being alive," Brian said. "And we wouldn't go to heaven if we killed ourselves."

"So a technicality then," I said, and began to well up.

"I can't tell if you're being ridiculous or not," Brian said.

By then I was really crying, though that sort of thing was normal in an ER waiting room.

"I'm not trying to be ridiculous."

He moved forward, to hug me perhaps, but resisted. I let out a small laugh.

"I'm not going to, like, attack you," I said.

"I know."

A patient came in with his hand wrapped in a towel, moved nonchalantly to the admissions desk to tell them he'd sliced one of his fingers. He unfolded the towel. I wanted to see, but couldn't from where I was sitting.

"I'm not worried that you'll throw yourself at me," Brian said.

We drank hospital coffee, its heat snaking down my chest. Brian's left heel tapped against the floor.

"I would hug you for telling me that," I said. "But that's just what you don't want."

Brian might have thought of me over the years, wound up each time with worry and lust and shame. I thought about him rarely, and then only as an anecdote.

"And the me from back then would have hugged you too hard," I said.

I waited for him to talk about the path to damnation I'd forged and followed. But he smiled, and asked, "What about you now?"

"You're probably safe now," I said.

"Probably?" he asked.

The wounded man sat across from us, wrapped hand in his lap. With his free hand he picked up a copy of *Good Housekeeping*, which I found funny, though I find everything funny.

"Yes," I said. "But you know, I can always change my mind."

Esophageal spasms, the doctor told Brian and me. "Your father's body has been through a lot with his surgery. But he isn't in danger. Just discomfort."

Brian drove us home. He helped Dad out of the car with a graciousness I found annoying. Inside, June had wound herself into hysterics. Brian said he'd leave us to it.

"Why didn't you call?" she asked.

"I did."

"There's no message on the machine."

"I called your job. Someone named Michele said you were out but that she'd tell you."

"Michele hates me," June said.

I wanted to ask why.

"It's just his esophagus," I said.

"What's wrong with his esophagus?" she asked, pitch rising with worry.

"Just some basic discomfort," I said, and added, mimicking the doctor, "Should pass sooner rather than later."

June asked if he could still eat, given that his esophagus was an important part of that process. I handed her his discharge papers and said, "Some light reading."

In my room I thought of Brian. But each time I went to undo his belt or stick my tongue down his throat, he looked like he was being injured. And when I told him he wouldn't go to hell, wanting this dream version of Brian to say he didn't care if he did, he told me instead, "You don't know. We might end up there together."

———

A week later, Dad wanted to go for a drive. It was one of his first times behind the wheel since his surgery. I sat in the passenger seat, listening to a story about a camping trip I had zero memory of.

"Lake Superior," he said.

"I've never been there," I insisted.

"There are pictures somewhere, maybe with your mother."

"She doesn't hold on to pictures."

Dad gave me an exasperated smile, and I told him we should call her and ask, beginning an improvised version of that conversation in which Mom had the pictures and had quit smoking and admitted everything was her fault. Dad's rattling laugh filled the car.

"You were right about everything, Bob," I said, in imitation.

A cat darted into the road. Dad slammed on the brakes. They worked, and the cat made it to the street's far side. But rather than continue, Dad's hands squeezed the steering wheel. His stomach rose and fell. I put a hand on his forearm; he moved it away. As cars gathered behind us in a honking line, he said, "Gordon, you shouldn't have distracted me."

The accident years before happened when Dad sped through a stop sign he insisted wasn't there. I'd seen it, though, from the passenger seat, and pulled in a startled breath when we blew through it and into an oncoming car.

As we waited for police and paramedics to arrive, Dad

kept saying, "It wasn't there." Blood gushed from his already swollen nose.

"I know," I said, the ache from what turned out to be my broken arm so strong I grew woozy. But I turned my head and saw the sign he claimed didn't exist, looked back and saw that he'd seen what I'd seen. Dad started to cry, his hands squeezing the steering wheel until his knuckles whitened, purpled. For a long time I imagined that, had I not looked back at the sign, not made it so clear I was on to his bullshit, Dad might have stuck around for a time. Later, I tried to see my turning around as a public service, an animal's labored breathing stopped with a clean shot from a steady hand.

A coworker named Duncan and I started to take smoke breaks together. I'd mistaken him for boring in my early shifts, was thrilled to learn that he had an amazing memory for minutiae, could mimic our manager's affect so perfectly I kept asking him to say ridiculous things in his voice.

One evening, Duncan invited me out to drinks after work. "You can meet some of my friends," he said. "I've told them about you." When he mentioned the gay bar we were going to, I looked at him with surprise.

"Don't ask, don't tell," he whispered.

"We're not in the army," I said.

In a bar filled with loud music and interested men and eye contact, I grew shocked at what I'd forgotten.

Duncan's friends were fine. One was a hairdresser who had things to say about the hair of most people in the bar. Another talked mostly about his nemesis at his office job, Sheila.

A man came over to me. The sharpness of being wanted filled my mouth. He was a dentist, he told me, pointing to his perfect teeth, as if I'd asked for evidence. An hour later, I went to find Duncan to tell him I was leaving, but he was occupied with a man who looked twice his age. The dentist and I left. When I told him I had my bike with me, he laughed sweetly, sweetness something I hadn't realized I'd missed. We drove to his place with the bike perched in his trunk, its back wheel out and spinning.

The sex was nice, not otherworldly, though I liked how he looked at me. I like being looked at too much.

He asked me to stay the night. I told him I wasn't looking for anything serious. He answered back that it was just a night and I agreed and conjured an excuse to tell Dad and June.

The next morning I put on my stinking uniform from the day before. And just as I was leaving, the dentist said, "It's still not serious if you come over again tonight."

He gave me his card. Told me to come to his office after work.

"You are kinky, doctor," I said, imagining us in one of his exam chairs, drills and posters on flossing in the background.

At work, one of my colleagues told me I was being weirdly chipper and asked if I'd gotten laid.

"Bingo," I said.

For the rest of the shift, we used that word. *Bingo* when the line got long or when one of us needed to use the bathroom. *Bingo* when the old man came in who always complained that the coffee wasn't hot enough, as if we were keeping the hotter coffee from him.

"You told me you hadn't had your teeth cleaned in years," the dentist said, when I made it to his office. We stood in his waiting room, with its matching chairs and magazines fanned out on a table. I wondered if he needed a receptionist.

"Why are you being nice to me?" I asked.

"I'm trying to woo you." His face fell as he added, "Though I imagine you're not looking to be wooed."

I was probably, not by him, though in the years since I wished I'd remembered his name.

"Come," he said, and cleaned my teeth, moving close so I could hear the gentle whistle of his breathing.

I stayed the next night, then Sunday, which I had off. The dentist drove me to Dad's when he and June would be at church so I could leave a note (*Staying with a friend for the weekend*) and get more clothes. Back at the dentist's, we cooked together. I put together a salad I'd learned to make from Philip. The dentist ate it as if it were some great delicacy, and I stayed another night.

After my Monday shift, I biked back to Dad's, rehearsing a story about a friend from work, the fun we'd had, whittling the last days down to an innocuous childhood sleepover. I can leave and come back, I thought, especially for a few days.

But walking inside, I found my packed bags just inside the door. Seeing them, I regretted the dentist, regretted the either/or my father demanded of me, regretted coming back at all.

Dad got up from the golf he wasn't watching. I could

see the sadness weighing him down, wishing I wasn't so expert in translating what it meant when his blinking sped up and he knotted his mouth so that his lips turned close to invisible. I wanted to scoff at his hurt, to tell him I'd done nothing wrong, but he had taken me in when I'd needed it. Dad stopped in front of my duffel bag.

"We can't have that kind of behavior in this house," he said.

"It didn't happen in this house," I answered, a sincere statement, though he seemed to take it as sarcasm. I tried but failed to catch his eye.

Dad asked me for my keys.

"Thanks for packing my bags," I said.

"What a thing to say," Dad said.

I'd meant it. He'd been kind to me, even though I'm not sure he wanted to.

I stepped close, to hug him goodbye, but Dad shook his head, an action that allowed anger to creep in, though as he kept shaking his head so that his jowls trembled and with the edges of his eyes ringed in red, any anger lost its traction, especially when he tried and failed to pick up my bag.

"I'm sorry," I said.

I was about to explain that I wasn't sorry for the dentist but for the mutual injuries he and I were expert at inflicting, but didn't know if that distinction mattered.

I walked until I found a pay phone. When Duncan answered, he sounded surprised.

"Is it okay that I'm calling?" I asked.

In the background, TV or the radio. The reality that I had nowhere to live again crowded the booth I stood in.

"Sure," Duncan said. "I just didn't remember giving you my number."

Duncan lived with his mother. They offered me the couch in their basement, a space with a carpet remnant and a rumbling hot water tank, boxes labeled with things like *Sweaters* and *Holiday*. Niceness permeated their house. They refused the rent I offered, told me I could get groceries from time to time. When I came back from work with a hundred dollars' worth of food one night, his mom said, "This is too much," and the three of us ate dinner from the overabundance.

Duncan and I went back to the bar where I'd met the dentist. He found another older man and I went back to his house without him, embarrassed when his mother, Lois, heard me and walked out of her room. She had on a bathrobe, her hair flattened on one side. I told her Duncan would be home soon. She smiled and answered that I was a good friend, though Duncan had been the good friend, me the beneficiary of his kindness. I asked Lois if I could use their computer to check my email.

There was a message from Janice, asking how Mexico City was going. Despite my promises of steady friendship, I'd let her drift into the distance. I began to write back, but the last, colorless months were too much to rehash, so I told myself I'd finish it later, hoping I would. I went to the basement and slept hard, was woken up the next morning by Duncan when he came down to do his laundry.

———

One night, Lois out and Duncan at work, I called my mom.

She talked about her job at the Y, then asked where I was.

"Milwaukee," I said.

"With your father?" she asked.

"For a while, but that didn't work out."

"You thought it would?"

Her question was fair, even if magical thinking was a trait she and Dad had taught me.

"I'm staying at a friend's now," I said. "On a sofa in his basement." I talked about the chatty hot water heater, the dryer so close I'd felt its heat.

"The way you sound," she said. "Talking about it like it's a good thing."

"A place to live," I said.

"Barely."

I asked about her apartment. She told me it was a studio, warding off the possibility that I'd ask to stay. I talked next about Mexico City.

"Why did you go there?" she asked.

"I was invited."

"What sort of invitation?"

"One that was offered and accepted."

There was quiet for a while, a sucking sound. Maybe she was smoking again. Maybe it didn't matter. Just as I was about to sign off, Mom said, "You can't act like some scared child forever."

I wanted to bang the phone against the wall, for her to hear each hard sound. But that feeling came and went, leaving behind a reminder that she could do nothing for me, that even as a child my sore throats or questions were puzzles she wasn't up to solving.

"That's true," I said, "but I can be a scared adult."

"Not everything is funny," she said.

I was deciding whether to retreat or engage, whether to tell her she was right, that most things were only pretend funny, or funny if you didn't think too much about them, when Mom told me she had to go, finishing with, "Let me know where you end up."

I didn't talk to her for months. Even then, I did so begrudgingly after several emails from her, each progressively more hysterical. The last one ended in all caps: *I DON'T EVEN KNOW WHERE YOU ARE.*

———

I was making lattes for women with their work IDs on lanyards when my father appeared. He moved slowly. I steamed milk and called out orders. Dad waited in line. When his turn came, he dropped mail onto the counter.

"This is for you," he said.

"How are you feeling?" I asked.

"You should tell people this isn't your address anymore. I don't want to keep you."

He turned around and walked out the door.

I went into the back room, dropped the mail into my satchel, and returned to my post. But instead of taking the next order, I asked Duncan to cover for me. Dad was only a few steps out of the store. He walked carefully, as if navigating an icy sidewalk.

"You didn't answer my question on how you're feeling," I said.

"How do you think I'm feeling?" Dad asked.

"I don't know. That's why I asked."

"There are some bills in that mail," he said.

On the street beyond us, his car sat double-parked. Wanting to end this on my terms, to fulfill the role he'd assigned me, perhaps, I said, "You know Brian at your church? He's like me. Brian who you rely on, who you called when you needed to be taken to the hospital."

"He's not like you," Dad said.

I outpaced him and turned to block his path. He kept his eyes on the ground.

"I spent those nights when I didn't come home with a dentist," I said. "He even cleaned my teeth, which was nice of him. Hot in a strange way."

"Gordon," he interrupted.

"After I slept with him the first night, he wanted me to stay. I probably could have turned into his wife or something. Wouldn't that have been a thing, me and my dentist lover living just a few miles away from you? Maybe he's your dentist. That would be an amazing coincidence, him checking your fillings and gums with the same hands he did things to me with."

"Gordon," Dad repeated.

"All sorts of things."

"Why are you like this?"

I could have answered that his coming and going had shaped me, though there was a hardness in me I remembered even before he'd found the Lord, when he and I were, as Mom said, "quite a pair." Could have told him that I also wondered why I jumped into uncertain waters only to flail once I reached them. How giving up felt good, the way it did when a man grabbed my throat or went at me with teeth, with force, and I didn't have to try, just to let him. How it was sometimes only in those moments of abject pain or failure or with a pillow over my mouth that might not get lifted in time that I felt something close to better.

But instead I said, "I'd love it if he were your dentist. That would make me happy."

Dad got into his car. He pulled onto the street without looking to see if anyone was coming.

When June called me eight months later to tell me Dad had died, she kept saying, "If only you'd seen him again." I had seen him though. Living in their guest room, there'd been moments of loveliness, most in remembrance, what was left for us to share outside of nostalgia a shrinking patch of ground. The version of him I'd miss had left long ago, existing even more as what I'd hoped he might be. "The funeral's Friday," June said. I told her I'd book a flight, though I didn't and on Thursday called and said that my flight had been canceled, that I didn't have money for another one. I wanted her to offer to pay, or admit she wouldn't, but she said she was sorry to hear that, and asked that I go to church the next day. "While his service is happening. So you can be with him." I went out that night, felt lucky when someone reasonably attractive took me home. Early the next morning I stopped by a church—a Catholic one, with flickering candles, everything there plated in gold—and felt only the discomfort of the bench I sat on, a wish, too, to have felt more. I lit a candle, paid for it, and thought about the sex I'd had the night before, how it always took me by surprise when a stranger ended up being careful and attentive and looked at me with something like love, for a few minutes anyway.

Back in Duncan's basement after Dad had come to the store, I went through the mail he'd brought me. There was a postcard from Janice, a credit card bill I couldn't believe had found me. The last was written on thick card stock, a handwriting I recognized right away as Philip's. I hoped he was writing with forgiveness, that his note explained how he'd kicked Nicola out and was hoping I'd return. I ripped the envelope open.

Philip's note was brief. He mentioned the work it took to find me, that he wished me the best. Accompanying it was a check for five thousand dollars. In its memo Philip had written *Arrears*. I didn't know that word then and had to look it up.

It wasn't the forgiveness I wanted. And not getting what I wanted left me embarrassed at the way I clung to a vision of the world as I wished it to be. But the money was a lifeline. And as I lay there, the check written in Philip's elegant hand resting on my stomach, I thought of Dad that afternoon when he'd pulled into traffic without looking, certain all he needed then was to get away from me.

I put the check in my wallet.

The next morning, I walked for an hour to get to my bank. The woman behind the counter accepted the check as if that much money were no big deal, so I pretended it was no big deal, too, and took a taxi back to work with its coffee smells and line of customers, and waited until the end of the shift to give notice to my manager.

PART FOUR

19

The shift had been busy. One patient moved toward a surprising recovery, but an old woman who seemed to have beaten the odds was back, resigned in a way that often signaled the end. She remembered me, told me about a Gordon she'd once known, admitting that he, too, was, as she said, "A homosexual. Though he'd had to hide it."

"What happened to your Gordon?" I asked.

Her serious face gave me the answer. I held her hand until I was needed elsewhere.

The shift done, I passed any pertinent information on to the next nurse, then went to find my friend Susan. Since nursing school a decade before, she'd been one of my people. We'd sat together in the back of our classes, whispering and writing on each other's notebooks, though we always knew the answers when we were called on. People sometimes took Susan's refusal to engage in bullshit as meanness. I saw it as the opposite. She made me laugh until I cried and told me with blunt kindness when I was engaging in what she called my "Gordon nonsense." I sometimes spent Christmas with her family at the far edge of Brooklyn, her aunt joking that I was the white devil each time I showed up. But now Susan and her husband were struggling. That morning she texted me, *Need to tell you things.*

When I got to her ward—one that catered to leukemia, larger than the blood cancers one I worked on—Susan was busy, so I waited at the unit desk. I talked to a PA about a TV show we both were ashamed to love, then Obama's chances for reelection. Another nurse, Rueben, short and fit, someone Susan and I wondered about in terms of his area of interest, joined us behind the desk. He took a sip of his coffee, telling us he was on his way to check on "His Highness."

"The old queen actually isn't that bad," Rueben added, his word choice making it clear what team he was on. "Just the way he talks makes him sound like he's giving commands, even when he's, like, asking politely for some water. And his name: Philip Belshaw."

Susan and I went to the cafeteria. I listened over scalding coffees as she told me how her husband suddenly didn't know if he wanted kids when kids had always been their plan.

"Maybe the two of you should talk to someone?" I asked.

"Try getting Kevin to do that," she said.

Kevin was quiet and proud, my friendship with Susan a strange amusement to him.

I went back upstairs when Susan's break was done, telling her I needed to ask Rueben a question.

"Like if he's a top or a bottom?" she asked. It was nice to see her smile for a moment.

The elevator dinged, one floor, another.

"Rueben's definitely a bottom," I said.

When Rueben came back to the desk, he said, "Still here?"

"How was Philip Belshaw?"

"Good memory."

"I used to work for him," I said, and asked if anyone named Nicola had visited. "Italian and fancy."

"Fancy people have visited for sure," he said.

A doctor appeared, a resident, I guessed, from his baby-faced determination. He went to a computer, typing fast and loud.

"You were his nurse?" Rueben asked.

"This was before."

"Let me guess," he said. "You were in art school, maybe wrote poetry. I dated one of those once. He sat in coffee shops all day and his parents paid most of his rent."

"I wasn't a rich kid," I told him.

I wanted to find Philip's room, to see his spark of recognition. But it was late and this wasn't my ward, so I told Susan to call me later. She went into the room of a young woman whittled down by sickness. The young ones still startled me, even though I'd been working there for years.

After Philip had given me the money, I took a day-and-a-half bus trek back to the city, sleeping so hard and long that a man across the aisle shook me awake to make sure I was still with the living. I found a cheap room so far out in Brooklyn that I had to take a bus to the subway, in a house rented by three PhD students. I wanted to sleep with one of them, though I knew better than to try. That felt like growth to me.

I found a new temp agency and somehow did well enough on the typing test to qualify for non-receptionist jobs. A few weeks into working for them, I got a shift in the billing department of a Manhattan hospital. The woman who ran its HR office was a lesbian named Carol. She took a shine to me and kept me in billing for three days. The next morning the temp agency told me Carol had requested me again. That day I covered the desk in the ICU. The first few hours, with the combination of my inexperience and the high stakes, I was terrified. A man died. His family left his room, arms linked and mouths open as they wailed, too run over by grief to notice me. Knowing I wasn't the center of things made that job easier. And I liked its busyness, calls to answer and people to give directions to and forms to complete.

I became Carol's regular temp. One day, I was assigned to the hospital's main information desk. People came in rattled and confused. I looked up room numbers, told them how to make their way to the ER. Carol brought me a coffee, told me the ICU had an opening for a unit secretary. "You need to apply."

"And if I don't get it?" I asked.

"Why is that the first thing you ask me?" she said.

I spent the lulls between visitor questions completing the application.

I got the job, its shifts so busy I had little time to think about Pavel or Philip or my father's death. I worked the day of his funeral and told no one about it, though in its quiet moments I couldn't escape the thought of his body in a box being lowered into the ground.

At work I answered phones and held the hands of

women whose husbands had had strokes or heart attacks, and anything outside the hospital walls fell away. After each shift, exhaustion won out. I was glad for its bossy company.

Carol invited me to her house for dinner. She lived in Queens with her girlfriend, a nurse named Liz. We ate pasta and drank wine. I told them about growing up in Minnesota and my PhD roommates who might have been communists, but avoided talk of Philip or my dad. When it got late, they insisted that I spend the night in their guest room. I agreed, thinking of the collection of sofas and air mattresses and floors I'd laid claim to. A month later, at their house again, Liz gave me the card of a friend of hers who ran the nursing program at the city university. And though I felt ashamed at the way I let others lead me to things, I thanked her and called, kept my job at the ICU while I went to school so I was always busy, always tired. While people talk about this job as a calling, for me it's truer to say that it fulfills a need I have for motion, a satisfaction in tackling tasks that matter, with a clear beginning and end. I show up in rooms to worried faces and see hope that I'll be able to take some of that worry away with an injection or a few softly spoken words. A hand on an arm to let them know they're less alone, at least in that moment.

After I graduated, I ended up at a hospital specializing in cancer. I bought an apartment in a Brooklyn neighborhood just before gentrification had dug its claws in (though I was part of that gentrification, or as Susan liked to say, "Its poster boy"). I ran in the park and saw art house movies and went to dimly lit bars where I found it easier to pursue men than I once had, telling them what I wanted almost as thrilling as when we finally yanked off each other's clothes, or when they pressed their weight onto me so for a moment I couldn't breathe. I had a boyfriend for a time, smart and funny though I always worried he was one step away from leaving. We got as far as moving in together. But in the end, he told me something was missing, though he couldn't or didn't explain just what, which broke my heart, turned work into a necessary narcotic, a break from thinking of the mistakes I had made and would keep making without meaning to.

At the end of my next shift, I stood outside Philip's room. I was debating whether to walk in when I heard him say, "Yes?"

His eyebrows were wilder and whiter than before. I wondered if my scruff or the gray that had begun to populate my hair, the laps I ran through the park most days, made me unrecognizable. So I said, "I'm not sure that you'll remember me."

"I'm not here for dementia," Philip said.

Flower arrangements crowded his windowsill. Beyond it were buildings, evening's last light lava on the river.

"You still wait until you're invited to do things," Philip said. "Sit down. Come in. Et cetera."

"I work here," I said.

"Gordon, I know how to put two and two together."

His face was all teeth and bones, and skin sagged off his arms, like an overworn sweater. Liquid fell from his IV in bright blips.

"Perhaps not where you expected me to end up," I said.

"I saw you walking past a few days ago," Philip said.

"You still walk the same way. And I don't know if it's surprising. You were always most comfortable caretaking." He added that I'd grown into my face, asked if I'd forgotten to shave or if I was doing what so many young men seemed to be then. "Perpetually as if they shaved two and a half days ago."

"I guess I'm doing that."

An orderly came in with dinner. Philip ignored it.

"You should eat," I said.

"The food isn't good," he said. "And eating just delays the inevitable."

"Starving yourself is an especially unpleasant way to go."

He rearranged food with his fork.

"I've often wondered about you," he said. "I wanted to tell you about the plate." I worried that he'd gotten some memory tangled. "Shortly before Nicola moved out for the final time, I'd grown jealous and distrustful. I was going through his things and found a plate he'd insisted you'd stolen. It was the reason I'd agreed to fire you. It had value, sentimental and otherwise."

He rested one hand, blotched in bruises, on top of the other.

"But when I found it," Philip went on, "I wondered about other things Nicola had accused you of. You'd had friends at our place, irresponsible though not so unexpected. And he kept going on about the clothes of his you'd taken, though I'd practically encouraged you to help yourself. It was the plate that was our end. That's when I started looking for you."

"I was in Mexico City for a time," I said.

"This was after Pavel got tired of you as he gets tired of

most things. That money I'd sent. A sliver of the commission we got for the paintings of you."

"I didn't paint them."

"No need to be coy, et cetera."

"I'm not," I said. "Et cetera."

"I never heard from you after I sent that money."

I'd drafted several versions of a thank-you note. Some were too effusive, others came off as cold. Another so pathetically apologetic that I ripped it up before I finished. After a while I stopped trying, told myself I'd send one soon, but then a few years passed and embarrassment erased any possibility that I'd answer. But as Philip stared at me, my excuses felt piddling, so I said, "I didn't think you'd want to hear from me."

"I sent you five thousand dollars."

Philip's eyes and gums were a raw red. He had a week, I guessed, two if his body stubbornly dug its heels in.

"It allowed me to come back here," I said. "To get an apartment. To do everything, really."

"I'd wanted to hear from you."

"You should have said as much."

"I thought I had."

He made a huffing noise then fell asleep. I stayed and read a magazine.

When he woke up, he said, "Always waiting. Remember those dogs we had?"

"You're still mean," I said.

"Honest," he said.

"Both."

"I don't know how you still are," he said. "Haven't seen

you out in the wild, as it were. I hope things are easier, though."

"Easier than what?"

"The way you were when you worked for us, any attention was a necessary sunshine."

Tiredness raked his throat. I helped him sip water. His tongue curled toward the straw. I held a hand behind his neck, felt the sharp turn of his bones.

"I don't know that I'm that way still," I said. "I don't know if it's easier either."

Outside, a boat floated up the East River. I told him he must be tired.

"Dying will do that to you," he answered. I held his hand, my fingers rested across his hard-wormed veins.

"I'll let you sleep."

"Not yet," he said.

Rueben had told me there'd been no record of any Nicola visiting.

"You still talk to Rebecca?" I asked.

"She was so sad that I'd fired you. Told me I'd let Nicola win. I tried to find you," he said again.

"I guess I didn't want to be found."

"I have a painting of you still, that Pavel did. It's one of the few pieces in my bedroom."

He turned toward the window, a shyness in him that I hadn't noticed before. I wondered what else I'd missed then, when all I could consider was what he thought of me.

"That makes me happy," I said.

I asked if he still lived on Morton Street. He told me he'd given that up for an apartment years ago. "A famous actor lives in that house now. I imagine he has parties there all the time. Not that any of it matters. I won't be going back to my apartment either, I imagine."

"That's probably right," I said.

"I appreciate your lack of bullshit. But tell me. Besides working here. Tell me things."

"I went to Mexico City after."

"Things I don't know."

"After that I had nowhere to go and stayed with my father for a time. He was dying, though I didn't realize. It was nice until it wasn't."

"A thing to put on a tombstone," he said. "May I ask you something?"

"You want to smell me?"

His smile showed off his swollen gums.

"I'm guessing you don't smoke anymore," he said. "But I want to ask. It's strange, but I don't care. This might be my last chance to have someone lie next to me."

I closed the door to his room, took off my shoes, and climbed onto his bed. I rested a hand on his chest. Breathing and bones. He put his hand on mine and said, "There's still time."

I was going to ask what that meant, but I liked the vague hopefulness of those words, hope at its most potent without specifics to knock it back to earth.

"When do you work again?" he asked.

"Two days," I said.

"Come back then," he said. "I have more things to say to you. But stay until I'm asleep, if you're able."

"I'm able," I answered.

He closed his eyes. I rested my hand on his arm and his

breathing slowed. I hoped I'd be with him when he went from living to gone, his body losing color without blood's animating traffic. I wanted that more than I'd wanted anything for a while. "I'm here," I whispered, embarrassed at my earnestness, though I said those words again, letting sincerity win. When it was clear he was asleep, I got up and found my shoes. And just before I left, I leaned down and kissed Philip's mouth.

The next time I visited, Philip was asleep, so I found Susan and we went to a Mexican place we loved for its kitschy décor and strong drinks. She told me how she'd suggested to her husband that they talk to someone and he answered that he'd think about it. "But he never thinks about it," she said. "Once he says those words, he never thinks about the thing again."

"Maybe this time he'll be different," I said.

"Why would it be different this time?" she asked.

I didn't have a good answer.

Two days later, when I tried to visit Philip again, I found the bed empty, Rueben undoing the machinery.

"You missed him," he said.

The narrow indent of Philip's body still lay across the sheets. I touched them, no heat left to feel.

"By how much?" I asked.

"An hour officially. But he hadn't been awake in a while."

"Since the last time I was here?"

"I'm not sure."

I wanted that to be true, for the last thing he felt to have been my arm across his waist, my mouth on his. Tears began. I didn't fight them. Rueben said he'd give me a minute.

I hadn't been there when Dad died, imagined it would be the same for Mom, who was now married to a man who listened to conspiracy theory talk radio and lived in Tallahassee. The heaviness I hadn't felt for some time returned, though I knew it would pass. One of the benefits of aging, I suppose, is to know that most feelings aren't permanent fixtures.

On the table next to his bed lay a large, shiny watch. He'd worn that same watch or one almost identical years before. I slipped it into my pocket and walked outside. Rueben was waiting for me. He told me his shift was done, that we should get a drink.

The wind outside was insistent and cold. Rueben complimented my coat. I told him I'd had it for ages, didn't mention that I'd bought it with money Philip had given me, that I wore it so often I'd had its lining replaced.

In the Irish pub next to the hospital, as we ordered beers, I turned shy. But I took a few sips then told Rueben that Susan and I had been unsure of what team he was on. Rueben laughed and closed his eyes. I wanted to touch his face, his mouth.

"Yours, of course," he said, then asked how I knew Philip. I told him about that job.

"But then I did some dumb things," I said.

His face lit up at gossip's possibility. I talked about the party and the man I'd had to their house, the name of the actor who owned it now. Rueben ordered us more beers.

Hope that this was more than a friendly drink quickened in me.

"I did another dumb thing," I said, and pulled the watch from my pocket.

"That's his?" Rueben asked. I nodded.

"Somebody might get in trouble. One of the orderlies," he said. "Fired or worse."

Rueben moved his finger across the rim of his pint glass. The shortsightedness of that party I'd had years before, the things I'd taken from Nicola, some of which I still had, pulled me back into what I thought I'd gotten away from. I stood up.

"What are you doing?" Rueben asked.

"Bringing this back," I said. "I wasn't thinking clearly before. Grief, et cetera."

Rueben's face stayed serious. Mine warmed with stupidity. I asked him not to leave.

I returned to Philip's empty room and placed the watch on the table by the bed, just under a box of tissues so that, when it was found later, it would look like an oversight. For the elevator ride back down, the walk toward the bar, I hoped Rueben had stayed. He could report me. I could lose my job and have to sell my apartment and scrape by, my needling, juvenile impulses knocking down what had taken years to carefully construct.

Rueben sat where I'd left him, my beer next to his. I thanked him for waiting, told him where I'd left the watch, how the room hadn't been touched since we'd left it.

"It was dumb," Rueben said. "But you fixed it."

I wanted to believe that, so I smiled and asked if I'd repaired things enough to go back to flirting with him.

He answered that he had a person, that they weren't open that way.

"Tell me about your person," I said.

"I would," Rueben said, "but I need to get back. He's probably starting to wonder."

"He's the jealous type?" I asked. It came out cattier than I'd meant.

"I'm sorry about Philip," Rueben said.

He told me he'd paid our tab, then kissed my cheek and headed out the door.

After I got off the subway, I stopped to buy a pack of cigarettes. I hadn't smoked in close to a decade. At my apartment, I climbed onto the fire escape. It was cold out. I lifted up my coat's collar. A delivery person zipped by on a bike, and a sparsely populated bus rumbled past. The first inhale startled me. I held in its smoke and picked up my phone. Janice answered after one ring.

"Like you were waiting for me," I said.

"Always, sugar," she answered.

She lived in Cape Cod with her wife and family. Her wife taught elementary school; Janice managed a restaurant. They had a small house and two daughters, the complicated older one still alive then, already causing trouble. Janice told me she was driving back from the restaurant, the moon on the water, almost like it was following her.

"Guess who I ran into," I said.

"You know I'm bad at this game."

"Philip Belshaw."

"He's still alive?"

"Until a few hours ago. He was in the hospital. I found out accidentally and got to spend a few hours with him." I told her how he'd asked me to lie next to him, how I'd kissed his sleeping mouth and hoped that it was the last thing he felt. "That's probably bullshit, though."

"Speaking of bullshit," she said. "Are you smoking?"

"I don't know."

"So much bullshit," she said.

"Bullshit's why you like me."

She asked me to describe the cigarette's taste. I closed my eyes, pretending she was on the fire escape next to me.

"But I wanted to be there," I said. "When he died. It felt important."

"He was already gone, I'm sure," Janice said.

"Even so. It's quieter now on your end."

"I pulled over. Didn't feel like a driving kind of conversation."

"You're too good to me," I said.

"Just good enough."

I began to cry, was sure Janice could hear it, but she didn't say anything. I got it together enough to tell her about the watch I'd taken and returned, wondering if my reckless impulses would ever settle down. Thought, too, about what might still change for me, what would stay the same. Janice and I would have these same kinds of conversations for years. When her daughter died and I tried to get her to slow down her breathing. When the virus appeared a few years after that and I talked to her about how tiredness was the only thing that kept me from freaking out as I intubated one patient then another, most soon joining the morgue's riot of bodies.

But that night, she just said that it was good that I'd returned the watch, added that I should focus on that decision rather than the taking and asked if I was going to start smoking again.

"I'll throw this pack out as soon as we get off the phone."

I took a drag, felt the awful burn.

"You sound sad," she said.

"I am," I answered.

"Tell me what you're looking at right now."

I described a man walking his dog, the airplanes angling into LaGuardia in a blinking row. Also the people in the apartments across the way watching television and folding laundry on unmade beds, a woman awake who was often sleeping. Janice asked for more. So I told her about the cars parked close and the haze from nearby Manhattan, the bodega on my block, the *L* in its sign blinking, beginning to waver. Also more about Philip, and what it was he might have wanted to tell me.

ACKNOWLEDGMENTS

Thank you to the brilliant readers and friends who gave me invaluable feedback on early drafts of this book: Anne Ray, Cathrin Wirtz, David Horne, Marie-Helene Bertino, Melanie Martinez, and Lesley Finn.

Thank you to the community of writers and friends I'm lucky to be a part of, particularly Amelia Kahaney, Amy Fox, David Ellis, Elizabeth Logan Harris, Elliott Holt, Helen Phillips, Megan Murtha, Michael Cunningham, Mohan Sikka, and Ted Dodson.

Thank you to all of the writing teachers I've had over the years, particularly those at the Brooklyn College MFA program.

Thank you to my intrepid agent, Jody Kahn, for her insight, wisdom, support, and friendship.

Thank you to my brilliant editor, Jackson Howard, for honoring what I was trying to do with this book while also pushing me to make it better at every turn. Thanks, too, to the entire team at Farrar, Straus and Giroux and MCD, especially Sean McDonald, Mitzi Angel, Flora Esterly, Brianna Fairman, Sophie Albanis, and Patrice Sheridan. Thanks to Alex Merto for another perfect cover. Thank you to Patrick Harbron for the lovely author photo.

Thank you to my family, particularly my sister, Anna; my brother, Christian; my nieces Katarina and Anika; my nephews Max and Lukas; and my cousin Bastian. Thank you to Nancy and Ed Lynch.

Thank you to my partner, David, for his unwavering support, humor, and patience.

Finally, a huge thank you to my mother, Christine Demmer Grattan, who passed away shortly before *In Tongues* came out. She was my biggest cheerleader, a person whose warmth, creativity, and generosity shaped me in more ways than I can know. She left us too soon, and I will miss her forever.

A Note About the Author

Thomas Grattan is the author of the novel *The Recent East*, which was a finalist for the *Los Angeles Times*'s Art Seidenbaum Award for First Fiction, was long-listed for the 2021 PEN/Hemingway Award for Debut Novel, and was named a *New York Times Book Review* Editors' Choice. His writing has appeared in several publications, including *The New York Times Book Review*, *One Story*, *Slice*, and *Colorado Review*. He lives in New York City and upstate New York.